Outstanding praise for Stephani...
ARE YOU IN THE MO...

"*Are You in the Mood?* I certainly was after reading Stephanie Lehmann's wonderful, witty new novel. Meet Camille, an aspiring actress in New York City. Can she finally make it in such a tough industry? Or should she settle for marriage and motherhood? Will she ever find contentment with her life and resolve her issues with her mother and deceased father? Camille took me on an exhilarating, emotional rollercoaster ride—I simultaneously laughed and cried as I read this new page-turner from the author of *Thoughts While Having Sex*."

—Michelle Cunnah, author of *32AA*

"Take this book to bed to find yourself in the mood . . . for laughter, love, and sex! A delightful, revealing portrait of women edging toward marriage and motherhood. I couldn't stop reading!"

—Josephine Carr, author of *The Dewey Decimal System of Love*

"In an honest and bittersweet look at fantasy and reality, Stephanie Lehmann shines a spotlight on real life and exposes what it takes to live, love, and act honestly. *Are You in the Mood?* is a heartrending, fulfilling novel about trying to survive motherhood, marriage, and life's disappointments before the curtain falls and the audience goes home. A highly recommended read."

—Karen Brichoux, author of *Coffee and Kung Fu*

"Are you in the mood for fun? Then Stephanie Lehmann's got just what you're looking for."

—Jennifer O'Connell, author of *Bachelorette #1*

"*Are You In The Mood?* is a darkly compelling portrayal of what happens when two roads diverge in the wood, and you try to take both of them. Stephanie Lehmann is brilliant."

—Cathy Yardley, author of *L.A. Woman*

"Lehmann's sly wit takes center stage once again in this wicked-funny send up of urban angst. Loved it!"

—Liz Maverick, author of *What A Girl Wants*

"Droll and dead-on, Stephanie Lehmann will make you laugh and cry. For anyone who has ever dreamed of living a different life. A sure-fire hit!"
—Carole Matthews, author of *For Better, For Worse*

"I love this book! Finally an author who tells the whole truth and nothing but the truth about ambition, sex, babies, mothers, and the ambivalence of love. Stephanie Lehmann is funnier, smarter, sharper, more insightful, and a lot more honest than your ideal best friend."
—Pamela Redmond Satran, author of *Babes In Captivity*

Books by Stephanie Lehmann

THOUGHTS WHILE HAVING SEX

ARE YOU IN THE MOOD?

Published by Kensington Publishing Corporation

Are You in the Mood?

Stephanie Lehmann

KENSINGTON BOOKS
http://www.kensingtonbooks.com

KENSINGTON BOOKS are published by

Kensington Publishing Corp.
850 Third Avenue
New York, NY 10022

All Kensington titles, imprints and distributed lines are available at special quantity discounts for bulk purchases for sales promotion, premiums, fund raising, educational or institutional use.

Special book excerpts or customized printings can also be created to fit specific needs. For details, write or phone the office of Kensington Special Sales Manager: Kensington Publishing Corp., 850 Third Avenue, New York, NY 10022. Attn. Special Sales Department. Phone: 1-800-221-2647.

ISBN 0-7582-0335-7

First Kensington Trade Paperback Printing: August 2004
10   9   8   7   6   5   4   3   2   1

Printed in the United States of America

*To Minnette,
otherwise known as Malka,
otherwise known as Mom*

Acknowledgments

Thanks to John Scognamiglio, Barbara Lowenstein, Amanda Selwyn, Franny Silverman, Charlotte Hampden, Marc Geller, Julie Carpenter, Wendy Walker, Heather Berman, Michael Gnat, Mark Lang, Gita Redy, Christopher Moore, Helene Goldstein, and Deanna Carlyle.

Special thanks to Elizabeth Kandall for cheering me on, Leah Pike for being so generous with her time and comments, Karin Sibrana for her inspiration, and Anne Galin for keeping me honest—or trying to.

And, finally, for living with dishes in the sink, piles of laundry, cereal for dinner, and the accumulation of things occupying every available surface in our apartment, I want to thank my wonderful family.

Part One

Chapter One

Camille knew what she wanted. The beet, endive, roque-fort, and walnut salad. But her friend Lisa was still obsessing over the menu, so Camille sat back and took a look around. Small wooden tables, mosaic floor tiles, large mirrors, tall windows. Pretty. She liked coming here. It was like being transported to a bistro in Paris.

The restaurant was actually on the main drag of the meat-packing district in downtown Manhattan. Just outside the louver doors, carcasses hung in a double-parked truck. But even that didn't seem real. Two blocks away there were chic West Village shops and three-million-dollar townhouses.

"Everything looks so good," Lisa said. "I can't decide."

"I'm getting the beet salad."

The proximity to slaughtered animals gave the restaurant that extra layer of appeal to "well-heeled" New Yorkers who wanted to pretend to be slumming. Not that Camille and Lisa were "well-heeled." They were actresses. The struggling kind. So they were happy to pretend to pretend to be slumming.

"I'm thinking maybe a burger. I just don't know . . ."

It was mid-afternoon and not very crowded. A woman sitting near the back . . . she looked familiar. "Oh my god."

Lisa looked up from her menu. "What?"

"It's Meg Ryan."

"Are you sure?"

"Definitely."

Camille couldn't stop her eyeballs from darting from Lisa to Meg, Lisa to Meg. "She doesn't look so good."

"I'm turning around."

"The deuce behind you to your right, near the bar. Be subtle! She's with a man; his back is to me. Can't tell who he is."

Camille watched as Lisa twisted her head around as if she had a crick in her neck, stretched out her shoulders for added effect, cast a glance back, snagged a look, then forced her face forward again. "She looks so old!"

"That woman never made an interesting acting choice in her life."

"I saw her bio on E! She was a journalism major in college and then got on a soap and never stopped working."

"It's so unfair."

"But I have to say, I did love *When Harry Met Sally.*"

"Mmmmm." Camille took a sip of wine. Maybe she had felt guilty pleasure watching that movie when it came out, and then on video, and at least once on TV, but she wasn't going to admit it. Still, her eyes couldn't help but find their way back to Meg, who was laughing now, but how could she be happy? Her best parts were behind her. She did have a child, but her marriage was over and her stalker was in jail. Starring in TV movies was the next inevitable step in her fall from grace.

The waiter came, and they both ordered the salad. Of course it was ridiculous to feel bad for Meg. Camille would be thrilled to get paid to do a TV movie. She'd be thrilled to do a commercial that aired during a TV movie.

"So," Lisa said after the waiter took their menus, "I had a big talk with Wally last night."

"And . . . ?" Lisa had been toying with breaking up with Wally for months. Maybe she'd finally gone through with it.

"He asked me to move in with him."

"Really."

"And I don't know what to tell him."

"You're actually considering it?"

"I know I'm always putting him down," she said, hooking her dirty blond hair behind her ears. "But he really is a nice guy."

Lisa was looking at her with . . . could it be . . . pity? They'd lived two blocks away from each other for years. It was the perfect arrangement—always there for each other, but with their own spaces for when they got on each other's nerves.

"I just don't seem to be able to end it," Lisa said.

Camille did her best to sound supportive. "So maybe you should move in with him."

"But he's so boring."

"Then maybe you shouldn't?"

"You aren't helping!"

"I'm sorry. I don't know what you should do!"

Camille could never be with a man who bored her. She was amazed that Lisa could. Of course, Wally the Wallet earned hundreds of thousands of dollars a year as an investment banker, and that part wasn't boring. But. A man with lots of money had expectations. At least her flaky and broke artists, actors, and musicians had all been incapable of long-term commitment, leaving her free to put her own ambitions first.

Lisa took a piece of bread from the basket and then put it back. "I can't believe I'm actually considering it."

"He is crazy about you."

"And he's very sweet."

"He's very sweet."

Camille checked back in on Meg and her mystery date. He was talking to the waiter. She could just about get his profile. . . . "Oh my god."

"What?"

"It's Eric Hughes."

"You're kidding." Lisa turned around and stared at him like a tourist.

"It's not fair." Eric Hughes was incredibly handsome in that Laurence Olivier-Leslie Howard-Richard Harris-Richard

Burton-Cary Grant-Hugh Grant British sort of way. Why did he have to waste himself on Meg?

"Maybe it's the first time they've met," Lisa said. "And he's realizing right now that she's a bore. And when he gets up to go to the bathroom he'll pass our table, and see you . . ."

"Or you . . ."

"And he'll say, *Pardon me. I couldn't help but notice how lovely you are. Would you like to star in my next movie?*"

Camille took a swig of wine. Of course, Eric Hughes would never know she had worshiped him ever since she saw him in the movie version of *Hamlet*. And she didn't even hold it against him that he'd left his wife for that twit Mimi Tyler (and where was she now?) who co-starred with him in *Bombshell* and then made that trashy thriller with Harrison Ford even though she couldn't act to save her life.

"So tell me." Lisa leaned forward onto the table. "What's happening with you and Daniel?"

"He called the other night." Daniel was an old friend of the Wallet's. Lisa had engineered an introduction, and Camille had gone out with him, once, for coffee the week before. "I haven't called him back."

"Why not?"

"I'm just not sure he's my type."

"I think he's sexy."

"Do you really?" Daniel was a psychiatrist on staff at Bellevue, the famous state-run mental hospital. The depository for all the crazies in the city. The joke. The place you don't want to end up in. "I just don't see myself dating a shrink." She'd never even been to one as a patient. Her acting had always seemed like enough of an outlet for her emotions, and who had the money anyway?

"Wally says he's very into you."

"He's nice. But he was so quiet."

Except that he kept asking her questions, and listening very attentively to her answers, and encouraging her to talk.

By the end of the date she'd practically told him her entire life story! And he'd revealed hardly anything about himself.

"He's shy. Give him a chance!"

"I will, but I have to tell you my really exciting news. I got an appointment to see an agent!"

"Really? That's great!"

"Norman Freed. Ever heard of him?"

"I've seen his name around for years."

"Me too, but I don't know who he represents. Anyway, I'm seeing him next week."

"Good luck."

"Thanks. God knows I'm overdue for some luck." Camille raised her wine glass. "To us. For not giving up."

Lisa seemed to hesitate before raising her glass. "To not giving up."

As they clinked, Meg and Eric got up from their table. "They're going," Camille said, "don't look!"

"I have to."

So they both pretended not to watch Meg and Eric leave. And everyone else in the restaurant pretended not to watch Meg and Eric leave. And Meg and Eric pretended that everyone in the room wasn't pretending not to watch them leave.

The pair snaked their way through the tables past the hostess who smiled graciously and nodded. It was as if all the patrons had become extras, and their conversations were merely dubbed-in background noise to give atmosphere to Meg and Eric's exit. The door closed behind them. And there was a communal pause for a moment of self-importance and glee, as if the entire room of people had shared dinner with the two stars.

Chapter Two

Maybe it was the threat of Lisa's defection. Maybe it was the fear that Norman Freed would have no interest in her and she needed someone around who did. Maybe it was because she was about to open in a lousy play in a run-down Off-Off-Broadway theater for no pay after five weeks of rehearsals for a showcase which would last only sixteen performances that no one would bother to come see and what was the point of her life? But when she got home, Camille called Daniel.

He sounded happy to hear from her, and she apologized for taking so long to call back. He was writing a paper, "Mental Illness in the Cinema," and had a list of old movies to see, so she agreed to meet him that Saturday evening at a video store near her apartment.

During the next few days she fought the temptation to cancel on him. Rehearsals were stressing her out. She felt inexplicably tired. Would he expect her to tell him more about herself? At least they would have the video to watch. There wouldn't be so much pressure to talk, and maybe she'd learn a little more about him this time.

She was tempted to call it off right up until the moment she walked into the store and found him in the suspense section. He was intently examining a row of boxes, leaning forward slightly with his hands clasped behind his back. There was something very reassuring about his presence. And he was handsome enough, with small delicate lips, sweet little arched eyebrows, and nice thick wavy brown hair.

Though his hair was starting to recede. And he was only about five foot ten. She really preferred tall men.

But he did have a good build.

But how could he wear that tweed suit and tie in this heat?

He picked up *Vertigo.* "Is this okay with you?"

She eyed the box: Jimmy Stewart holding on to a ledge for dear life. She'd seen it before and wasn't particularly in the mood, but he was the one writing the paper. And it did take place in San Francisco, where she grew up. And Jimmy Stewart did make her feel like the world was a better place. So she agreed.

At the check-out counter they went "all out" and bought Twizzlers, microwave popcorn, and soda. As they stepped out of the air-conditioning into the summer heat, she wondered why she'd been so nervous about seeing him. After all, they were just watching a movie together.

On the way to her apartment in the East Village, they passed through Astor Place, one of the most chaotic intersections in the city. Two huge avenues crisscrossed and a subway station disgorged endless streams of people. Someone was playing bongo drums on the traffic island and hordes of NYU students, Goths, and neo-punks overflowed onto the streets. She felt self-conscious next to this tweed-suited man who looked older and more conservative than everyone else. Of course, she was older than most of them too, but not by as much, and she knew how to dress the part in her bell-bottom jeans and lilac stretch top that revealed her flat belly and just a bit of cleavage.

"Welcome," she said, "to DisAstor Place," as she liked to call it. She was pleased when he laughed.

Then he nodded toward an elderly man in white pants and a white shirt with stringy long white hair who was holding up a sign: SECRET TO THE UNIVERSE! 25 CENTS! "One of my ex-patients."

"Really?"

"Just kidding. If he'd been to see me, he'd know to charge more than that."

Daniel did have a sense of humor. And a very dry delivery.

The scent of incense was in the air as they passed down St. Mark's Place with its tables of sunglasses, cheap jewelry, and marijuana pipes for sale. "So do you like living down here?" he asked as they passed the third piercing parlor on the block. His apartment was on the ultra-high-rent Upper East Side.

"Oh, you know. It's home. Really hasn't changed that much over the years other than all the Starbucks, of course."

She'd loved the liveliness of it all when she'd first arrived over ten years ago, but it *had* recently begun to feel a little old. Or was she the one feeling old? Most people did tend to move out once they hit their thirties, but she was glad to have her own place and the only other neighborhood she could afford would be out in one of the boroughs.

"To be honest," he said, "this part of town always makes me feel very 'uncool.' "

"No one is cool enough to live in the East Village. Even the people who live here. That's why we stay. We're in an eternal quest to achieve ultimate coolness."

"Well," he teased, "I think you're 'cool.' "

She wondered what it would be like having sex with a psychiatrist. As soon as they were done, would he ask, *So how did that make you feel?*

When they reached her block on Ninth Street and First Avenue, Camille started to feel more insecure than cool. She shoved open the heavy black metal front door to her building and was hit with an unexpected feeling of shame! This had to seem so shoddy to him. The dark narrow lobby; the worn, yellowed linoleum floor; the slanted, warped stairs . . . it probably looked like she was living in poverty. She wanted to explain to him that she wasn't. But then it occurred to her. Maybe she was!

After the opening credits, they leaned back on the sofa, not touching, feet on the floor. (She wore black Italian sandals. 75-percent off on Eighth Street. He wore brown suede Wallabees.) His body next to hers made it hard to relax. She was glad to have the bowl of popcorn and tried not to shovel it into her mouth.

Jimmy Stewart was hired as a detective to follow Kim Novak, who played the blond, cultured, uptight Madeleine. He fell in love with her, and about halfway through the movie she faked her own suicide. Jimmy was devastated.

At that point, they'd been watching for well over an hour, but there was still a long way to go. She remembered how the second half was almost like a whole additional movie. They decided to take a break.

She put a new bag of popcorn in the microwave and watched him take in her living room. Did he find her taste bohemian? Or eccentric? Or just plain tacky. Maybe the pink walls, red trim, and antique gilded mirrors did scream "cheap bordello." And a matching deco vanity and bureau from the flea market—a bargain at $350 including delivery—would've been elegant if the wood wasn't chipped and a drawer handle wasn't missing. Almost every surface was crammed with makeup, jewelry, books, magazines, and a collection of old perfume bottles that she was always on the verge of getting rid of but couldn't, quite. "It's always a mess," she said. "I won't even pretend otherwise."

"It's got a lot of personality. I like it." Daniel nodded toward a photo on the mantle of her faux fireplace. "Is that your father?"

"Yes."

It was taken before she was born, when her parents lived on a commune in Marin County in the sixties. He wore jeans and

a black T-shirt, and cowboy boots. He looked like a cross between Cary Grant and Peter Fonda. He was gorgeous.

"I see the resemblance," Daniel said.

She liked hearing that. But Daniel was staring at her with
an intense look of compassion that he'd undoubtedly per-
fected for his patients. He already knew that her parents had
divorced when she was five, and her father had died when she
was sixteen, and she felt like he wanted her to cry about it all
right then and there. "I think the popcorn is ready," she said,
and went to refill the bowl.

In the second half of the movie, Jimmy Stewart happened
to meet Kim Novak on the street. But now she was a brunette
named Judy from some hick town in Kansas. Jimmy didn't realize she was the same woman.

By then, Camille was getting used to lounging next to Daniel.
Their shoes were off. Their thighs were touching.

Jimmy tried to get Judy to look exactly like Madeleine. He
bought her the same expensive clothes, made her dye her hair
blond, and had her pin it up. Finally, he succeeded in getting
her to look amazingly, incredibly . . . just like Madeleine!
They kissed, and the camera panned around them both in or-
giastic triumph.

It really was a good moment.

When the movie ended and the credits started rolling,
Camille decided she'd better get up and put the empty bowl
of popcorn in the sink. Not that she thought Daniel would actually try to make a move on her. But it seemed like a good
idea to head off the possibility.

"So this was nice," Daniel said.

"I thought so too."

"Maybe you'll come watch a movie at my place next time."

"I'd love to."

Before he left, he gave her a very gentlemanly kiss on the
cheek.

As soon as Camille shut the door behind him, she realized
she was going to have a hard time falling asleep. She wished

she could call Lisa and fill her in on how the evening went, but Lisa was undoubtedly with Wally, and maybe they were having sex that very minute. So she went back to the TV and flipped channels until her eyes started to droop. It was three in the morning when she finally turned off the TV. As she got into bed, she wondered if Daniel could love her the way Jimmy Stewart had loved Kim Novak. As she drifted off to sleep, she wondered if she wanted him to.

Chapter Three

From the moment she opened her eyes, the day was all about Norman Freed. A grapefruit for breakfast and then to the gym for a half hour on the Stairmaster, a steam to get the bags out from under her eyes, then home to give herself a bath, and put on clothes and makeup. Her standard favorite for summertime auditions and first meetings was a royal blue slip dress that came to just the right spot above her knees—attractive but not slutty—with matching white thin-strap sandals. Luckily her hair was nice and thick this morning. She wore it down and blow-dried it with the diffuser to keep the wave. Then came base, blush, concealer, a bit of mascara and shadow, and her favorite shade of Sugar Plum lipstick. A day full of promise. Not a pimple on her face.

West Eighty-first Street was not exactly a happening location for an agent. It seemed he worked out of his own apartment. That wasn't necessarily bad, but it wasn't good either. Chances were he didn't have the best contacts. Still. A month ago Camille had sent her headshot to every franchised agent listed in *Ross Reports*. Then she'd made follow-up calls. He was the only one who'd called back.

She went down a few steps through an arched doorway with a black iron gate that looked like the entrance to a dungeon.

"He'll be right with you," the receptionist said, hacking between puffs on a cigarette, "take a seat." She was a woman in her fifties with red hair and dark roots. Before she could sit, Norman Freed popped out from his office as if he'd been anxiously awaiting her. That creeped her out. Why wasn't he busy with phone calls and other clients?

He was short, pasty, gaunt, with a moustache that covered the top portion of his upper lip. His hair was greasy and had dandruff along the middle part. He wore a navy polyester suit with fat lapels, a fat light blue tie, and aviator glasses.

Don't make any quick judgments, she reminded herself. Just because he was interested in her didn't mean there was something wrong with him.

"I'm Norman." A thick Brooklyn accent. "Nice to meet you."

"Nice to meet you."

She smiled graciously at the secretary (whose look said stay away from this man) and followed him into his office.

After all, this man could help her career. Theoretically. And it didn't have to be a bad thing that he didn't keep her waiting. And his pasty appearance could have to do with the fact that he was always inside, on the phone, working hard for his clients with no time for grooming or the whims of fashion.

He sat behind his desk. She sat opposite him in a low green armchair that forced her to look up at him. "Do you need another copy of my résumé?"

"I have it right here." As Norman studied it humming some non-tune, she checked out his office. Behind him was an abstract painting of mustard yellow blobby shapes on a blood red background. Stacks of headshots covered a brown corduroy sofa with dirty, frayed armrests. So even this guy got inundated with pictures and résumés. It was distressing. Maybe even Norman Freed didn't want her. . . .

Finally he threw her résumé on top of his desk, sat back, and looked at her. "So tell me, why should I sign you?"

This was the part of the interview she hated most. "You can see by my résumé that I've had excellent training. Studied Meisner, Linklater, took classes with Uta Hagen for two years . . ." She blathered on. It was all on the résumé, but one had to say something. "I spent a wonderful year in England at the Royal Academy of Dramatic Art and had the chance to perform Rosalind in *As You Like It,* Helena in *All's Well That Ends Well,* and Kate in *Taming of the Shrew.* . . . I have a Broadway credit, done lots of regional theater—Kitty in *The Time of Your Life* at the Dorset Playhouse, some great reviews last summer as Billie in *Born Yesterday.* . . . But of course I'd really like to expand into television, film, commercials. If you'd like to hear a monologue, I've prepared something from *Three Sisters*—"

"You need to lose ten pounds."

"Excuse me?"

"How tall are you?"

"Five foot eight."

"You wear a size six?"

"Yes." Verging on eight . . .

"Okay, you really need to fit into a size four. For theater, maybe you can get away with a size six, but if you want any TV or film work—and let's face it that's where the money is—then you have to get down to a four. And if I were you, I'd have some work done on your teeth. That little space next to your canines is a problem. Have you ever considered going blonde?"

"Excuse me?"

"The brunette thing really isn't doing anything for you."

"I'm a natural blonde," she lied. "I dyed my hair brunette for a play I'm rehearsing."

"Are you taking this personally?" He chuckled and shook his head. "You have to get over that. This is a business. You girls don't understand that. I've been doing this for twenty years, and let me tell you, if you want to succeed, you have to understand that you are the product."

"I do understand."

"Good. How old are you? Twenty-eight? Twenty-nine?"

None of your business. "Twenty-seven."

"Already past your prime. You'll be lucky to find anyone to represent you. Let me tell you, I'd be doing you a favor. I'm just telling you the truth. I look at you and I see someone almost impossible to cast. This city is swarming with girls like you, and you're all competing for jobs that don't exist!"

Camille considered fleeing out the door and ending this odd form of torture but was too curious to see where it would go.

He leaned forward on his desk as if he was about to be intimate. "I'm just being honest with you, okay? I know it's unpleasant, but you'll thank me later."

Later. What did that mean? Even though this idiot was making her feel like a piece of shit, she would still sign with him given the opportunity.

"Do you know how many résumés I get every day? Twenty, thirty, forty, fifty . . . People dying to get work. Everyone and their mother wants to be an actor! They would pay to get the chance to be in a movie! Who has time to look at all those pictures? Who has time to open the fucking envelopes, excuse my French. What can you tell from a goddamn picture anyway?"

"Not too much," she gave him. "If you'd like to come see my show, it's opening next week—"

"Do you know how many lousy Off-Off-Broadway plays I've seen? Enough to last twenty lifetimes. If I never had to see another Off-Off-Broadway show in my life, I would jump for joy."

"I know what you mean," she said, suddenly wanting very much to get out of this room. "So . . ."

"You've got talent, that's obvious, or I wouldn't have agreed to see you."

He thought she had talent?

"So I'll send you a contract. That's the next step. And we'll go from there."

He stood up. She stood up too. "That's great."

"Thanks for coming in," he said, and held out his hand. She didn't want to touch it. She shook it. Of course. Cold and clammy.

As she said good-bye to the receptionist, Camille marveled that this man hadn't even seen her act. He wasn't even asking her to go freelance. And he was sending a contract! She wasn't sure whether to jump up and down with joy or hurl herself off the George Washington Bridge.

Chapter Four

Her last student was Vin, a young actor with a thick Brooklyn accent who was coming to her for the first time. "I hate de way I sound," he said. "Too lowah class. And it keeps me outta de runnin' for lotsa good parts."

Camille helped people who had accents get rid of them. Some were aspiring actors with regional accents they wanted to lose; others were foreigners trying to assimilate. She saw them in a building on Eighteenth Street that rented out rehearsal spaces. The room she used was only ten dollars an hour because it was tiny and windowless, as if the architects had made a mistake when they designed the floor and ended up with this little space left over. But it suited her needs perfectly. She advertised in *Backstage* and posted fliers on bulletin boards, and managed to get a steady stream of clientele. She charged forty dollars an hour, and it allowed her to keep her schedule flexible for auditions, rehearsals, and performances. With a small inheritance she'd gotten from her father that kicked off eight thousand a year in interest, no health insurance, and watching every dollar she spent, she got by.

"Of course lots of actors like Joe Pesci, Al Pacino, and Billy Crystal wouldn't have their careers without their New York accents," Camille said.

"But at least I wanna be able ta *know* howta speak right."

"And you're right. But you shouldn't think of your accent as 'wrong.' It's just the way people in the community where you grew up speak. This non-accent you're trying for reflects no origin at all."

"It doesn't?"

"It evolved out of Madison Avenue and Hollywood. You know. Broadcaster-speak. Bland. No character."

"I nevah thawtavit dat way."

She showed him her diagram of the human mouth, vocal chords, lungs, and diaphragm. Talked him through the basics of how different sounds are articulated.

"So, uh, Miss Dinsmore?" Vin asked. "I'm just wonderin. Where'd ya learn all dis stuff?"

Miss Dinsmore was the name of the voice coach in *Singing in the Rain,* the one who tries to teach Lena to drop her squeaky Brooklyn accent when she's trying to transition into talkies. Camille used this alias because she was "not really" a vocal coach. "Miss Dinsmore" was the vocal coach. A rather severe tight bun and faux glasses completed the illusion.

"I got my training at The New York Language Institute and The Announcer Training Studio." She'd always been good at accents and foreign languages. When the indignities of waitressing had started to wear her down, this had seemed like an attractive alternative.

Camille spent the last part of the hour drilling him on his *r* sound. "The sides of the tongue are pressed up against the side top teeth. The tongue tip is pointed upward behind the top teeth. It should not actually touch the palate. The lips pucker and protrude slightly."

She demonstrated for him. "Can you picture that?"

"I guess."

"Then give it a try. Say *hear.*"

"*Hea.*"

"Try not to drop the *r* sound. Say it again. *Hear.*"

"*Hear.*"

"Good. We're going to concentrate right now on words that

have the *er* sound at the end. Repeat after me. *Dinner. Happier. Murder . . .*"

He repeated diligently. It touched her. He was so eager to learn. So innocent about his chances. Obviously intent on becoming the next DeNiro. People worked so hard—and for so little payoff! She tried not to let it make her feel sad. Success wasn't impossible, after all. She had an agent, now, didn't she? Maybe he *would* be the next DeNiro. Anything was possible, as long as you still had hope. *"Theater, ogre, defer, differ . . ."*

The other actors weren't at the theater yet when she entered the "dressing room," a brightly lit narrow space that was hardly bigger than a walk-in closet. She put on her makeup, glad to be alone after working with students all afternoon. It was opening night and she wanted to get into her character's headspace.

Home at Home was set to run for a month in this seventy-five-seat theater. It was on the ground floor of a tenement on East Fourth Street and had that inscrutable scent that, like a fine wine, was hard to break down but was reminiscent of piss and mold. The production had no money for advertising. The writing was mediocre. And she wasn't thrilled with her part— a frumpy character named Mary Ann with no sex appeal. At least, not until the last scene when she got to strip down to her underwear. She wasn't sure if she'd allow anyone she knew to come, but not because of the underwear. She hated how she looked in the brown floral dress they made her wear in the first act.

Camille stared into the mirror and took a good look at herself. Her father had told her many times that an actor needed to know his own face like the back of his hand. She most certainly did—every angle, every contour, every inch of skin. And for the most part, her face did please her. Today there was one blemish on her chin, but at least she wasn't bloated. She got out her makeup and applied base, then powder to even

out her complexion. Because her face was a bit long, she
shaded the sides of her nose and the top of her forehead.
Then she added some blush for definition on the underside of
her jaw. And, because Mary Ann was very innocent, she chose
a delicate pink lipstick and gloss. Then some darker pink liner
to define the shape of her mouth. She brushed light pink eye-
shadow on the inner lid and darker pink on the outer, then
took a good look at herself. She added some dark eyeliner on
the outer third of her upper lid for an open, doe-eyed look.
Took another look. Done.

The three other actors started to filter in. Other than saying
hello, Camille ignored them and did her breathing exercises.
She didn't want to relate to anyone before going on stage. It
was distracting, and anyway, they were all on her nerves. A
bunch of losers for wasting their time on a production like this,
but then so was she, so how could she judge them, but she did.

At least Norman Freed might rescue her. She'd been looking for his contract in the mail and was getting nervous it was
never going to arrive. *Please, God, let him rescue me.*

Once Camille went out on stage with the hot lights warm-
ing her skin and all eyes on her, she felt good. The play was a
comedy about a newly married couple living next to an obnoxious neighbor who used to be a major league baseball player.
Camille played a repressed kindergarten teacher whose sex-
crazed yoga instructor mother becomes romantically involved
with the neighbor. At best it was like an updated *Barefoot in the
Park*. At worst it was like a bad episode of *I Love Lucy*. But it
was better than the alternative (nothing) so she allowed herself to be exploited (felt grateful for the part).

Some of the sorry few who'd shown up were laughing. After
four weeks of rehearsing to silence it was nice to hear that
sound. There was something so innately satisfying about
laughter. So seductive. Affirming. Even if she didn't write the
lines, she felt brilliant and funny to be delivering them. And,
when the actors took their curtain call, the applause lasted
until after they left the stage.

Back in the "dressing room" Camille felt warmly toward everyone. She hadn't realized how nervous she'd been, maybe because it was demoralizing to feel anxiety over this meaningless little production. "That went well, don't you think?" she asked to the room in general. It would've been nice if they all told her how brilliant she'd been. Of course, all they wanted to hear was how brilliant *they'd* been.

"You were marvelous as usual." It was Eddie, who played the obnoxious neighbor. He'd been trying to get Camille into bed since the first rehearsal. Eddie wasn't bad looking for his age, which had to be around fifty, and she did have a thing for older men, so she couldn't resist having a mildly antagonist flirting relationship with him. But she really had to stop getting involved with flaky artist types. Eddie was a stand-up comic who used to live out of his car.

"Thanks," she said. "You were marvelous as usual too."

"Coming to drown your sorrows tonight?" he asked.

"Considering the state of my career, I'm ready to drown myself."

She took off Mary Ann's dress (which she'd just slipped on for the curtain call) aware that he was enjoying a free look. Under the circumstances modesty was a waste; after all, she'd just paraded on stage in her underwear. She put on her black Anna Sui top rescued from Loehmann's at 70-percent off.

"You're breaking my heart," he said. "Let me buy you a drink."

She turned to Anita. "You'll come too, won't you?"

"I'd love to, but I have to take the train back to Jersey." Anita sighed. "Maybe Saturday."

Like Camille, Anita was a devoted actress. But the once gorgeous woman worked full-time as an administrative assistant, never married, never had kids, and was still doing shitty Off-Off-Broadway plays hoping she'd get some kind of break that would finally catapult her to the next level.

Camille dreaded becoming Anita.

"I thought it went very well," Paul piped up. He played her

husband. He was gay, disturbingly skinny, but was able to pass as straight (on stage at least). He was also a bit young at twenty-three to play opposite her. But she seemed to be able to get away with mid-twenties (on stage at least). "The audience really seemed to be enjoying it."

"Yeah," Eddie said. "Both of them."

"Come on, Eddie," Camille said, "there were at least ten people out there not including your parole officer."

She brushed out her hair but the humidity was making it frizz, so she decided to put it up. She swirled it into a loose twist, pulled it halfway up the back of her head, tucked the ends under with bobby pins and left a few free tendrils near her face.

"I love how you do that," Eddie said.

"I love how the drool drips down your chin," she said.

"I'd love to show you some of my other fluids. . . ."

"Would you two please shut up," Paul said. "Please?"

It was two in the morning when she pushed open the door to the vestibule of her building. The light bulb was burned out again. What if a mugger or a rapist was lurking? She headed past the super's ground-floor apartment. He was just coming out. She could smell the liquor on his breath. Or was that her breath?

"Hello Sheila," he said.

"Hi Jimmy!"

She should really mention the light bulb. And her leaky faucet. But would he remember in the morning? Best not to bug him. She hated dealing with these things. Maybe next time, in the light of day. She climbed the creaky stairs.

Maybe her building was old and decaying, but she did love her apartment. Living on her own. What it lacked in glamour, it made up for in character. Sometimes she imagined an immigrant family from a hundred years ago crowded in here, all ten of them sharing the one toilet and doing piecemeal sewing to put food in their mouths like in that movie *Hester Street* with Carol Kane, before she was in *Taxi*.

She lived here courtesy of Sheila Thompson, an old friend from acting class. Sheila had inherited the lease (after major legal wrangling with the managing agent) from a grandmother, but never moved in because she lived in Soho with her boyfriend. But a rent-controlled apartment like this—$500 a month—was too good a deal to let go. So Sheila made this arrangement with Camille, who paid her $600 a month. The Con Ed, phone, and cable bills came to the apartment addressed to Sheila Thompson. Camille forwarded them to Sheila (with checks made out to Sheila) and then Sheila wrote out checks to pay the bills. Camille had her own mail sent to a post office box.

She would've preferred to have an apartment in her own name. It was unsettling that her security was dependent on Sheila's relationship with her boyfriend, a flaky musician. If Jimmy or the owner ever figured out the truth, they'd get rid of her immediately and jack up the rent, and then where would she go? But she tried not to dwell on it. Everyone's situation was precarious on some level, wasn't it?

She checked her messages (none) and decided to take a shower before going to bed.

Chapter Five

"I got a lawyuh," Wanda said.

"And?"

"We're gonna meet next week."

Wanda had a plan. Leave her no-good husband after getting a promotion from secretary to executive secretary. But her thick Queen's accent held her back.

"That's good. Good for you." Wanda talked about her marriage problems every chance she got. Camille didn't want the lesson to turn into a pseudo therapy session. "So let's start. Relax. Straighten your spine. Relax your jaw . . . shoulders . . . let's hear some quick breaths from your chest to release the tightness . . ."

"I dunno if I'll go through with it, but I set it up anyway. Whenever I think of leaving my husband, I feel sorry for 'im! I'm sorry, Miss Dinsmore, you've hoid all this before. I must drive you crazy."

"No!"

"You must think I'm an idiot."

"I don't, really. I know how hard it is."

"You been a doll, Miss Dinsmore."

"Thanks. So did you have a chance to work on your vowels?"

"Shuaw."

"Ok, let's work on the *ah* sound. Repeat after me. *"Father, park, star, calm . . ."*

There was a line at the post office and she regretted not having gotten coffee first. But it had been a week since the meeting with Norman Freed and she was anxious about that contract. By now, she was getting used to the idea of "settling for" him. After all, his smarminess was typical of all agents. And she was fortunate to sign with anyone. And he did seem to be legitimate—had been listed as a "franchised agent" in *Ross Reports* for years. So he had to have at least *some* contacts. Had she imagined he had said he would send that contract? Finally it was her turn. The postman handed her a small stack of mail. When she saw Norman's return address on a business-size letter, she ripped open the envelope while still at the window. A woman behind her said a grouchy, "Excuse me," and Camille shimmied to the side.

She removed the contents. A cover letter and . . .

This was it.

She had the contract.

The contract was in her hands.

She met Lisa that evening at the Odeon, a Tribeca restaurant with white tablecloths, beveled mirrors, and fifties diner details like a pink and green neon clock over a mahogany bar. The place was packed. They settled into the banquette against the wall and Camille checked out the fashionable mix of loft-living artist types and after-hours Wall Streeters. "This place manages to be classic yet trendy," she said. "It's been around for years, but it still draws a crowd."

"I used to be classic and trendy," Lisa said. "Now I'm just classic: a single woman valiantly carrying on with life in the face of fading looks and dwindling prospects."

"Are you going to be depressing? Because we're supposed to be celebrating here."

"You're right. I'm sorry. I'm so happy for you! Norman is going to do amazing things for you!"

"Finally I've had some luck."

"First of all, it wasn't luck. You worked hard for this. Second of all, he's the lucky one to snag you as a client."

Third of all, Camille thought, he was creepy, slimy, and annoying. But Lisa didn't have to know that.

A busboy placed a breadbasket on the table and asked if they wanted bottled water or tap. They both said tap was fine.

"Who cares about water?" Lisa said after he was gone. "I need alcohol for god's sake."

"And food." The waiters were walking briskly back and forth past their table with very important business to attend to everywhere else. The busboy filled their water glasses and Camille finally let herself take a thick sourdough slice from the breadbasket. She tore out some of the middle and dipped it into a saucer of olive oil. "This is so good. Don't let me take a second piece."

"Excuse me," Lisa said to a waiter passing behind her. "We'd like to order some drinks."

"I'll be right with you," he said over his shoulder as if they were two toads sitting on a log.

"He hates us," Lisa said.

"This bread is really good. Are you having any?"

"Maybe later."

The waiter, who had a carefully manicured goatee, returned and asked with absolutely no fanfare, "What would you like?"

"A glass of wine," Lisa said. "Merlot."

"And for you?"

"Cabernet." Camille smiled at him and wished for his approval even though he most certainly didn't deserve hers. The small smile he returned was curt, and he left without ceremony.

"So I was going to wait until they brought the food," Lisa said, "but since it's taking an eternity . . ."

Okay. Here it was. She was going to move in with the Wallet.

"Wally asked me to marry him!"

"What?"

"You know. As in, 'I now pronounce you—' "

"How did this happen?"

"I told him I didn't feel right moving in with him . . . making such a big commitment at my age, you know . . . unless it was for real."

"Wow." That was practically a marriage proposal in itself.

"I didn't give him an answer yet. I don't know what I'm going to do. But let's face it. I haven't been in a play for an entire year. And I'll be happy to stop temping. And I mean, really! The last thing I want to be when I'm sixty years old is a woman living alone with her cats on welfare regretting the fact that she ever had stupid fantasies of being an actress."

"Don't call your fantasies stupid."

"You're right. I know. I mean it's not like I have to stop working. If you can call my acting work. As if I ever made any money at it."

"That doesn't mean it's not work." Camille could hear her father's voice in her head. Lecturing her about "the arts." *Just because most artists in our culture don't get paid for what they do, that doesn't mean it's not important.*

"On some level, the whole acting thing is so trivial," Lisa said. "Who cares? I want to do something *meaningful* with my life."

"Marrying Wally is so meaningful?"

"I'm talking about having kids."

"Kids?"

"Those people who come out from between your legs?"

"I'm sorry. But I don't see you as the motherly type."

"Are you sure you aren't talking about yourself?"

It was true. She had never once had a craving to shop in Baby Gap. Children seemed like they were from another species, or possessed by the devil, like in *Rosemary's Baby*.

Although Elizabeth Taylor *had* made a fetching mother in *Daddy's Little Dividend* and she *had* always wanted to wear one of those shirtwaist dresses with the high heels and a string of pearls.

The waiter set two bulbous glasses of wine on the table. "Are you ready to order?"

"I'll have the duck," Camille said, hoping he would support her choice, but he turned to Lisa without a word.

"I'll have the duck too." He took their menus and left. Lisa looked around the room as if she was worried people were going to eavesdrop. "Since I know you're probably mad at me considering all the not very complimentary things I've said about Wally," she began. "I'm going to tell you something highly confidential, okay?"

"Okay."

"As far as the general public is concerned, I turned thirty this year. But the truth is . . . I'm thirty-three."

"Excuse me?"

Lisa held her chin up. "I might as well admit it. What the hell. I'm thirty-three years old."

Camille's eyes widened. "You've been lying to me about your age?"

"To you, to everyone!"

Camille considered telling the truth about her own age. She wasn't really thirty, as Lisa believed, but thirty-four. Ten years earlier when she'd decided to use the professional name of Chaplin instead of Chiarelli, she'd decided to start telling people she was twenty. And why not? Everyone said she looked young for her age. At this point she'd been pretending to be four years younger for so long, she almost believed it. When it had been her real thirtieth birthday, she didn't even pay attention since everyone else thought she was only twenty-six. "Well thanks for telling me after all these years."

"Don't take it personally. I started lying about it long before I met you."

"So you're actually older than me."

"Uh-huh."

"My god. This is so disorienting!"

"I'm a bitch, aren't I?"

"Did you tell the Wallet your real age?"

Lisa looked at her with surprise. "Of course. I couldn't lie about that with *him*. It wouldn't be right."

"Of course not."

Since when did Wally rate knowing the truth while she'd been kept in the dark? Camille managed a stiff smile. "Well, ya fooled me."

"By the way, I'm thinking we should drop the Wally the Wallet thing."

"Of course."

"You should shave a couple years off," Lisa continued quickly. "No one will ever know."

"I'm not going to lie about my age," Camille said proudly. What age had she given Norman Freed? "Maybe I can fool Joe Schmo, but I'll never be able to fool myself."

"Fine." Lisa leaned forward in her chair. "So are you seeing Daniel again?"

"He left a message on my machine."

"And?"

"I don't know." She couldn't deal with him now. Not if Norman Freed was going to finally make things happen. Not that the two men had to be mutually exclusive. "So that's great news about Wally," she finally said, unable to completely omit the sarcasm from her voice. "Congratulations."

"Well don't plan the shower yet, I haven't decided anything."

When the waiter finally appeared from the kitchen carrying two big plates of food, Camille slid back in the banquette to give him space. At least she would get her duck. It sounded warm and succulent. Her stomach growled with hunger.

That night she lay in bed awake for hours. Her thoughts would not let her fall asleep. It now seemed quite possible that Norman Freed would be an incredibly positive development in her life. So what if he wanted her to lose weight? How could she have felt prickly about that? He had film contacts for god's sake! And it would be easy to lose the weight with this kind of incentive. Never mind that it would make her look gaunt. Everyone knows film puts on ten pounds. And film was where the money was, and if she started making money, she could retire Miss Dinsmore and achieve immortality at the same time!

She convinced herself so thoroughly that she was lucky he wanted her that by three in the morning she started to think there was no reason to waste money on a lawyer to check it over; she really should just get that contract back to him as quickly as possible. By next week, he could be sending her out for auditions.

When she finally drifted off to sleep, she was rocketing into outer space farther than anyone had ever gone and all the stars were glittering and she just kept soaring to new heights in the universe. Then the phone was ringing.

She checked the clock. Six in the morning. Something was wrong. Her mother sick? Lisa had a fight with Wally?

The machine answered, and she listened anxiously as the message broadcast to the room.

"Camille Chaplin?"

It was Norman.

"That's a damn good name. I liked meeting you very much. You're a very beautiful woman. And I hope you weren't offended by what I said. Believe me, you look great. So I just wanted to say . . ."

He sighed audibly. Camille pulled her blanket up over her chest.

"I liked meeting you very much. And I know you're not a blonde. You're as brunette as they come. And you're meant to play brunette parts. Every woman wants to be a blonde, but believe me, it's not you. You see, what actors don't know is this. It's not about pretending to be someone else. In the end, you have to find yourself in any role you play. And I like you. So I guess I really shouldn't be calling. But you see, I have a lot of trouble sleeping at night. Are you there? Are you listening to me? Because I really thought we made a connection. Am I right? God. I don't know. I've had too much to drink, that's the problem. But you see, when I can't sleep at night, I start to drink. . . ."

Camille turned the sound off on the machine. Norman Freed kept going. For twenty minutes. She had a digital machine that didn't cut people off. Not that she was planning to listen. Luckily, she could erase the message just by pushing one little button. And then it would be gone. As if it never happened.

Chapter Six

Camille climbed the stairs out of the subway station. It was a hot, humid Saturday afternoon and she started to wilt on the short walk up Lexington Avenue to Daniel's apartment. She felt nervous about seeing him again. But she was curious to see where he lived, so she didn't cancel. She fantasized an elegant old pre-war building with high ceilings, original details, and views of the park. Or, at the very least, a nice brownstone like Holly GoLightly's in *Breakfast at Tiffany's*. So it was disappointing to find he lived in a white brick post-war building. It reminded her of Jack Lemmon's apartment in *Prisoner of Second Avenue*. No character, cheap materials, designed to contain as many people as possible.

Not that this was cheap real estate. At the entrance she was stopped by a rotund, mustached doorman who wore a military-looking gray suit with a matching gray cap and maroon tie. He asked for Camille's name, and then called up on an intercom to get the okay from Daniel before letting her in. The mirrored lobby had huge gaudy chandeliers and white marble floors. It screamed wealth without taste.

His apartment, at least, was not hopeless for a bachelor. The furniture was modern cherry wood from someplace like Pottery Barn, and hanging over the black leather couch was a nicely framed Rothko print with a huge square of watercolor gold melting into a magenta square. Not her taste, but not a disaster.

"So what movie are we going to see?"

"It's a surprise," he said, and she was pleased—very pleased—to see him wearing blue jeans and a blue T-shirt on this weekend afternoon. Much better than his musty old suit. Though she still wished he was a little taller. "I thought we'd get some lunch somewhere first. Or we could bring it up here and watch while we eat."

"Let's do that," she said, suddenly feeling shy and worried about conversation.

"There's a bakery on Lexington that has good sandwiches. Is that okay with you?"

"Sounds perfect."

They walked to the Patisserie Margot and ordered turkey sandwiches and coffee. Daniel asked if she wanted to get a dessert, and she smiled at the glass case filled with fruit tarts. They had apple, apricot, plum, strawberry . . .

"What kind should we get? Your choice."

"Oh, god, it's so hard. Strawberry," she finally said. "They look so beautiful."

Camille held the box as they walked back. "So how did you come to live in your building?"

"My ex-girlfriend had the lease. Plastic surgeon."

"Ugh. I can't imagine you dating a plastic surgeon."

"They get a bad rap," he said. "But they aren't just about tummy tucks and face-lifts. People get disfigured in accidents. Birth defects. Their work can be very important."

"I didn't mean to offend your ex-girlfriend." And how "ex" was she?

"I didn't mean to *defend* her." Daniel nodded to the doorman as they entered the lobby. "She was very into her work, and we ended up having different . . ." He was silent for a moment as they got onto the elevator. He pushed the button for his floor. "Basically it boiled down to I wanted a family and she didn't."

"How long were you together?"

"Seven years."

"Wow."

"She kept leading me to believe that by the next year she'd be ready. But she wanted to build up her practice. And it's hard in this city—a lot of competition. Then she was offered a great position in Boston. 'Couldn't turn it down.'"

He sounded pretty disgusted. They were silent as the elevator went to the tenth floor. Was he looking for a wife to buy his groceries and bear him children? She hoped he wasn't seeing her that way. Like the ex, she was bound to disappoint.

"I grew up just around the corner." He put his key in the door. "On Park Avenue."

That would be pre-war. Elegant.

"Both my parents were psychiatrists," he said wryly, "with offices in the lobby of our building."

"Both? Wow. So, what . . . are they retired?"

"My mother passed away five years ago. Breast cancer. My father is retired and lives in Arizona now." Camille felt some relief. She wouldn't have to face dinner out with all three shrinks staring into her soul and intuiting all her flaws. "I'm sorry about your mother," she said as they entered his apartment.

"Thanks."

He turned up the air conditioner and they spread their meal out over the glass coffee table and she settled into his couch. Daniel was suddenly full of excuses for having made his choice. "I saw it a long time ago. It's not really a very good movie. But I think it was good in a bad way."

"Bad movies can be good."

It was pretty bad. *Final Analysis*. With Richard Gere playing what had to be the sexiest (no wonder Daniel picked it) psychiatrist ever portrayed in the movies. He falls in love with Kim Basinger, who plays the sister of Uma Thurman, who plays one of his patients. It was all pretty trashy, but in a fun way, and, to their surprise, it ended up being a brilliant choice because it had all sorts of references to *Vertigo*, from Kim Basinger wearing a gray skirt suit, gloves, and updo just like

Kim Novak to a climb up a spiral staircase when she falls to her death. It even took place in San Francisco.

"Of course a psychiatrist really shouldn't sleep with his patient's sister," Daniel frowned when it was over.

"It's sexy! You aren't really offended by that, are you?"

"I suppose," he said, making himself look a bit tortured, "if the patient was attractive enough."

"Do all your patients want to sleep with you?" she asked.

"If you were my patient," he asked, putting his arm around her, "would you want to sleep with me?"

"If I was your patient," she asked, cuddling up to him, "would you want to sleep with me?"

He leaned over and kissed her. She made a mental inventory of her body. There was a large bruise on her leg from walking into the corner of her desk the week before. It refused to go away and no amount of makeup would disguise it. But her underarms and legs were shaven and she didn't have her period and she'd made sure to wear a black lace bra and panties.

She felt him pull away from her and opened her eyes. His face was so close he was slightly out of focus. Looking straight at her.

"Hi," he said.

"Hi."

And then he kissed her again. And her eyes closed again. And his arms were around her and he was Richard Gere. And she was his patient. And she trusted him completely. And he was doing this even though he really knew he shouldn't, and it could get him in a lot of trouble—cost him his entire career—but he couldn't help himself, he just couldn't help himself, she was so goddamned beautiful he couldn't pull away. . . .

He pulled away.

"Are you okay?" he asked.

"Mmmmm." She opened her eyes again, pouted like Kim Bassinger, or no, make that Uma because she was the better actress. "Are you?"

"Yes." He leaned over and kissed her again.

And she melded into his arms. Surprised at how well she fit there. How sure his touch was. But then, Richard Gere was a very confident man. She pulled off her shirt. He unhooked her bra. She leaned back on the couch, and he leaned over her, kissed her breasts, made his way up to her lips. If he fell for her, that was too bad for him because he really should not be doing this and she started to pull her pants off, but he took the moment to sit up. "Maybe we should stop."

She wasn't sure what to say. Didn't he want her? Richard had rejected Uma, but she was a psychopath! "Yes," she said. "We probably should."

Camille went to use the bathroom, reapplied her lipstick and put her hair back up. As she looked in the mirror, she couldn't help but feel rejected.

But when he walked her to the door, she could tell by the way he took her in that she was not being rejected. "So let's get together again soon," he said quietly, drawing her to him, kissing her lightly on the lips. "Okay?"

"Okay."

He went down to the lobby with her and waited while the doorman flagged a cab. But when the doorman went to open the door, Daniel slipped in front of him so he could open it for her. They all laughed, and she slid inside.

As the cab made its way past the shops on Lexington Avenue she speculated, with a little smile on her face, that Daniel probably advised his patients not to sleep with their dates too soon. So he had to uphold the standard. So he had to wait, too.

Chapter Seven

Camille ate a bowl of borscht at the Odessa Coffee Shop. She had an hour before she had to be at the theater, but she really was not in the mood to perform. After teaching all day, she just wanted to go home and relax. Audiences had been so small. It was a drag doing comedy to empty seats.

She thought of the lesson she'd just had with Wanda. As soon as she walked in the door, Wanda had announced "So I'm doin' it!"

"Moving out?"

"Found a place; put down a deposit!"

Camille had wanted to congratulate her, but Wanda sounded wary. "Did you tell him yet?"

"It isn't even furnished. I'll tell 'im when it's all set up, so I can make my getaway."

As she opened her copy of *Backstage*, Camille wondered if Wanda would actually go through with it. She sighed. Life was so hard. The paper was no comfort. It was chock-full of listings for auditions that were preordained invitations to rejection, articles that gave advice to do things she'd already done that hadn't worked, and profiles of other people's "inspirational" stories of success that only made her burn with jealousy. Still, she couldn't resist scanning the auditions. She saw

that the Roundabout was doing a production of *Uncle Vanya*.
She'd always wanted to do that play.

They were seeing people the following Friday at the
Gramercy Theater at eight o'clock in the morning. It would
be freezing cold. There would be a long line. They would give
each person two minutes to perform and barely pay attention.
In other words, it would be a complete waste of time.
Everyone knew these auditions were bogus. The only reason
this casting call existed was because the actor's union insisted
these theaters at least pretend to make the effort. The producers already knew who they wanted, and that was most
likely someone with movie credits because no one wanted to
go to a play these days if there wasn't a Hollywood star in the
lead. Five years ago, even two years ago, Camille would've
made herself go to that audition. Not anymore. Why waste her
morning? Forget it. She turned the page.

That night there were only ten people in the audience and
not one of them had a sense of humor. The complete lack of
laughter threw the actors' rhythm off. The lack of rhythm
caused Paul to completely blank out on his lines during the
final scene. Eddie panicked and jumped in with his own line,
which actually came a page later. A key plot point was left
out. The audience filed out as if they'd been to a funeral and
were relieved to go home to a nice snack in front of their TV sets.

As she walked home (and looked forward to her own snack
and TV) she wondered if Lisa was right. What the hell was she
doing with her life? This was not why she had become an actress. Even if she could be working in better theaters in better
productions, the truth was, she was too old for all the good
parts. Desdemona, Juliet, Ophelia, Viola . . . All that was left
were those horrible old-lady parts written by playwrights who
hate their mothers.

Well, that wasn't completely true. There was still Blanche
in *Streetcar.* Martha in *Who's Afraid of Virginia Woolf.* Hedda

Gabler. Everything Jessica Tandy ever did. Lady Macbeth . . .

But she could never be Juliet, only hope to be the nurse; never be Laura, she'd have to be her mother.

Camille heard her father's chiding voice. *Is Sarah Heartburn expecting star treatment? Acting isn't about getting attention for yourself. It's about being a character in a story.*

Well, okay. Maybe the size of the part didn't have to matter so much. Ingenue or grandmother, lead role or character part, she needed to act. She needed to be on stage. She couldn't imagine life without it.

Though she certainly would prefer to remain an ingenue.

Old age. It scared her. Who would love her when she was old? Looks gone. A failure. Nothing to show for her life. She waited for the light to change at DisAstor Place. Maybe she should throw in the towel; marry Daniel. If he'd have her. But what then? Would he be flexible enough to live with her? What if she was in a play and had to be out every night? What if he wanted to get her pregnant right away? What if she found it impossible to have sex with the same man for the rest of her—

"MOVE!"

A maniac bike rider whizzed past inches from her face.

"Asshole!" she yelled after him, jarred by the sudden blast of her own unladylike voice. But what could you do? She hated those bicycle people. They appeared out of nowhere traveling against the flow of traffic and were always ready to blame you for being in the way.

She ran into the super in the vestibule.

"By the way, the landlord? He tells me your check is late this month."

"Really? I think I sent it."

Sheila Thompson must've spaced out.

"You better make sure."

"I will," she said. "Thanks."

As she dragged herself up the stairs to her apartment, Camille wondered if she'd lived her life entirely wrong. Been naïve in imagining that the world provided possibilities to everyone who tried hard. Now she knew better, but it was too late. And the rest of her days would be a downhill slide of paying for her foolish mistakes.

Chapter Eight

"So how are your patients?"

She liked to ask about his patients, though he wouldn't usually tell her much. Daniel was very conscientious. But sometimes he would share a little nugget.

"I saw a very interesting woman this week."

She quietly ate her gnocchi to give him space to continue. They sat up front in an Italian restaurant on Third Avenue. It was a warm, humid evening. All the windows were open, and they watched people passing on the street.

"Came on her own. Wanted to be admitted. Says she's hearing voices."

"What kind of voices?"

"Voices saying she's a bad person. Doesn't deserve to live."

"Why?"

"When she was very young, she was riding in a car with her little brother. They were next to each other in the back seat. He opened the door and fell out. Died."

"God. That's so sad." Camille speared a gnocchi and rubbed it in the sauce.

"She feels very guilty."

"But it wasn't her fault."

"From a child's point of view . . . she feels like she made it happen."

Camille shook her head.

"She was able to function all right for years. Worked as a bookkeeper for a car dealership."

"That's ironic."

"But recently both her parents died."

"Please don't tell me it was a car accident."

"Natural causes. Her father had liver cancer. A year later her mother's kidneys failed. But it seems to have pushed her over the edge. She became depressed, stopped going into work, and ended up living on the streets. Tortured by these voices . . ."

"Is there anything you can do for her?"

"Medication might help."

"If only she could see that it wasn't her fault."

"Hopefully she'll start hearing different voices in her head," he said. "Encouraging voices. Nice voices. People can be so hard on themselves."

"I hear mean voices in my head sometimes. They tell me I'm a failure."

"Don't listen to them. Tell yourself what a good job you do."

"Do you have mean voices?"

"Sometimes. But if they start talking I tell them to stop."

"You make it sound simple."

"If it was simple, I'd be out of a job."

They left the restaurant and strolled over to his place. It was a beautiful, soft evening. The kind of evening that makes you happy to be alive, happy just to have the chance to visit this earth, and who could complain about anything? But still. Was she falling for Daniel? He was smart and sweet, and treated her well. He could give her a comfortable life on the Upper East Side. She almost felt like she was living one of those New York existences people fantasize about.

Too bad it didn't happen to be her fantasy.

"So how did you get your name?" he asked.

"My father chose it. He loved the movie with Greta Garbo. You know, based on the play by Dumas."

"What's the story?"

"She's a prostitute with tuberculosis in the 1700s who falls in love with a man named Armande, who comes from nobility. And he falls in love with her too, even though according to society, he shouldn't feel anything for a whore, but he wants to marry her, and his father disapproves. So the father convinces the prostitute—her name is Marguerite—to turn Armande away even though she's madly in love with him. And then she gets really sick—"

"So who is Camille?"

"There is no Camille, actually. Her name is Marguerite. American audiences mistakenly called her Camille because the original title was *La Dame aux Camellias*, because she loved the flowers."

"Do you love the flowers?" he teased.

"Yes, as a matter of fact. I do."

They were in front of a Korean grocery store that sold flowers. The rows of summer blossoms were lush with color. Pink peonies, purple hydrangeas, white lilies, orange zinnias. No camellias, though. He picked out a mixed bouquet and handed it to her. She accepted it with feelings that were also mixed.

They settled in on his couch to watch *Now, Voyager.* His choice, again, because of the paper he was writing. Camille wanted to warn him she might not go for it. "I once saw the beginning of this on TV. Bette Davis had the most unflattering heavy eyebrows pasted on by some sadistic makeup artist. And her mother was a bitch. I couldn't watch it."

"Give it a chance," he said. "I think you'll get into it. This was one of my mother's favorite movies."

"Why?"

"One of the few positive portrayals of a psychiatrist in a Hollywood movie."

But it was hard. There was Bette Davis with those horrible eyebrows. And her character, a depressed woman from a

wealthy New England family, was referred to as a "spinster."
A spinster? Bette Davis had to be in her thirties when she did
this movie! What a turn-off.

Charlotte Vale's father had died long ago; her mother was
the queen of mean voices who scared Bette into being a
mousy woman totally alienated from her own sexuality. A psychiatrist played by Claude Rains came to her rescue. Camille
thought Bette would fall in love with Claude, especially when
she'd stayed in his mental institute and started to feel better.
But Claude was not a leading man; he was too short.

Bette went on to meet Paul Henreid on a cruise. She appeared from her cabin for the first time with her eyebrows
waxed—a huge relief—and a wide-brimmed hat demurely
tilted to the side. She looked stunning for the rest of the
movie.

Paul Henreid was the one she fell in love with.

And then came a pleasant surprise. She introduced herself
to him as Camille, because she was pretending to be a French
passenger so she wouldn't have to socialize. "Another Camille,"
Camille said, wondering if her own father had ever seen this
movie. Paul Henreid said she was like a chameleon and continued to call her that for the rest of the movie, even after she
admitted who she really was.

Though Bette fell in love with Paul Henreid, Camille
found herself resisting. She was too used to thinking of him as
Victor Laszlo in *Casablanca*, which also had Claude Rains as
the chief of police. (Ingrid Bergman wanted to leave Paul for
Humphrey Bogart, so Camille was used to thinking of him as
the less attractive alternative.) In any case, Bette never did get
to marry Paul Henreid because he was trapped in an unhappy
marriage but was too noble to leave his wife.

In a scene toward the end, after the mean mother died,
Bette Davis sat on a train feeling miserable. She sobbed over
the fact that she'd never done anything to make her mother
proud. Camille started crying too. "I can't believe I never saw
this movie," she said, wiping her tears with her fingers.

"Another Camille! And she has a bad relationship with her mother, just like I do! And her father is dead, like mine."

Daniel turned off the TV. "Your Dad . . . he moved to New York when you were how old?"

"Ten."

"Did you ever visit him here?" Daniel handed her a tissue.

"Once. I was sixteen." She blew her nose. "He took me to see *Chorus Line* on Broadway. It was amazing. The first time I ever went into a Broadway theater. I stayed with him for two whole weeks. He lived in the Manhattan Plaza, that high-rise complex on Forty-second Street. Lots of theater people live there, and I thought it was the most glamorous thing in the world. I remember he took me to that little French restaurant across the street. It's still there, the Madeleine, and I still remember what I had: a chicken dish with cream sauce and Tarte Tatin for dessert. I was never so happy. Just walking down the streets with him, I felt so grown-up and sophisticated." She sighed. "That was my only visit."

Daniel still stood next to the TV, observing her on the couch. "Did you want to move here and be with him?"

"I was dying to, but my mom wouldn't let me. But I knew, as soon as I graduated from high school, I was coming. I couldn't wait. And then . . . he died. I moved here anyway, but . . ." She was about to say it was too late. But if it was too late, why was she still here?

He sat down next to her and put his arm around her. "I'm sorry." His jeans had a rip on the knee. She could see his leg hair peeking through.

"Sometimes I think I came here looking for him," she said. "I'll be walking down the street and think I see him down at the other end of the block coming toward me."

"Uh-huh."

"It's funny how people can look fuzzy off in the distance. And you make yourself believe it's who you want . . . and then they get closer and it doesn't look anything like them."

Daniel didn't say anything.

"I mean, of course I know perfectly well he's not dead and it won't be him."

"He's not dead?"

"What?"

"That's what you said. 'I know perfectly well he's *not* dead.' "

"No. I said 'I know he's *dead*.' "

"Did you?"

"Yes."

"Okay." His tone insinuated that he was right and she was neurotic. "Maybe it was my mistake."

"Of course," Camille pulled away from him, "I imagine it's him because I wish it was him, obviously, and I just can't help myself."

He removed his arm. She pressed her lips together and turned to stare out his window at an identical building across the street. Someone was watching *Frasier*.

"That must've been hard on you," Daniel said.

"When he died?"

"That too. But I was thinking about how he chose to move so far away when you were young."

"If you're really passionate about acting, you have to be in New York." She was aware of sounding like a cliché, but couldn't help feeling defensive. Really, it had been her mother's fault. Her mother should've been more supportive of her father. If she had, maybe he never would've left. But her mother had never understood his ambitions. Or Camille's. Her mother thought their heads were in the clouds.

But Camille had been seduced by the acting bug ever since she was four years old and saw her father doing a Noel Coward play from backstage. He was so handsome in a black tuxedo and bow tie with his hair slicked back! Watching him go out on stage with a wink, being in character for everyone else, then back to her all himself again—it was just too much fun! Where was the joy in her mother's life? Camille would take the clouds any day.

When they made love that night, Camille felt confused. At

first she tried turning Daniel into Claude Rains, which didn't really turn her on, so then she tried Paul Henreid, but she kept seeing Ingrid Bergman rejecting him for Humphrey Bogart. She'd never found Humphrey physically attractive, so she switched to Richard Gere. But by then she just wasn't really into it and though Daniel started a trail of kisses that was heading south, she pulled him up when he got to her inner thighs and told him she just wanted to go to sleep.

"Are you sure?"

"Yes. I'm fine. Just tired," she lied.

Camille fluffed her pillow, snuggled deeper under Daniel's blanket, and stared up at the square glass light fixture on the ceiling. He fell asleep moments later. But she couldn't. His mattress was too hard. She missed her own Posturepedic. If this went on much longer, she'd have to take him to Bed Bath and Beyond for a makeover.

She turned onto her stomach. She still wasn't sure if she should let this get any more serious. If only she could fall in love with him in the insane, passionate way Bette Davis fell for Paul Henreid. After all, Daniel was a good man. He could take care of her financially. She could have his baby. Life could be simple.

She shifted to her side. His clock said one A.M.

Simple seemed so boring.

She drifted off to sleep.

Daniel woke early to get to the hospital. He told her she could sleep in if she liked. "Mmmkay," she said without opening her eyes, and he kissed her good-bye. She woke up a couple hours later, dressed, and left without showering.

The doorman opened the heavy glass door. She stepped out on the sidewalk and was bathed in warmth. Inside, with all the air-conditioning, you could forget the summer sun was baking the streets. She took a stroll down Madison Avenue. All the designer clothing shops were here. Donna Karan, Versace, Armani, Givenchy, Barney's . . . Once she reached Fifty-fourth

Street, she decided to duck in to Gucci. Too bad she was only wearing a rayon skirt from Urban Outfitters and a Gap tank top. Think Jackie O. Think Madonna. Think Britney, for god's sake. She deserved to browse just like anyone else, even if the stuck-up salesgirl was giving her a look. Okay. Suede jeans, $2,850. Silk amethyst top, $1,550. Black pigskin and suede bamboo-handle bag for $1,300. Don't worry, she nodded at the salesgirl, I'm going.

Getting out of the subway at Astor Place, Camille felt culture shock. Had the East Village gotten worse? She didn't want to look down on her little neighborhood and wished she could remember how it made her feel when she'd first arrived in New York City. It had all seemed so incredibly exotic. In California, the architecture seemed old if it dated back to the fifties. Here, it had always amazed her that people still lived in these run-down old tenements, like they were all dwelling in living museums.

But at the moment it just seemed like a slum.

Chapter Nine

It was a Wednesday night. The second to last week of performances. Marie, the director, a perpetually upbeat woman with large square glasses, appeared backstage after the show. "Guess what, ladies and gentlemen? We had someone interesting in the audience tonight!"

"You're kidding," Paul said. "My mother finally came? Was she proud?"

"Someone, believe it or not, more important than your mother."

"My mother?" Eddie said. "Did Sing Sing give her a pass?"

"Certainly not mine," Camille mumbled. God forbid she fly all the way to New York to see her in a show.

"My mother is dead," Anita said. "So I hope it wasn't her!"

"Nobody's mother or father, because as far as I know Jeb Sanders is a bachelor."

"From the *New York Times?*" they all said at the exact same moment.

"Yep."

"Oh my god," Paul said. "Oh my god, Oh my god . . ."

Eddie went back to the mirror and combed his hair. "So we all get to enjoy being publicly humiliated."

Marie put her hands on her hips. "Come on. Tonight was great. And we had a good audience."

Meaning the theater was half-filled. Maybe Mr. Sanders

would take pity on them. "They did actually laugh at the right places," Camille said, which was after many of her lines. This could be very good news. "Thank you for not telling me he was here." She would've been a nervous wreck.

"I wouldn't dream of it, my darling."

"This is unbelievable," Paul was practically yelling. "The *New York Times!* I'm going to be a star!" He launched into song. "I did it myyyyyy wayyyyyy. . . ."

Anita looked anxious. "Did he seem to like the show?" Anita really shouldn't worry; her career wasn't exactly going anywhere at her age, no matter what the review said.

"I couldn't tell what he was thinking. But he was very friendly. Thanked me on the way out."

"He stayed for the whole thing?"

"Even clapped during the curtain call."

That was good. The only other time she'd performed for a *Times* reviewer was when she'd had the lead in an Off Broadway play called *The Burial.* She'd won the part in an open casting call, a miracle in itself. The production was booked in a beautiful theater on Upper Broadway. The playwright, a man in his fifties, was a well-known novelist with a good publicist who promised reviews in all the major papers. The raves would get her an agent who would get her auditions for other shows, television, commercials. She was twenty-four years old.

The reviewer left at intermission.

He called it "one of the worst plays on the boards that year." He mentioned her along with the other actors as "bravely carrying forth." After six weeks of rehearsals and hype, it was over in one week and her big break turned out to be a big nothing.

No one knew exactly when (and if) Jeb Sanders's review would run. It could take days, a week, even two. Or it might not run at all. Camille wished she could be cryogenically frozen until it came out.

*   *   *

Camille met Lisa at the gym, and they found two empty treadmills next to each other. Their attention quickly focused on the row of TV sets mounted to the ceiling. Camille bounced back and forth between a *Friends* rerun about Phoebe's plan to have a baby, and a news report on CNN about Al Qaida plans to nuke the United States. Then she noticed a *Law and Order* rerun on the TV down at the far end. She couldn't watch that show without fuming because she'd never managed to get seen by their casting agent. They were one of the few shows filmed in New York and everyone, including Lisa, had gotten at least one line on *Law and Order.* Even Eddie! But not her.

Dripping with sweat, they headed over to the weight machines. Lisa sat at the hip-adduction machine. Camille sat at the hip-abduction machine. They pushed their thighs together and apart in unison.

"So how are things going with Dr. Kessler?"

"Good."

"He's treating you well?"

"Yes . . ."

"And you aren't holding that against him?"

"Trying not to."

"There are benefits to marrying a doctor," Lisa said.

"A dermatologist would be more useful. . . . I could get lasered every night before going to sleep."

"Are you suggesting you aren't in dire need of mental help?"

"If I could stay young forever I'd be perfectly happy."

"If you got married, you wouldn't have to worry about staying young."

"Because it's all over after you sign *that* contract."

"Are you really *so* against the idea of marriage? I know your parents didn't do too well with it, but—"

Camille let her weights drop with a clang. "Can we switch machines please?"

They traded places. Now she was pressing in.

"Sorry," Lisa said. "I guess I'm trying to figure my own stuff out."

"I guess." Camille decided to change the subject to something more fun. "Do you think Jeb Sanders might give us a good review? I mean, the play is funny, don't you think?" She ignored the tense smile on Lisa's face. "And it's very New York. . . . It could be really popular in a Neil Simonesque sort of way."

She was so caught up in the fantasy, she was ready to convince herself *Home at Home* could win the Pulitzer . . . Outer Critics Circle . . . a Tony. There'd she'd be in a Gucci gown accepting the statuette from Bernadette Peters. . . .

"Why don't you wait to see if you get a good review," Lisa said, "before you start planning your acceptance speech?"

"I'll pretend you didn't say that."

"Just a little dose of reality."

"If I was being cynical you would tell me to be more positive."

"I just don't want you to set yourself up for disappointment."

"You think the play is bad?"

"No."

"You think *I'm* bad!"

"No! I just remember how hard it was when *The Burial* tanked. You can't keep hanging all your hopes on some stranger out there to realize how great you are."

"Did my mother coach you?" Camille flapped her knees together. The weights flew up and down. "Because it sounds like you two are conspiring in some mission to get me to—"

"Never mind! I'm sorry. Maybe the review will be great. You want to take a steam?"

Camille felt pretty steamed already, but she agreed. At least they could end this conversation. It wasn't that she didn't know where Lisa was coming from. Sometimes she felt amazed that she still could get her hopes up so high.

In the locker room, she peeled off her sweaty clothes. Kate

Hudson happened to be a few lockers down changing into her yoga clothes. They saw her there occasionally. Camille glanced straight through her. The woman was democratic enough to go to a public gym; she deserved to be left alone. Camille wrapped herself in a towel and followed Lisa into the steam room.

They spread their towels on the tile ledge so their heads met at the corner and splayed out at right angles to each other. Camille lengthened her body—her arms tucked in by her sides on the narrow ledge—and put another towel over her face. She breathed the hot wet air. Tried to let her worries ooze out of her pores. And allowed herself the luxury of thinking about nothing at all.

Hector Munoz was a short man in his thirties, born in Puerto Rico, intent on assimilating—especially since he'd gotten a good job as a salesman at a camera store.

"Spanish doesn't have a *z* sound like ours, so it can be hard to get the hang of it. So you're used to saying words like *is*, *was*, and *has* like *ihss, wahss, hahss. . . .* You hear the difference?"

"Yehss," he said.

"So we're going to practice. To make the sound, put your tongue behind your bottom teeth and make a continuous sound like s, but you have to voice it. From your voice box." She indicated his Adam's apple.

He tried. *"Sssssss."*

"Put your fingers against your throat while you say it. You can feel the vibration."

"Sssssss."

"Keep your hand on your Adam's apple and really make it vibrate."

"Sssss . . . sssszzzzz. Zzzzz."

"There you go!"

He smiled with a proud look of achievement. *"Zzzzz!"*

"Great! Now repeat after me. *Husbands . . . busy . . . crazy . . .*"

* * *

She put the plastic containers of broccoli, brown rice, and sesame chicken onto Daniel's coffee table while he set up the plates. "I wonder what Lisa's going to do."

"You mean with Wally?"

"It looks like she's going to say yes. She wants to quit acting and have babies."

Daniel went into the kitchen to get beer.

She waited for him to return. "I guess I shouldn't be surprised," she said, "but I am."

"Do you ever think about quitting?"

"No." She sat down on the couch. These days it seemed like all she *did* was think about quitting. And frustrations with her career, as if experiencing frustration had become her career and the acting was just a sideline. "If I quit, I think I would feel like I didn't exist anymore."

"It's important to do what you feel passionate about."

"So you don't think Lisa should quit?" she asked.

"I don't really know her well enough to say."

She sensed that they were testing each other, but were dodging answers, not yet knowing if they wanted to pass or fail each other's tests.

"But," he said, dishing rice onto his plate, "I can see how it must be very frustrating. Other professions, after you train you can be fairly sure you'll get a job. But acting . . ."

Camille dished herself a generous portion of chicken. Fuck dieting now that she didn't have to lose ten pounds for Norman. "You must think I'm an idiot to waste all this time and energy. Acting is so much about vanity," she heard herself say—the same thing she'd resented Lisa for saying. "The kind of work you do is much more important."

"I don't know about that."

"You actually help people live their lives."

"So do you."

"But if you screw up, a patient might commit suicide or do

something violent. The worst thing that can happen at an evening in the theater is we bore everyone to death."

"I'll never forget the first time a patient of mine killed herself."

"After going to a boring play?"

Daniel grimaced.

"Sorry. What happened?"

He stopped eating and stared down into his food. "I was a first-year resident. For years I thought it was my fault."

Camille kept her eyes on Daniel and stayed quiet. He was opening up—a rare occasion—and she wanted to encourage him.

"You always wonder," he went on, "if there's something else you should've done or said. I'll never forget having to tell her family. She was on the lock-in ward against her will. Ended up stabbing herself with sewing scissors. I always wondered if we'd let her go, maybe she'd be alive."

"Or maybe she would've left and killed herself and then you'd be mad at yourself for letting her go."

"Maybe." He looked at her. "Then you have the people who never *want* to leave. They stay inside for years, struggle with their problems, never get any better, but never give up. . . ."

Camille forked a piece of chicken. She could relate to that. How she refused to give up acting even though it was obvious to everyone else in the world that nothing was ever going to happen and she was over the hill and should really find something else to do with her life. . . .

"So," he asked, "are you going to let me come see your play?"

"No."

"But I want to see you on stage!"

"I'd rather you wait till I'm in something better."

"Will you at least think about it?"

"I suppose." But she didn't have much to think about. There would be nothing to be gained from letting him see her performing to an empty audience in a frumpy dress. She'd sooner invite him to watch her legs get waxed. "Shall we start the movie?"

It turned out to be amazing. *The Three Faces of Eve*. Joanne Woodward (one of her favorite actresses of all time) played a frumpy, depressed woman named Eve White who goes to a psychiatrist played by Lee J. Cobb. It emerges that she has a second personality, a floozy named Eve Black who has a much better time. (She's constantly trying to get Lee to sleep with her, but he won't; he just keeps smoking his big cigars.) Both Eve White and Eve Black can't stand her husband, who's always threatening to beat her up. Then she develops a third personality, Jane. Jane seems sane. She gets a handsome boyfriend who looks like Rock Hudson. By the end of the movie, Jane reigns. And the two Eves "die." Jane presumably enjoys sex with the Rock look-alike.

Camille felt such envy for Joanne Woodward. What a wonderful part—to be able to make those transformations from one character to the next. And she did it so convincingly! Camille's stomach ached with longing. (Or maybe it was too much Chinese food.) If only she could have the chance to do parts like that. She wouldn't complain or be bitter about anything ever again.

After the movie, they cleared the table and then Camille settled back into the sofa, leaned back into the cushions, and closed her eyes. Daniel sat down and put a lock of her hair behind her ear. "You are so pretty." He kissed her. And she closed her eyes. She was Eve Black, the floozy; he was Lee J. Cobb, finally succumbing to her irresistible beauty. At least he didn't smoke cigars.

Chapter Ten

A few days later. Early morning. She was home alone in her apartment. The phone woke her out of an exhausting dream featuring a woman in a red flouncy dress who was dancing and twirling and dancing and twirling, and it was a relief to leave that dream behind. Unless it was the return of Norman. She didn't pick up and waited to hear the incoming message. It was Paul, and he was screaming.

"It's in the paper! The review is in the paper! Wake up already!"

Camille's adrenaline surged because she knew, by the way he was screaming, that it was good. She grabbed the phone. "What does it say?"

"Get out of bed!"

"Why?"

"I want you to be awake when you hear this."

"Is it good?"

"Just get out of bed."

"I'm out." She sat up against the pillows.

"No you aren't, you creep."

"Okay." She touched one toe to the floor. "I'm out."

"All the way!"

"Do you have a hidden camera?"

"Inside your little brain, now get up!"

She groaned and sat on the side of the bed with both feet on the floor. This was as far as she was going. "Okay, I'm out. Would you tell me what it says?"

Paul cleared his throat. "An amusing though broadly drawn comedy about newlyweds, an ex-major league baseball player and an eccentric mother . . . blah blah blah . . . directed at a fast clip . . . blah blah blah . . . but the *best reason* to see *Home at Home* is actress Camille Chaplin. Managing to be both hilarious and heartbreaking as Mary Ann, the uptight kindergarten teacher turned sexpot, this vivacious actress . . ."

Camille slowly started to stand.

"Lit up the stage . . ."

By now she was fully erect.

"With charm and sophistication. It would be hard to say if it was her beauty or her wit that brought more oomph to the part. This reviewer was left to wonder why she isn't performing on Broadway instead of this small Off-Off-Broadway theater with questionable indoor plumbing. . . ."

"Oh my God!!!!" She realized she was jumping up and down hysterically. "I don't believe it! Oh my God! Oh my God! Oh my God!"

"Can you believe it?!"

"I don't believe it!"

"It's incredible!"

"It's a rave! I got a rave!" Camille screamed. "In the *New York Times!* This is incredible!"

"And you were ready to give up!"

"I was not!"

"Yes you were!"

"No I wasn't!"

The phone rang all morning. Twenty-three messages came in while she went out to get coffee and scrambled eggs at the 2nd Ave. Deli. And a bouquet of flowers! At first she thought they were from Daniel, but they were from Marie. Did Daniel even read the Arts section? Probably not. She'd call him later, tonight, because she didn't want to page him at the hospital.

But one call she did want to make—at least thought she did—was to her mother.

Her mother.

Her mother would be having breakfast now, San Francisco time. Sitting in the kitchen reading the *Chronicle* having a piece of toast, psyching up for work. She was, as usual, suffering through summer school. None of the other teachers wanted to spend their vacations in the hot, stuffy school building, but Polly always took the job. If she didn't call now, it would have to wait till tomorrow because she'd be at the theater by the time her mother came home; she didn't want to leave a message.

This was the big call. The call she'd been waiting to make for years. Mom, I got a rave review in the *New York Times*. Now, today. She could finally justify her life.

Camille decided to take a shower. After drying off, she considered running out for a second cup of coffee. Forget it. The last thing she needed was coffee. The phone was ringing again. Lisa. She didn't pick up, just listened. "Hey, sweetie, saw the review. You so totally deserve it. I'm proud of you! Congratulations! Call me!"

She felt proud of Lisa for successfully editing out any jealous, competitive bitchy comments. Could she have done so well?

But she really should call her mother.

She turned on the TV. A rerun of *ER* was on. A younger Anthony Edwards was saving the life of a child who had fallen into a lake ice fishing. When Dr. Green took charge, you knew the child was going to get the best care. The guy playing the father was doing a good job. The show went to a commercial as he prayed over his child, and her eyes filled with tears.

This was ridiculous. She had to call her mother.

She turned off the television.

Dialed. Half wished her mother wouldn't answer.

"Hello."

Polly would be wearing her usual plain, boring straight-leg Levi's and pullover sweater. No makeup. Long, thick unabashedly gray hair that had never seen a drop of Loving Care. It wasn't that her mother was unattractive. She had a good figure for her age, good skin, and a pleasant if not pretty face. But put on some lipstick for god's sake!

"Mom?"

"Camille?"

"I know it's early. I have some news." Pause. "I got a great review in the *Times*." (Why did her voice sound disappointed?) "For this play I'm in."

"Oh. Good for you. How exciting!"

"Isn't that great?"

"That's marvelous! I didn't know you were in anything."

"Just a small production, a showcase, you know, so it's amazing we actually got reviewed. I'll e-mail a copy to you."

"Please do. I'd love to read it. So what is this play?"

"It's a comedy called *Home at Home*. It's not bad, actually. But the reviewer really singled me out. I think it could really help my career."

"You never know."

"No, I mean really. It's incredibly good."

"So e-mail it. I can't wait to read it."

"At the very least I should be able to get an agent now."

"Maybe. But you know how things go in that world."

"Mom, can't you just enjoy this with me? Good news like this doesn't happen very often."

"I'm just saying, don't let it go to your head."

"You think I'm making too big a deal out of it?"

"No, but I wouldn't flaunt it too much. The other people in the cast are bound to be jealous because you got singled out."

"You think I'm going to rub it in?"

"Just be gracious."

"I am gracious! And it's not like I could control the fact that he singled me out!"

"I'm not saying everyone isn't happy for you, but there's bound to be some resentment, that's all, so just be aware."

Typical that her mother had to point out the one possible negative. Of course, Polly hated the whole acting profession, thanks to her father, so *she* was the one with the resentment. Probably hated the fact that she'd gotten this encouragement.

"So of course," Camille said, "you don't want to come see it."

"Oh, honey, you know I'd love to. But I have a zillion papers to correct and I'm supposed to get the kitchen painted. . . ."

"Forget it. It's fine. I didn't think you would, I just . . ."

Why did she even ask? Her mother hated New York. The crowds; the people. When she came to New York, someone—a cab driver, waiter, another pedestrian, a daughter—inevitably made her cry.

"But you will be coming out here in August, won't you?"

"I don't know yet, Mom. We'll see. Anyway, thanks for enjoying this with me."

"Congratulations."

She hung up and stared at the wall mirror, which reflected a row of empty perfume bottles, and tried to get her mother's voice out of her head.

Her father would be so happy for her. He would understand.

Or maybe he'd just be jealous. He never got a rave in the *Times*, though he did get some nice mentions. She had them in a scrapbook.

No, he wouldn't be jealous of her. His own daughter. That was ridiculous.

Or was it? Maybe her mother was jealous, too. Living her depressing life in San Francisco with nothing to look forward to but what? Retiring? Her mother had retired years ago, really. Retreated from life, never remarried, settled for what she had with no ambitions for anything more.

Why shouldn't she have the chance to bask in her success? Maybe she *was* a cut above all the others. And Jeb Sanders had simply recognized that. Paul was just a novice, after all, and Anita was over the hill, and Eddie, for god's sake, was an ex-stand-up fucking comic! She had far more training than the others and certainly more range. Plus she was pretty. Pretty enough to be a leading lady. Idiosyncratic enough to do comedy. Goddamn it, she was a find. And they'd been lucky to cast someone of her caliber in this stupid little production. The whole thing probably worked *because* of her!

Oh god, she thought, as she went to the bathroom to pin up her hair. I'm starting to believe my own press. (But how delightful to *have* press!) What to wear, what to wear . . . (Too bad she had to be Miss Dinsmore today, how would she be able to concentrate?) It would be nice if Daniel happened to read her review. She picked out a short black skirt with a pink and white striped top. But he was probably too absorbed with whatever the hell shrinks read to bother with the Arts section.

She smiled into the bathroom mirror. Anything could still happen. Life was wonderful!

No. Calm down. Relax. A good review was a guarantee of nothing. She couldn't let her ego get so pumped. Lipstick. Just a dab of blush. One thing was for sure. She wouldn't have to spend the rest of her life wondering if she had talent. The truth didn't matter anymore, because the ultimate judgment had now been documented in the *Times*. The paper of record. "Vivacious . . . charming . . . witty . . ." This was tangible. No one could take this away.

Now it was up to her. She got the list of agents in *Ross Reports*. Settled in at her desk. Forced herself to go down the list, called every single one, mentioned the review as soon as possible to every receptionist she reached.

Most of the agents were out of the office. Of course. On a Friday in July they were likely to be on the beach in the Hamptons. But she was determined to go through the entire list no matter what. After ten calls, no one was interested. She kept going. She was not going to take it personally. This was business.

Call number fourteen was the lucky one.

"May I speak to Sylvia Hopkins?"

"May I ask who's calling?"

"Camille Chaplin. I'm in *Home at Home* at the Maverick Theater. We just got a rave in the *Times* this morning."

"Hold please."

Camille held. Sylvia Hopkins got on. "Hello, Camille? Saw the review. Wonderful write-up!"

"Thanks."

"Don't thank me; I had nothing to do with it! Why don't you come in Monday morning so we can chat. Around eleven?"

"I'd love to."

"Great. See you then."

She hung up. And just like that, Camille knew. She was on her way.

Everyone at the theater had a smile for her. And of course, everyone did hate her. But at least no one had been dumped on. And it would help them get audiences. Maybe the play could be extended, and they could take out some ads. If performances started to sell out and a buzz got going around town and some producers came to see what the fuss was all about, they might even move the play to a larger theater Off Broadway. This would mean new contracts, pay, and exposure that would bring in even more reviews, agents, and producers.... This was how it worked. This was what you needed. One good write-up from Jeb Sanders and all their lives could change.

After the initial flurry of congratulations all around (no one gave Camille any special attention) the actors didn't refer to the review again. Just put on their makeup and waited for their entrances with pleasant anticipation. After all, on some level it wasn't cool to give the review too much credence. That gave the reviewer too much power.

But it did affect their performances. They did the show that night with renewed energy. And the audience—about fifty people!—laughed much louder than ever before.

Of course, they'd all read the review. They'd all been alerted to the laugh lines. It was like they were puppets, and the review had told them what to think. So maddening (even though for once it had worked in her favor) that a review could make this much difference.

She wondered what Jeb Sanders looked like, and if he was single, and if he would like to have an affair with her. Maybe his praise was his way of making a pass, and she should call him up. What a weapon to have: a powerful theater reviewer on her side. Like Eve Harrington and Addison DeWitt in *All About Eve,* her favorite movie of all time.

At the curtain call, Camille got the loudest applause. She bowed and grinned from ear to ear. Lisa could quit. *But I can never leave this. Nothing gives me a high like this. I love the theater.* She resolved to remember this feeling. Nothing else in life came close. If only her father was here to see this.

After the show, they all went out for drinks at the Holiday. Motherly Anita (hooray for her, sticking it out this long!), bitter Eddie (he was an artist—couldn't force him to take a conventional job!), innocent Paul (just don't think it will always be this easy!). Marie, who was talking too loud and too fast because she'd had too many drinks, could very well be a genius. And that woman who did the lights—what was her name?—she was always on time and reliable and she wasn't even being paid (or was she?). Even the costume designer was brilliant. Yes, in the theater, you have to let everyone do his or her job. It takes a community of people working together. And what a special thing, in this cold and cruel world, where it's so easy to get lonely and depressed. Everyone needs something like this that gives you a chance to play with other people. And now, finally, she didn't have to feel bitter. She didn't have to throw all her dreams away!

When she got home at two A.M., she played some new messages. Maybe one would be some director or producer calling to tell her she must do his next play because she was so fabulous.

The first was another actress who she hadn't spoken to in years. "I saw the review. Congratulations. That's so cool. Maybe we could get together for lunch sometime."

If you think I'm going to do something to jump start your career, forget it. Erase.

The second one was Flora, her cousin in Philadelphia, full of congratulations. No longer would she have to face her relatives and feel like a complete loser. Erase.

The third was from Daniel. "Hi. I have a good movie picked out for Sunday. Call when you have a chance."

Obviously, he didn't know about the review. She wished she felt happier to hear his voice. Was he going to take up her valuable energy while she really needed to focus on her career? She hesitated. Erase.

Chapter Eleven

Neither of them had ever seen *The Snake Pit*. Depressing. But Olivia de Havilland, who Camille could not watch without thinking of Melanie in *Gone With the Wind*, was great as a woman who has a nervous breakdown. Her husband put her in a state mental institution populated by wacko women, mean nurses, and benevolent god-like psychiatrists. "Is that how your patients see you?" she asked. "The kind, wise man with the ability to save souls?"

"I *am* kind and wise, with the ability to save souls."

"I think you're spending too much time around unbalanced women who inflate your ego."

"Everyone needs their ego inflated now and then," he said.

"I suppose." Thanks to the *Times*, her ego was nicely inflated at the moment, as a matter of fact.

"Congratulations again on your review," he said, kissing her on the cheek.

"Thank you."

"Maybe I can come see you in the play now."

"Maybe," she teased. "If you're good."

The Snake Pit was practically an infomercial for Freudian psychiatry. Olivia thrived in her sessions with Dr. Kirk, played by an actor Camille didn't recognize. But then Olivia made the mistake of accusing one of the mean nurses of being in love with Dr. Kirk, and the nurse stuck her in the craziest ward—the "snake pit" of mad women. Lots of them were talking to themselves. Others were catatonic. Or hostile. Or friendly but afflicted with tics. Most annoying was the woman who kept dancing around the place as if she'd escaped from a Martha Graham performance.

"Are these the kind of people you hang out with all day?"

"It's not that far off, really."

"Isn't it depressing?"

"It can be."

As the movie came to its triumphant resolution, Olivia came to realize that she had idealized her father, who died when she was six, and hated her cold and distant mother. Finally, the psychiatrist helped her unearth one of her last memories of her father before he died, when he took sides with his wife against his little girl. Olivia had gotten so angry, she'd smashed a doll he'd given her to pieces. And then he got sick and died. And she felt like it was her fault. And she felt guilty and unlovable.

Reassured by Dr. Kirk that the illness would've killed her father whether she'd had the tantrum or not, Olivia come out of her funk. At the end, Olivia said to the doctor as she was being discharged from the hospital, "Do you know how I know that I'm cured? I'm not in love with you anymore."

He replied to her: "You never really were."

And she smiled and got on a bus with her husband to go home.

The credits came on and Daniel rewound the tape.

"Do all your patients fall in love with you?" she asked.

"I don't consider them cured until they do."

"They'd be crazy not to, right?"

Did she almost say she loved him? Time to change the subject! "So do you still want to go to my show this week?"

"I'd be honored. What changed your mind?"

"The review, I guess. And now we're getting great audiences. People are laughing even when it isn't funny. Just be warned: I have to wear an ugly, totally unflattering dress."

"I'm sure you look beautiful," he said, sitting back down next to her and putting his arm around her.

She nestled into his shoulder. "How can you be so sure?"

"Don't all your audience members fall in love with you?"

He kissed her. They were sweet, gentle kisses. He was too nice to her. She didn't deserve it.

But she didn't make him stop. He wanted to kiss her, and she wanted him to want to, and she let him.

After all, this was the routine. Every evening they were together.

Talk, eat, watch a video. Talk some more. Kiss. Get undressed—the exact same way every time.

He would take off her top.

Then his shirt.

Kiss some more. His warm hand cupping her breast. Made her feel so safe, so secure. She knew he loved her body, and now she knew he loved her.

He would start to take off her jeans.

She would take them the rest of the way off.

They would kiss some more.

Then he would take off his own pants. By the time they were in their underwear, they'd make their way to the bed. The underwear came off when they were in the bed. Then he would put on his condom while she waited on the bed.

Daniel loved his routines. Not such a bad thing, really. As a matter of fact, it was incredibly reassuring. He knew where to touch her. She knew where he wanted to be touched. He would have his orgasm. She would have hers. Safe sex. In every way.

But when they made love that night, Camille just couldn't get into it. She had no wish to imagine herself as Olivia, who seemed like such a little girl in the movie and, even at the end, still did not really seem like a full-grown "woman." What would Olivia's life be like post movie? Would she be able to love her handsome husband? Would she allow her husband to love her? Would they have a good sex life? It seemed unlikely. But the movie had to end on a high note. So no one would ever know.

Chapter Twelve

She went underground at DisAstor Place, reached her stop in ten minutes, and walked up the stairs to emerge through Grand Central Station at Forty-second Street. She felt good in her royal blue slip dress, apart from unpleasant memories of the last time she'd worn it for Norman.

Sylvia Hopkins had an office in 1401 Broadway, a building that was famous for having many "show business" people as tenants. She entered through a revolving door into a deco lobby with marble floors and an old-fashioned newsstand and passed—it was unbelievable—Leonardo DiCaprio! He was coming out of an elevator just as she was about to go in! This was a good sign. Not that she was particularly superstitious, but there was some good karma happening here.

She took the elevator to the tenth floor and walked down the hall feeling like Katharine Hepburn in *Stage Door*. SYLVIA HOPKINS TALENT AGENCY was stenciled on the glass door. Even though she'd been around too long to be seduced by stenciled letters on a glass door, the sight made her heart flutter. She turned the knob and walked in. A pretty, young (frustrated actress?) blonde sat behind the reception desk and looked her over with obvious disdain. "May I help you?" Southern accent. Gold charm bracelet. Coral sweater set.

"Hi, I have an appointment with Ms. Hopkins. Camille Chaplin. Eleven o'clock."

"Picture and résumé?"

Camille held it out.

"Take a seat," she said, not taking the résumé. "You can give that to her." She nodded toward Sylvia's inner office.

Camille nodded and smiled, sat down on a chair, and ignored the stack of *Hollywood Reporter* magazines on the glass coffee table in front of her. Fifteen minutes passed. Finally a very tall, broad shouldered young man wearing jeans, a T-shirt, and a baseball cap emerged with Sylvia Hopkins.

"Thanks," he said. "So if they need any ball players for the shoot, think of me. The lefty with a great knuckleball."

"I'll be in touch." It was obvious by her tone that she wouldn't.

The three women watched him leave (he did have a nice ass) and then Sylvia Hopkins turned to Camille.

She was a bottled redhead in her sixties. Her skin was too freckled from too much sun. She wore a tight orange dress—too loud for her figure, which wasn't what it used to be—and matching orange heels.

Camille held out her hand. "Hi, I'm Camille Chaplin."

Sylvia Hopkins took her hand, hardly even grasping before letting it go, and said, "So nice to meet you. Come into my office. Did you bring a picture?"

"Yes." Camille handed it to her before sitting down.

"Good. I know you mailed one, but I can never keep track."

Camille had not mailed one since they'd just spoken on the phone, but it seemed unnecessary to mention. Indeed, Sylvia's desk had the usual piles of headshots. On the floor to the side of her desk she had more stacks of headshots. And a wastebasket next to her desk overflowed with them. On the wall were posters of various recent Off Broadway shows, some signed by the actors.

"So," Sylvia said, studying the headshot. "You got a great review."

"Yes, I did." Camille knew she sounded stiff. Like she was manufacturing enthusiasm. She took a few deep breaths and tried to relax and think of something to say. "Everyone in the show is very excited."

"You should be more excited. You were singled out. Congratulations."

"Thanks."

Sylvia Hopkins rubbed her chin. Looked her over. Sized her up.

Camille smiled. Big. Her mouth was one of her best assets. Julia Roberts, Cameron Diaz, Calista Flockhart—all had big mouths. Jumbo smiles conveyed jumbo happiness.

"Would you like to hear my monologue?"

"That won't be necessary," she said, reading through Camille's list of credits on the back of the headshot.

Not necessary? Oh yes. Sylvia Hopkins had read the review, could see her résumé, *knew* she was good. Camille sat erect. Maintained her smile. All these years of paying her dues were going to pay off now. I'd like to send you out, she would say. We'll build on this review in the *New York Times* and get you in to see the top casting directors; I'll have you working in no time.

Sylvia put Camille's résumé down on the center of her desk. "So," she said, "I have to be honest. I have ten more just like you."

Her big smile froze.

"You're pretty. Talented. And so are lots of other girls. I wish I could tell you otherwise. But the supply exceeds the demand. Disappointed?"

"Oh, no . . . Really. I don't have any illusions left about this business."

Don't cry.

"A good review is a good review. But it won't get you anywhere in itself."

Do not dare, under any circumstance, cry.

"The truth is, even good reviews in the *New York Times* don't mean all that much anymore. I mean, who doesn't have one at this point. How old are you?"

Camille couldn't remember what the hell age she was. Thirty-four? Twenty-eight? Five? "With all due respect, even if you have ten more who seem to be just like me . . . they aren't just like me."

"So how are you special?" Sylvia Hopkins could not have sounded more bored.

How do you tell a stranger how special you are? Especially if you aren't feeling particularly special. Especially if you're feeling pretty goddamn cliché. "I can do comedy. I can do drama. When I was at the Royal Academy of Dramatic Art, I was Rosalind in *As You Like It*, Helena in *All's Well That Ends Well*—"

"Anyone can take a class. Tell me why I should sign you."

Because you would save my life? Rescue me from bitterness? Keep me from abject failure?

"I noticed in *Backstage* they're casting for a production of *The Seagull* at the Vineyard."

"Yes."

"I want an audition."

"So do hundreds of other actresses."

"If you could just send me in. Give me that one opportunity . . ."

"I don't sign people for just one shot. It takes time to build a career."

Okay, calm down, she told herself. This woman wanted to be convinced. It was her job to find talent. And it's your job to figure out a way to convince her you have it. "You read my review. You see me in the flesh. What's not to believe in? I'm a cut above the rest. All I need is a chance to get seen by the people who cast the plays. If I had that chance, I swear to God, I would blow them away. I've used Nina's monologue as an audition piece for years."

"Aren't you a little old for Nina?"

She blanched. "Well . . ." If Norman Freed thought she could be twenty-seven, it wasn't that big a stretch to see her as a few years younger than that. . . . Was it?

"Never mind. Go ahead. Do Nina. Blow me away."

Standing up raised the energy level. So she rose, flexed, took a deep breath, closed her eyes.

She was Nina. Romantic, restless, theatrically ambitious Nina. She opened her eyes. Began.

"He doesn't believe in the theater. He laughed at my dreams con-tinuously to the point I didn't believe in them either or believe in myself. . . ."

The phone rang.

"Hold that thought."

Camille held.

"Hello. Uh-huh. Uh-huh. Uh-huh. You listen to me. Are you listening to me? Then listen. You take what you can get, sweetheart. You know why? You're lucky to get this gig. I have someone in my office right this minute who would be thrilled to take that part away from you. That's right. Good girl. Listen, buy yourself some Ajax and a can of Raid and the place'll be good as new."

She hung up.

"Can you believe it?" Sylvia looked at Camille seeking sympathy. "I trouble myself to get this girl a part in the chorus of *Beauty and the Beast* down in Disney World and she has the nerve to complain about the motel they put her up in! People in this business don't know when they have it good, let me tell you. They read about the stars in *Entertainment Weekly* and think it's going to be the same for them and I'm the one whose gotta hear about it. Okay, I'm ready, hon. Got scads of people behind you, let's get on with it."

Camille tried to breathe. How could she find her way to Nina now? "If you don't mind," she said, "I'd like to do some-thing else. A woman playwright wrote it. The play hasn't been produced yet, but it deserves to be."

"Let her rip."

Camille didn't need a moment to get into the headspace; she was already there.

"You are a slimeball." She looked straight at Sylvia Hopkins. "Your cruelty would make anyone want to quit the theater. But I'm not going to let you get to me." Sylvia Hopkins was about to interrupt, so she raised her voice a notch. "I know what you're thinking! You know how hard it is to get anywhere in this business. And it's hard seeing me suffer all these years. But the truth is"—she got up and sat on the edge of the desk and leaned straight toward Sylvia—"you can't hurt me. Because I get to do something I love. While you are condemned to sitting behind a desk annihilating the self-respect of one creative person after another. And no matter how much you degrade me . . . no matter how many scummy, self-centered assholes like you try to make my life miserable . . . I will not let you get to me! Because I am better than you!"

Sylvia Hopkins was, for the moment, struck dumb. Was this a monologue? Or was this actress having a nervous breakdown. Camille didn't know herself. She took her picture and resume off the desk and tossed them into the wastebasket. This wasn't really what she wanted to do, but she couldn't stop herself. The emotional arc had to be completed with the action. Once she'd done that, there was nothing to do but exit.

So she exited. Took the elevator. Walked through the lobby. Now was when Sylvia Hopkins would come sprinting out of her office to find her. Dash frantically out of the building to catch up with her. Leap out onto the street to search desperately for her among the hordes of people walking down Broadway. She'd cuss at herself for letting this one get away, then she'd run down the street, run, for god's sake, dodging all the people in her way and, by some miracle, catch up, out of breath, to tell Camille that she had been fantastic. What a performance! She wanted to sign her then and there. And, by the way, she'd get her seen for that *Seagull* audition this week.

Camille exited the lobby.

Nobody followed her anywhere.

Forget the subway. She needed to walk this adrenaline rush out of her system. She had not blown Sylvia Hopkins away. She had simply blown it. A top-tier agent and she'd had a fit. Okay. It probably hadn't affected the outcome. But she could hear her father chiding. *Did Sarah Heartburn have a temper tantrum? This is not the way a professional behaves.* And she *was* a professional, even if she couldn't get cast in an Off Broadway production or get paid for the parts she did get. Even if she was too old to play Nina!

Chapter Thirteen

Lisa was waiting for her at a table by the wall at the Orlin Café. Camille dreaded this. A few days had passed since Sylvia, but it still made her ill and now she'd have to recount the gory details.

"So tell me! I've been dying to hear!"

Should she lie? No. She needed the emotional support even if, on some level, Lisa would enjoy her failure. "It was a catastrophe."

"I think you must be exaggerating."

"I think I must be losing it."

"Did you do your Desdemona monologue?"

"Not quite."

"*Private Lives?*"

"It was an improv, actually. I told her what an asshole she was."

"You're kidding, right?"

"I wish I was."

A waitress came and they both ordered salads with blue cheese on the side. The café was dark inside even though outside the sun was shining gloriously. When she'd first moved to New York, the Orlin was a small, intimate place, but a few years back the owners bought the space next door and expanded. It lost something. She never felt like she owned the place after that. Now it was just a restaurant that reminded her how much things had changed since she'd moved here.

"Well," Lisa ventured, "maybe it was a good thing to do. For once, you determined your own future, right? You took control."

"Or lost it."

"There's some relief in determining your own fate."

"It just wasn't the fate I wanted."

"She wasn't the right agent for you. Someone even better is going to come along, and one day she's going to kick herself in the ass for letting you go."

"Thanks for saying so, anyway."

"I'm sorry if I haven't been too available lately," Lisa said.

"That's okay."

"No it's not. But I think I've finally decided . . . and maybe this isn't the best time to mention it. . . ."

It was obvious what she was going to say.

"Okay. Yes, I'm marrying him."

"Lisa. That's great!" Was this how her mother felt when she had to congratulate her for the review? Hollow. Insincere. "I'm so happy for you."

"We haven't set a date yet. And I'm still moving in with him at the end of the month. I'd like to get married in a church, but everything books up like two years in advance, so maybe, I'm thinking, we should just go barefoot on the beach."

"That sounds romantic." Yawn.

The waitress brought their salads. There was a nice-looking wedge of tomato. Camille dipped it into the blue cheese and savored the sweet and tart. So it was settled. They would most certainly grow apart. And she would be jealous. Even though she didn't want the life Lisa was choosing. But still. Lisa's life was going to become so much easier. Not that easier was necessarily better. But it was easier.

"What are you thinking?" Lisa asked.

"I'm happy for you."

"You're pissed."

"I'm not."

"We'll still see each other all the time."

"Of course."

But of course they wouldn't. And when they did, it wouldn't be the same. Camille smiled again as if she was happy for her friend and then forked a piece of lettuce. Anything to avoid Lisa's look of pity. Pity! Who should feel sorry for whom? She dipped the lettuce in a dab of dressing and asked, curious to see how much Lisa had fooled herself, "Do you love him?"

Lisa attempted to smile but looked tense. "Yes. Of course. And he's crazy about me."

"Yes," Camille agreed. "Wally adores you." Well. Lisa never was that great an actress. And you can't expect to get anywhere in this business if you're ambivalent. And she did look old for her age. So maybe she was doing the right thing. Fine, quit, marry, have a baby. No one, she thought, is stopping you.

Chapter Fourteen

Saturday afternoon, the day of the last performance, Camille walked down to SoHo to relax herself by trying on clothes she couldn't afford. She wandered into French Corner on Broadway and thought how Daniel wouldn't be able to keep his hands off her if she showed up in one of their lace Dolce & Gabbana tops on display with a tight red skirt. She'd read somewhere J.Lo and Angelina Jolie were regulars in this store that catered to the bad-girl look. Well, she was a regular too, if "just looking" counted.

After checking out Label on Lafayette, Big Drop on Spring (the cutest little mod mini-dresses) and Rampage (affordable but disposable), she felt her optimism creeping back. At Scoop she paused in front of a rack of gorgeous, classic Michael Kors dresses all priced over $600. If she married Daniel, she could buy any one she wanted.

"May I help you?" There was doubt in the salesgirl's voice, as if she'd read Camille's last tax return.

"Just looking, thanks."

She left the store. She didn't need a $600 dress. A $600 dress was not going to make her happy. Why was she wasting her time? It was ridiculous to let Sylvia Hopkins—or Lisa's defection—destroy her good mood. She'd barely allowed herself to enjoy her review! She needed to take advantage of this good news, not sink into depression.

She walked back to her apartment, went straight to her computer, and wrote a cover letter that would go in a mailing with copies of her review to all the agents she'd already called. She printed out mailing labels and assembled everything while she blasted an old David Bowie CD. She worked so intently, she was almost late for her seven o'clock call and had to rush to detour to the post office, where she put forty manila envelopes into the mail. Who cared what Sylvia Hopkins thought? Or her mother. She was not giving up. And her father would be so proud.

Marie stood in the doorway of the dressing room and announced, "Completely sold out."

"House seats?"

"Nothing. You should hear the answering machine. It's filled with desperate people who suddenly have to see this show as if their lives depended on it. We already had to put in extra chairs. The center aisle is blocked. If the fire marshal comes, they'll close the show!"

Camille was glad Daniel was seeing it on such a good night. It certainly made her life seem more exciting than it was. She felt energized by the crowd and gave her best performance yet.

But she also felt the play could not possibly live up to the hype and that, on some level, everyone out there had to be disappointed. She imagined the audience collectively punishing them, in their minds, for duping them with the overly generous review and trapping them in the hot, stuffy theater.

But it was clear, by curtain call, that she was imagining this antagonistic relationship. The applause was genuine and sustained and the actors were compelled to take four curtain calls. What did Daniel think? She wanted him to be impressed. But she also wanted him to see that the play wasn't as good as people now seemed to think it was.

Or maybe it was.

Now she wasn't so sure herself.

After the show, Camille lingered backstage to soak in some
of the cheeriness. She changed into jeans and a black halter
top, let her hair down and fixed her makeup as everyone else
yakked on about how incredible it would be if the play moved
Off Broadway. She kept her mouth shut. Their enthusiasm
made her nervous. Nothing in the theater was real until the
moment it was actually happening. And the reality was that, as
it stood, they were all back to looking for the next part.

She hung her brown dress on the rack for the last time. She
would miss the innocent Mary Ann, especially now that she
didn't have to be her anymore. Eddie was just opening up a
bottle of champagne, but she had to go to Daniel.

"Aren't you coming to Ciao?" Anita asked. "It's not a party
without you."

"Maybe we'll meet you there," she said. "If not . . ."

"We'll see you when we move this runaway monster hit to
Off Broadway!" Paul said, and everyone cheered.

"You got that right."

She found Daniel coming out of the men's room carrying a
bouquet of pink and orange tulips. He wore gray flannel pants
and a navy blue suit jacket and seemed out of place. For a moment, she wasn't sure if she felt superior to him because he
looked so conventional or inferior because of how dingy the
theater was. He handed her the flowers.

"These are beautiful! You're so sweet!"

"You were great. Congratulations."

"Thank you . . ." She kissed him on the cheek.

"You were really great."

"Were you okay in there? It was so hot and stuffy. . . ."

"I didn't notice. All my attention was on you. Can I take
you out to dinner? Someplace special?"

"I don't know. The others are all going out."

"You want to go with them?"

"I'm not sure. . . ."

"It's your last night. You should be with them."

"But you'll be bored."

"No I won't."

They walked to Ciao. Her mind was replaying a loop of her finer moments. The audience had been great, laughing as if they'd been hired for a sitcom taping. It was intoxicating. "The audience seemed to enjoy it," she said, hoping to get him back on the subject of her performance.

"They were really laughing."

"I feel bad when everyone's all squished in like that, though they could've come when the seats were empty instead of following the review in like lemmings."

"You wouldn't let me come when the seats were empty."

"I didn't mean you, of course."

The restaurant was crowded. Marie had said she'd reserved a table, and there was an empty one up front, presumably for them, but it didn't seem like everyone would fit. "If you want, we could sit at our own table."

"You should be with the others."

"It's so packed. You won't be comfortable."

"It's up to you," he said.

She felt sure he wanted to be alone with her. So she asked for a table for two. They were seated in the back. She immediately regretted it. She propped up the bouquet against the wall and kept her eye on the door.

The noise level was really deafening. Everyone was competing, trying to pitch their voices over the manic chatter charging up the room. "It's loud," Daniel said.

"What?!"

Daniel yelled. "I don't usually like eating in loud places!"

"Sorry! Can't hear you!" She was teasing him, but he wasn't getting it.

"Never mind!"

Daniel ordered them two glasses of red wine. They both buttered pieces of bread. She wanted him to elaborate on how and when she was great, but he settled into silence, and she realized she'd have to get it out of him.

"So did you like the play?"

"It was good."

"You sound hesitant." He seemed tense about something, or was she the one who was tense?

"Well. It wasn't anything I would've chosen to go to on my own. I don't know."

"It's a comedy. It's not meant to be deep."

"I know."

"But you liked me?" She felt like a child.

"Yes. Especially considering the part you had to play."

She shot him a look. What did he mean by that?

"I mean," he said, "it must be fun."

"Performing?"

"Acting. Applause. Attention . . ."

"It's very addictive, it's true."

The waitress brought the wine and they sipped in silence. Did he sense she wanted to be with the others? He did seem subdued. "Is something wrong?" she asked.

"No."

"You seem quiet. More than usual."

"Well. I will say, it was hard to watch you kiss that guy on stage."

"Paul? He's gay. And don't worry. I'm not into trying to convert."

"You fooled me."

"That's my job."

"You're good at your job."

"So you really felt jealous?"

"Yeah, a little." He paused. "Did you feel strange being in your underwear on stage?"

"I wasn't in my underwear. Mary Ann was in her underwear."

"Sure, but . . . You know . . . it was your body in front of everyone like that. . . ."

"I didn't show any more than a bathing suit."

"I know, but—"

"You thought I looked fat?"

"No. You looked great. I just . . . it made me feel uncomfortable. I wanted to cover you up." Now he had a tense smile on his face. "But it was worse watching you kiss that guy."

"Come on, Daniel. You can't take it seriously."

"But still. You were kissing him."

"So are you saying this is a real problem for you?"

"I'm just telling you how I felt."

"So what are you saying?"

The crowd was coming in. Eddie, Marie, Paul, Anita, that woman who did the lights. Even the playwright, and he hadn't shown his face since dress rehearsal.

"You want to be with your friends?"

"No . . ."

"You want to move to their table?"

"I don't think there's room, anyway," she said, looking over at them with regret. Though there was possibly just enough room for them to squeeze in.

"So what will you do now?" he asked. "How do you deal with the fact that it's ending?"

She turned to him and shrugged.

"You don't have anything else lined up?"

"No! I don't! Would you stop asking me questions?!"

He couldn't possibly understand how hard it was to get cast, even in a shitty little production like this. And she didn't want to mention the chance of it moving. Didn't want to jinx it. "I'm just going to say hello to the others. Do you mind?"

"Go ahead."

Camille squeezed her way between the closely spaced tables. Why the hell was she dating a psychiatrist who lived on the Upper East Side? Did she think she was actually going to *marry* him and become a part of that world? That wasn't her, *this* was. This crazy bunch of people was her crowd. She stood behind Eddie. He turned his head up at her and asked, snidely, "You and lover boy have a fight?"

"Just saying hello."

"We miss you!" Paul said from the other side of the table. "Squeeze in with us! We'll make room for you and Dr. Freud."

"I think he looks more like Dr. Martin," Anita said, referring to one of the hunky actors on *All My Children*.

"He makes me think of Dr. Seuss," Eddie said.

Camille smirked. "That's because you have the maturity of a three-year-old. So Marie, I'm over there feeling sad we had our last performance. And you all seem to be so happy and celebratory."

Marie leaned back in her chair and pushed her glasses up her nose. "Well, my dear, there were some investors here tonight. For the second time. They love it. And they're interested in moving it."

"Really?" She felt a surge of adrenaline.

"Of course there are details to work out. But that's how they were talking."

"That's fantastic!"

"And of course, if that happens, we'll do everything we can to keep the same cast."

"So . . . they have money? That they're willing to invest?"

"They have money. And . . ."

"This is the best part," Paul interjected.

"One of them owns the Century Theatre. You know the theater—on Union Square?"

"Of course." She swallowed. The Century was beautiful. One of the few New York theaters that achieved just the right mix of grandeur and intimacy.

"He says the show there now is about to close, and he might be able to book us as early as August. Of course anything can happen, but I have a really good feeling about this."

"Just watch," Eddie narrowed his eyes at Camille. "She's going to say it'll never happen."

But the wine was kicking in, and she felt a wave of optimism. Beautiful, wonderful optimism. "Why shouldn't it happen? All the pieces are in place."

"It's going to happen!" Paul said. "It is fucking going to happen!"

Camille laughed crazily.

"Don't you think you should get back to Dr. Seuss?" Eddie asked.

Daniel was sitting by the wall. Quiet, somber, staring into space. Thinking about some patient? At that moment, with the promise of success in the air, he seemed like a bump on a log. She knew she wasn't being fair. But she felt it. She wished he hadn't come tonight.

She turned back to the table. Even Hank the playwright was drunk and singing like Frank Sinatra on uppers. "If you can make it there . . . you'll make it anywhere . . . !"

"This is incredible," she said to Marie. "Thank you so much."

"Don't thank me, thank yourself. Congratulations."

"Congratulations to everyone!" Paul yelled, holding up his glass but the racket in the restaurant drowned out his voice.

Camille laughed, shook her head, and squeezed through the labyrinth of tables back to Daniel. "This place is crazy tonight, isn't it!" she said, as she sat down.

"It's pretty noisy."

"So Marie says there were backers there tonight. They want to move the play to The Century, which is a really great theater."

"Great."

Did he care how fantastic this was or even understand?

"Of course it might not happen. But if it does . . ."

"You will be very happy."

"I will be euphoric!"

Daniel nodded and smiled, but with the distance of someone merely observing.

A waiter asked if they were ready to order. Camille hadn't even looked at her menu yet.

"We'll need a few minutes," Daniel said.

"No problem."

He looked down at his menu, but Camille looked back at the others. She didn't want to eat some big fattening meal. She wanted to jump up and down and dance and scream at the top of her lungs that something good was finally happening to her!

"Do you mind if we squeeze in at the other table? I'm not really hungry and . . ."

"Sure," he said. "No problem."

So he followed her—carrying her flowers—to the others, who squinched together to make room. As she got progressively drunker and giggly and high, poor Daniel gamely tried to make conversation with the dull girl who did the lighting. Camille imagined he must be delighted to be there with her (so animated and entertaining) as she told everyone a story about the time she did a production in Santa Rosa and her leading man did the entire second act of *The Iceman Cometh* with his fly down. When the waiter returned for more drink orders she was going to get another Cosmopolitan, but Daniel leaned over and said, "You know, it's so loud in here, and I'm beat. Do you mind if we head out?"

But she was having such a good time. Wasn't he? Maybe he wanted to make love with her. She wouldn't be surprised— she was feeling especially attractive—but she wasn't sure if she was in the mood. Though it wouldn't take much to get her there, and she would never sleep tonight anyway, she knew, she'd be replaying the high points of the evening over and over in her head. Anyway, Anita was leaving, and Marie seemed ready to go too. . . .

"If you want to stay with your friends," he said, "I understand."

Was he going to leave without her? That wouldn't look good. Oh well. It was late. "It's fine. Let's go."

Daniel threw two twenties on the table. Camille remembered to take her flowers and congratulated everyone once more ("You were wonderful, darling!") and kissed them, one by one, on the cheek. She hoped he was enjoying their good cheer. It had to be fun hanging out with the actors after the performance—to have the chance to take in this happy scene.

The street was quiet and the fresh air felt good. She wished he would take her in his arms and kiss her hard on the lips.

They reached her building. As she got her key from her purse, he said, "Thank you for inviting me tonight."

"I'm glad you could make it." She wasn't sure if she wanted him to come up. She wasn't sure if he wanted to come up. "Would you like to come up?"

"Do you want me to?"

"Sure."

When they were in her bed making love, she was somewhere else in her head. Sitting in a French bistro with Lisa. Eric Hughes at the other table. Meg was talking to him, but he ignored her and turned around to look at Camille.

Their eyes locked.

He got up from his table and came to her. Held out his hand. "Come with me," he said, in his upper-crust British accent. She put her hand in his and savored having all eyes on her—Meg Ryan livid—as he led her out of the restaurant. He took her to his black, no, white limo. No, black. His elegant shiny black limo, and she slid into the back seat, feeling guilty for leaving Lisa behind, but she'd understand. The limo pulled out and before she had a chance to take in the accoutrements like a mini-TV and bar, he put his arm around her. "Meg was boring me to tears."

She looked into her lap demurely.

"That woman," he went on, "has never made an interesting acting choice in her life. And then I couldn't help but notice you across the room."

She looked up at him with the tiniest bit of a smile because, of course, this happened all the time.

"You are absolutely stunning. I have to have you."

The limo sped uptown as he pulled up her dress, pulled down her thong. He kissed her hard as he eased her down so she was flat on her back. They started rocking together and she felt his hard penis, knew he was dying to be inside her, crazy for her, couldn't stop himself. "Now. Please ... I'm sorry ..." He slowly but deliberately entered her. "Have to have you ... Please ..." Then he climaxed with relief and looked straight into her eyes and almost pleaded, "I love you, oh god, I love you."

She waited for Daniel to finish having his orgasm, then waited patiently for him to remove his penis. He went to the bathroom to get rid of the condom. She got out of bed then, slipped a cotton tank and shorts on, and passed him on her way in to the bathroom.

After peeing, she got back into bed. They kissed gently on the lips. And she fell into a deep, exhausted sleep.

Chapter Fifteen

She woke up annoyed. She wanted her apartment to herself. She closed her eyes and turned away from Daniel. But then he cuddled up to her. She feared he was going to get aroused. She really just wanted to have a cup of coffee. "Morning," she said, wriggling out from under the quilt.

"Morning," he said without opening his eyes.

She was out of bread. But she did have eggs that hadn't expired. Maybe she would make him pancakes. He would like that. And it would relieve some of her guilt over wishing he wasn't there. She got out a bowl and some flour.

By the time he emerged from the bedroom, Camille already had a stack on a plate for him and felt in a much better mood. It was rather fun playing the good hostess. She reached to the back of her refrigerator. "And I think I have . . . Yes!" She found the glass bottle. "Some real maple syrup. I haven't used it in about two years, but it should be fine."

"Look at this," he said, sitting down at her table and letting her place the pancakes in front of him. "This is great. How did you know I love pancakes?"

"Who doesn't love pancakes?" she said, pouring him coffee.

"My mother used to make the best pancakes," he said. She watched as he took a bite of hers. "But these are better."

"Thank you. That's very high praise. But don't get any ideas about my cooking abilities."

"I'm sure you're a wonderful cook."

"Like the Big Bang, unproven."

She went back to the stove and stirred up the batter to make some for herself.

"I bet," he said, "you'll make a great mom some day."

The batter made a very loud sizzling sound as she poured it on her cast iron pan.

"Moi?"

"Why not?"

She poured one more puddle onto the pan. She could just make three fit. "I would not make a good mother. I have no maternal instincts. The idea of spending an entire day with a child is unimaginable. What does one talk about?"

"It's different when it's your own child."

"I don't know. . . ." She poured herself a second cup of coffee, aware that her stance on this might alienate him completely. But she couldn't pretend to be Suzy Homemaker—not now, not with her hopes so high about the play moving. He had to know how badly she wanted that, so why was he even bringing this up? She shouldn't have misled him with breakfast.

"Your pancakes are burning," he said.

She turned back to the stove. Smoke was seething up from the pan. "Shoot. You see . . . I have this tendency to keep the flame too high." She grabbed the spatula and got them onto a plate. The rims were burnt, but the middles could be salvaged. She sat down across from him and started trimming off the black edges.

He was done with his. Was he going to sit there and watch her eat? Nothing was right. If only she had a newspaper. "Sorry if I seem edgy," she said.

"You're probably hungry. Maybe I'll make myself some more." After pouring the batter, he turned around and asked her, "So what do you think about the institution of marriage?"

"What?"

"You heard me."

She speared a piece of pancake with her fork. "I think marriage is a lovely way to end romantic comedies."

"So you aren't really interested in that for yourself?"

She ate another piece. His eyebrows seemed arched even higher than usual. He was freaking her out. "What do *you* think of marriage?"

"Are you avoiding my question?"

"Are you avoiding mine?"

"I happen to think that even though it's not a perfect institution, it's the best thing we've come up with. Especially if you want kids."

"And you want kids."

"Yes."

"And you should have them. You would make a wonderful father."

"And you would make a wonderful mother."

"You're full of surprises this morning."

"How so?"

"I usually regard you as having good judgment."

"Maybe I do. . . ."

"I don't know." She nibbled one of the burnt rims of her pancake. The charcoal taste mixed with syrup wasn't bad.

"You would be an interesting mother."

"Interesting? Is that good?" *Interesting* was one of those words. If she wanted a part in a play, but she didn't think the play itself was very good, she would tell the writer the play was *interesting*.

"Definitely. Not boring. Not a boring wife, either."

So he wanted to marry her. And have a child with her.

He ate his second batch of pancakes while still standing by the stove. She dipped her finger into the syrup and licked it. Took a sip of coffee, washing down the sweet taste. Sunlight poured through the white lace curtains she'd bought in London. Glistening syrup was congealing on her plate. How do people do it? How do they commit to one person, one life, one future, forever? It felt like an ending, not a beginning.

"I can't think of anything right now except the fact that this play might be moving to Off Broadway. You can understand that, right? So why don't we have this conversation again later. Is that okay?"

"I just wanted to give you a sense of how I'm feeling. And get a sense of how you feel. And I guess . . . I got that."

He put his plate in her sink. And she had a sinking feeling. She didn't want to lose this man. She'd be lucky to have him. Have his child. Be secure with a sweet, sensitive man who loved her. She should want to live that life. But marriage should not be a should. Should it?

Chapter Sixteen

All she could think about was when and how the show would move. She tried to make use of her time by making follow-up phone calls to the agents. She hated doing this. All the assistants who answered the phones (undoubtedly frustrated actresses) took pleasure in brushing her off. She couldn't get an interview. Not one.

But she wouldn't give up. Not when this good thing was so close to happening. It was not time to give up. She told herself: *You are not allowed to think this is not going to happen.*

Even that was too negative. She tried again.

You must think this is going to happen.

Still not right.

This is going to happen.

It must happen.

It will.

She missed putting on her frumpy brown dress and being Mary Ann the kindergarten teacher. Could it be that the *Times* review was going to add up to nothing?

She took a walk. Maybe it would be better, she mused while checking out a rack of vintage clothes in a shop on First Avenue, if there was no possibility of anything happening. Then she wouldn't have to have her hopes up. She wouldn't have to worry about being disappointed, and she could just move on. But to what?

Maybe she should be happier than she'd ever been, but she just didn't know it yet. She couldn't really exist in the world until she knew.

Making things worse, Daniel didn't call. Maybe he needed her to call him. At first she didn't want to, didn't know what to say. Seemed easier to avoid the whole situation. But he was leaving for Arizona in two weeks to be with his father, so by Wednesday she wondered if they would have the weekend together before he went. She left a message on his machine saying only "So are we getting together this weekend?" After she hung up, she wondered if it sounded harsh. Oh well. At least she'd called.

"I told him I'm leaving," Wanda said as soon as she sat down.

"How did he take it?"

"Okay, I guess."

"What did he say?"

"Not much. He got quiet. I thought he might cry. But he didn't."

They were both silent. Camille considered starting the lesson, but she didn't want to seem insensitive. She took off her fake glasses. "Men will go to great lengths not to cry."

"And I've been crying like a baby. More than enough for the both of us! I know I probably sound like I'm okay, but the truth is, I'm a wreck." Wanda started to cry. "I'm sorry," she said, through her snuffles.

"It's okay. It's good to cry. It must feel sort of like . . . a death."

Wanda nodded, and that just seemed to make her cry more.

When Camille's father died, she hadn't been able to cry. That horrible day. She was in the eleventh grade. Home from school. Lying on her bed listening to her father's old album of *Camelot*.

She'd been cast in a production of *Camelot* at school and was going to be Guinevere. Her singing wasn't the greatest, but neither was Vanessa Redgrave's in the movie version, and she knew she could pull it off. After all, she'd listened to the album a million times. Had a crush on Richard Harris, who played King Arthur. Watched him win the Oscar. Her father would come see her—he'd promised he would fly out—and he would be so proud.

Her mother came in and sat down on the side of her bed. She had some bad news. Some very bad news. There was an edge of hysteria to her voice. "I don't know how to tell you this."

"What?"

"Your father."

"What?!"

"They found him in his bedroom. This morning. A heart attack."

It was irritating having her mother look at her with such concern. She was overreacting. He was sick. But he would be okay.

"He's dead."

Impossible. "Can't they do something? There must be something they can do!"

"I'm sorry, honey."

She imagined him in his dark little apartment in New York City on the floor not breathing, traffic passing outside the window . . .

She closed her eyes. Shut out her mother, the room. Richard Harris singing *"If Ever I Would Leave You."* Could not take this in. A stupid thought—*the* most stupid thought—kept going around in her mind. He would not be able to see *Camelot*. He would not see her as Guinevere. What was the point of doing the play if he couldn't see her?

She looked at her mother. "What do I do?" Not sure if she meant that day, that week, or the rest of her life.

"There'll be a memorial service in New York. I don't have any details yet. Oh, sweetheart. I'm so sorry."

Her mother felt sorry for her. The death was more important to Camille than to her mother. Polly wasn't married to him anymore after all. He was *her* father. This was *her* news. Polly didn't have to suffer.

She had an urge to make a scene. Fling Richard Harris across the room so the record would shatter into little bits. Sink to the floor and writhe and cry and moan and scream and make her mother see this was the worst moment of her life and it was happening right now and there was no way she was going to be able to go on!

But she didn't. She told her mother she wanted to be alone. And got deep under the covers. And kept listening to Richard Harris. That urge to cry transformed into a lump at the back of her throat. It was a lump that came and went for years—sometimes throbbing and ready to explode but never actually managing to—and just dissolved back down only to return again later.

She did play Guinevere. And didn't tell any of her friends about his death, just pretended everything was fine. What was the difference? Her father was never around anyway, none of her friends knew him. She didn't go to the memorial, either. She was busy with the play. Of course she did the play. The play was all she lived for, now. The memorial just would've been a room full of strangers.

And she was wonderful. Everyone said so. And why not? She now had a secret weapon. She could tap into this urge to cry for her father when she gave up Arthur and Lancelot to become a nun.

And she could carry that secret weapon with her for the rest of her life. Every time she got on stage. Could cry on cue time and time again.

But could not cry for her father.

Daniel didn't call back until Friday night. She didn't answer the phone. She didn't want to have an awkward conversation. Better just to hear what he would say.

"Sorry I haven't called. Things got really busy at the hospital. Summer brings the crazies out like cockroaches. . . . So . . . anyway . . . maybe you want to get together tomorrow night. Let me know."

She could hear a sort of exaggerated neutrality in his voice. Like he wasn't going to care too much if she wanted to come or not.

She immediately returned his call and got his machine. "Hi, it's me." He picked up. "I just got out of the bath." (Why not let him imagine her naked.)

"Hi."

"Hi."

"So . . . do you still want to come over?"

"Sure. Do you have a movie picked out?"

"No, but . . . I'll figure it out."

"Okay."

She hung up. Now she dreaded seeing him. They were in a limbo of ambivalence. It would be awkward. Tense.

She called Marie. Miraculously, she was there. Camille tried to keep her voice casual. "So what's new?"

"You know, I was going to call you!"

"Really?"

"Everything is still on track," Marie said. "We're still hoping to open soon. But the play that's in the theater now is extending, so it won't be as soon as we hoped."

"I thought they weren't filling their seats."

"Oh, evidently they got a new infusion of cash. So they're going to do a little advertising. But I think they'll be out of there in September, and then we'll be able to get the theater for October."

"Really?"

"Yeah."

"So they really are committed to us? It's still happening?"

"Oh yes. The investors are still very excited. Nobody is backing out."

"Good."

"Don't worry," she said. "And don't commit to anything else. I'm going to be sending you a contract."

Camille phoned Lisa as soon as they hung up. "Marie says she's sending me a contract!"

"That's great," Lisa said. "That's really exciting."

"You don't sound so excited."

"I am. It's just . . . I have my own news."

She almost sounded sad. Had she broken up with the Wallet?

"I'm moving in with Wally next weekend. Salvation Army is picking up a bunch of stuff tomorrow, as a matter of fact. You should come by and see if there's anything you want."

"Why didn't you tell me you were moving so soon?"

"It was sort of last minute. My lease is up in September and I thought what the hell, why not do it now, before we go away. I've called a couple times but got your machine and didn't want to leave a message. . . ."

"Where are you going?"

Lisa usually suffered through August in the city along with Camille. It was possible to enjoy Manhattan emptied out. If you had someone to enjoy it with.

"Didn't I tell you? Wally rented a house in the Hamptons. It's right on the beach. Gorgeous. If you want to come out one weekend . . ."

Camille could hear the guilt in her voice. Lisa most certainly didn't want *her* intruding on their romantic getaway. "That's okay. I'm heading out to San Francisco for the month." Maybe she would.

"That's great. Say hi to your mom for me."

"So that's it? Next week? You're out of here?"

"Wally paid for the movers and everything. . . . You wouldn't believe it. Over a thousand dollars just to cart my stuff twenty blocks."

"Sounds like a waste of money all right."

"Oh, and we set a date, by the way. His parents found this beautiful church on Long Island near their house. They just had a cancellation, so we got to book it for next August. The twenty-first."

"Great."

"His father is so sweet. And his mother is so lovely. I really like her. . . ."

Lisa never said anything negative about the Wallet's parents. Like they were perfect. Like they would never meddle or be difficult or get old and needy and crabby and would just baby-sit for the grandchildren all the time and then die and leave them a big inheritance.

"And Wally is so nice to his mother."

"Uh-huh." Maybe she should just hang up the phone.

"We went out to look at the church."

Pretend the line went dead.

"They have this incredibly gorgeous house. . . . It's almost like an estate, with stables just like in *Marnie*, do you remember? When Tippi Hedren shoots the horse? And his father barbecued for us. Isn't that sweet when the father cooks? And he helped clean up, too."

"Maybe you could get the parents to move in with you. Isn't there an extra bedroom in his loft?"

"Don't get catty. It just made me feel so good to be part of a family like that. They can't wait to have grandchildren. His mom already bought some baby clothes at Nordstrom. She said she couldn't resist."

"That's weird."

"I thought it was sweet!"

"To buy baby clothes before you're even pregnant?"

"They've had to wait so long for Wally to get married. He's thirty-eight years old for god's sake. They're chomping at the bit. . . . But I like it. We're going to try to get pregnant right away."

"Why wait for the wedding? You could have a baby shower and a bachelorette party all in one. It would certainly save on party favors. Not that you have to worry about economizing anymore."

"You're in a good mood."

She had noticed.

"Are things going badly with Daniel?"

"I think it's over."

"I'm sorry."

"It's fine, really. We just aren't in the same place right now."

"That's too bad. I was really hoping it would work out with you two."

This was too much. Why was she trying so hard to push her toward Daniel?

"Lisa?"

"Yes?"

"What is sex like with Wally?"

Lisa had never been shy on this topic when it came to other boyfriends but had never said one word about Wally and his talents—or lack of them.

"It's good."

"Really?"

"It's fine. Why?"

"Fine?"

"Sex isn't everything, Camille."

"So it's boring?"

"I didn't say that."

"And his personality is boring. And his looks are boring. That basically leaves the fact that he makes a lot of money."

"That is so incredibly out of line. Just because it didn't work out with Daniel does not mean you can dump on me!"

"Just because you're selling out doesn't mean I have to do it too!"

"You know . . . Camille . . . I think maybe we need to take a break from each other."

"Because you have no use for me now that you're getting married? Why depress yourself? I'm just a reminder of how horrible your life used to be."

"I'm going now."

"Or is it because I know how there was a time you could barely sit through dinner with the Wallet and now you want to spend the rest of your life with him. What was it you once said? He's consuming me! Well guess what, Lisa. You have been consumed. Bought and paid for. Just don't rip the tags off yet in case—"

Click.

A wave of heat went through her body. She hung up. Actually started to tremble. Well. She wouldn't be seeing Lisa for a while.

Chapter Seventeen

They met at Daniel's place. She knew he was more comfortable there, and it was easier for her to adapt to his surroundings.

Frances was Camille's choice. Jessica Lange played the actress Frances Farmer, who was successful in the late forties. She was smart, outspoken, and political, and hated Hollywood. She was committed to the theater, then was committed to a mental institution.

About halfway through the movie Camille regretted her choice. There was already tension in the air between her and Daniel, and the movie made her tense on top of that. Frances Farmer was a difficult actress and a difficult person. Camille felt annoyed with her for messing up her glamorous movie career even if she did do it because of her high standards.

Not that the movie could be trusted. It was, after all, made in Hollywood, and was sure to be distorting the facts in the same ways that had offended Frances Farmer. By the time Frances was escaping from the evil sanitarium, Camille suggested they turn it off.

Daniel agreed and Camille took the bowl of uneaten popcorn to the kitchen. Was Frances an actress who was crazy? Or was she crazy to be an actress?

At one point in the movie Frances Farmer met the playwright Clifford Odets and got cast in his play and had an affair with him. He told her, in an impassioned speech about acting (that was foreplay to having sex): don't *act* desperate, *be* desperate. Seemed to Camille that Jessica Lange had made that very mistake. "She didn't really transform herself. It was too mannered, like with the constant cigarette smoking. And all that shrieking and swearing. I always felt aware that I was watching Jessica Lange playing Frances Farmer and the whole time she was thinking *look at me in my big dramatic role sure to win me an Academy Award.*"

"And," Daniel said, "that psychiatrist had a creepy smile."

"The way he was so happy she was his patient because she was a movie actress. Very creepy. So do you favor your more attractive patients?"

"I don't have any attractive patients."

"That wasn't meant to be a trick question."

"Well. Psychiatrists are human. If a patient is attractive," he teased, "I might keep her from getting cured so she has to stick around longer."

She nudged him in the stomach. "I suspected as much."

But his smile faded quickly.

There was a lot unresolved from their last conversation. But she didn't want to talk about any of it. Though she couldn't resist mentioning Lisa, so maybe it was her fault the conversation went the way it did. "I can't believe she's going to be happy."

"Maybe you're a little jealous," he said.

"There's nothing to be jealous of."

"Maybe you feel rejected. Because it feels like she's leaving you behind."

"Dropping out is more like it."

"You think getting married is dropping out?"

"Don't pretend to be my shrink."

"If I was your shrink, I wouldn't be asking any of this. I'd be nodding my head and listening."

"Then *be* my shrink."

"I don't want to be your shrink."

"But you're saying there's something wrong with me because I'm not dying to get married and have a baby."

"No."

"But that's what you were suggesting."

"The truth is . . . there would be something wrong with me if I wanted to get married and have a family . . . but kept dating a woman who didn't."

That stung.

Then break up with me, she wanted to say.

But didn't want to say.

"Did you hear anything about your play moving yet?" he asked.

"No."

"I'm sorry. Maybe you will soon."

"Thanks."

This would have been when Daniel would start to kiss her. But even Daniel, it seemed, was not in the mood. Made no move. Maybe he even wanted her to leave.

"Maybe we should go to bed," she said.

"Maybe we should."

Another week passed with nothing in the mail. She called Marie. "What's happening?"

"We're having some more delays. That's why you haven't heard from me. Still ironing out some problems with the theater."

"I thought one of the backers owns the theater."

"He does. But evidently he got an offer. Somebody wants to rent it out for October and they're willing to pay top dollar, and he feels he can make more money renting it to them at a profit. . . ."

"And no risk to him."

"Exactly."

"So it's not going to happen."

"It is. But not as soon as we would wish."

Camille couldn't believe that she had managed to be such an idiot. Again! Believing . . . this time . . . it was going to go her way. Shit. Fuck. Damn.

"So how exactly does it stand?" she asked, continuing the charade. As if the coffin had not already been ordered.

"If that rental goes through, we have to wait until that show closes, or he might finance a production that would go up somewhere else. He really does believe in the show."

"Uh-huh."

Camille didn't know why he should. After all, it was a pretty mediocre play.

"So I don't want you to get discouraged. If this doesn't happen, something else will."

That was a nail. Right there. In the coffin.

"As a matter of fact," Marie said, "Hank is working on a new comedy."

Another nail. A new play meant he was already less invested in this play.

"It has a great part for you," Marie was saying. "And I know he'll want you."

"You don't have to say that, Marie." Hank probably hated her for upstaging him in the *Times* review. He would never want her in another play of his again.

"Don't be disappointed. I still believe in my bones that this is going to happen. It's just going to take longer than we hoped."

"Okay. Well thanks."

"By the way, I'm heading up to Cape Cod next week."

Another nail.

"I'm directing *Three Sisters*. Last-minute job offer."

"*Three Sisters?*" Her hopes rose like an involuntary reflex. Or was it acid reflux? God, she would love to do *Three Sisters* on the Cape. She didn't care if they didn't pay and she had to find her own housing. The Cape in August would be fantastic. She could spend her days on the beach and her evenings performing . . . But Marie had mentioned nothing about this to her.

"I would've cast you, of course, but I'm replacing a director who quit, so the thing was already cast."

"Of course."

"Now don't be glum."

"I'm not glum." Suicidal was more like it.

"You still got that great review." The final nail. "No one can take that away from you."

Yes. This was true. Especially since she had two hundred photocopies of it in her bottom desk drawer. When she died, someone would find them there. Evidence of how she'd over-reacted to her pitiful moment of glory. Whoever it was (her mother? the super?) would throw them into the garbage, her humiliation complete.

Camille got into bed, pulled the cover up to her chin, and closed her eyes.

If she did kill herself, who would notice? Her dead body would have to start stinking up the building before anyone would think to break down the front door. Maybe she should make friends with the old woman who lived above. They could have tea together every day and watch *Wheel of Fortune.*

That thought alone was enough to drive her to suicide.

Except . . . her apartment was such a mess. If she killed herself, she would have to clean her apartment first.

So forget it. She might as well live. The clutter was too overwhelming.

Not to mention the difficulty of allocating all her beautiful things. Clothes. Shoes. Her mother wouldn't appreciate her sense of style and there was no way the Salvation Army was getting everything. And who would get her perfume bottles? No one deserved them. Not that they were worth anything.

Maybe it was time to throw them out.

No. They were too pretty.

Lisa certainly didn't deserve anything since she was going to be rich. So she would have to stay alive if only for the sake of maintaining her things.

Enough of this. Camille got out of bed. What she needed was to take a walk and check out the summer sales in SoHo.

On her way out of the building she ran into the super. "Hi Sheila," he said.

"Hi Jimmy. How are ya?"

"Oh, not too good. How are you?"

She wanted to mention that dripping faucet but didn't have the heart. "Pretty good."

"Landlord says he still don't got that check for last month."

"Really?" She'd left a message on Sheila's machine. What was going on? "Sorry. I'll get it to him right away."

She headed downtown. Her existence. It seemed so tenuous. She was insignificant to everyone in the world, except her mother, and maybe Daniel. And even her mother didn't seem to care all that much. No, that wasn't true. Her mother cared. She did. In truth, she was the only one who did care. Even if it was in her uncaring way. She really should go to San Francisco for August. If her mother would pay for a plane ticket. One thing was clear. Nothing was keeping her here.

Chapter Eighteen

The small stucco house out in the Haight was always chilly, even in the summer, but that could be remedied with the space heater.

The old posters from the thirties on the wall were still there. The advertisements for Hershey's ice cream and Nabisco cookies. The set of mango-colored Fiestaware. The clutter by the phone. The birds tweeting outside. The complaints that would inevitably spill after each of them had consumed a cup of coffee. Yes, this kitchen could be counted on.

"So what's happening with the play?" Polly asked, putting the butter back in the refrigerator. Camille was sorry to see it go. She wanted more toast. But was full. Just craved the comfort.

"Nothing. I'm right back where I was. Nowhere."

Polly poured each of them half of the last quarter cup of coffee left in the pot. There was nothing Polly could say to help. Camille knew that. Whatever she did say would be wrong. Encourage her to quit acting? That was not supportive. Tell her to keep trying? That was sadistic. "I don't know how you keep at it," Polly said.

"Yeah." Camille smiled wryly. "I must be crazy." She took a sip of coffee and tried not to think about toast. "How are things with you?"

"The usual. More cuts. A new principal, no better than the last one."

"Have you been dating anyone?"

"Not really. But I did force myself to go to a single's event at Fort Mason."

"Really? How'd it go?" Camille had been thinking of doing something like that herself. If things fell apart with Daniel, she was ready to try Match.com.

"It was humiliating."

"Did you meet someone?"

"One man. We dated a few weeks. I broke it off."

"Why?"

"Seemed like he was ready to marry me. No thank you."

"Once bitten, twice shy?"

"No."

"No?"

Polly snorted. Bitter. "No."

Camille hesitated. But she really felt like she had to have it out. Whatever "it" was. "I know Daddy disappointed you. You think he was a bum. He put his acting first, and you've always resented him for that."

Polly shook her head. "That's not how it was."

"Then how was it?"

Her mother looked at her and shook her head. "Are you still seeing that shrink, by the way?"

"Daniel? He asked me to marry him. Sort of."

"Why didn't you tell me!"

"Don't get your hopes up."

"You like him, don't you?"

"Yes. I do."

"But?"

"I can't picture myself living that life. Upper East Side. Doctor's wife. It's not me." She paused, and then she said, "Or maybe I'm the one who's bitten. Shy. Or, I don't know. Fixated."

"On John?"

So odd to hear her mother call her father by name.

"On John. Yes. After all, I'm thirty-four years old and unmarried. Maybe no one can measure up to Dad." She noticed how easy it was to repeat Daniel's tidy summation of her mental problems, even though hearing him say it had been infuriating.

"Measure up to him . . . ." Her mother smiled and shook her head.

"Well. I know *you* don't see it that way. . . ."

"You know, I was the one who asked *him* to move out."

"Sure, because you wanted someone more reliable, who made a good living. . . ."

"You still believe that?"

"What else should I believe? That's what you told me. You were sick of being married to an actor and wanted stability. He was gone all the time and didn't make any money. . . ."

"That was a part of the story, yes. But . . . obviously I never did marry this reliable, stable, money-earning husband. . . ."

"Because you never found him. Because you were too bitter."

"What? Okay, yes, there was some bitterness. But not because he was an actor."

It was incredible to Camille that they'd never had a coherent conversation about this. But she'd never asked directly and Polly had never seemed to want to talk about any of it. "So . . . what? Tell me."

Polly searched Camille's face for a moment. "I don't know if we should go into this."

"Tell me."

Polly sighed. Frowned. Looked into Camille's eyes. Looked away. "Your father was unfaithful."

Camille crossed her arms across her chest. Her back was rigid. Lots of men, women, people—everyone—cheated. But her father? No. "So . . . you're saying . . . what?"

"He just . . ." Her mother said, "could not be faithful."

It was so annoying. Her mother was looking at her with pity, as if she was feeling sorry for *her*, as if he'd been unfaithful to *her*. "So you're saying he had an affair."

"I wouldn't put it that way, exactly."

"Then how would you put it?"

"He was with other women. More than once. A lot, as a matter of fact. That's all. But it would've hurt you to tell the truth. Seemed better to leave that part out. You know . . ."

Camille swallowed but her mouth stayed dry. She took a sip of cold coffee. The idea of an affair was bad enough. But more than once meant it wasn't like a huge emotional thing, like he'd made a mistake, found the right woman. . . . She didn't want to think about what it meant.

"I tried to deal with it. But he . . . well . . . he just wasn't committed to the marriage. So I told him he had to leave."

"That must've been hard," Camille said, not so much to be sympathetic but to get Polly to say more. This didn't feel real.

"Oh yes, let me tell you. I tried to work it out with him. . . . I gave him more than one chance to make it up to me, but . . ."

"There must've been a lot of tension in the house. . . ." Camille looked around the kitchen as if it was still there in the air. Not that she wanted to believe her father would cheat. But she did have memories of them fighting. Yelling. But all parents did that, didn't they?

"You were too young to understand, of course. God only knows what you thought. We tried not to fight when you were around but . . . I know we did slip sometimes. I felt horrible about it. That's why it was a relief when he finally left. Things got a hell of a lot more peaceful."

She could still hear it in her head, her mother shrill, crying. Her father defensive, belligerent.

"He was . . . it became clear. He could not be trusted," Polly said. "That's all. The divorce . . . it really had nothing to do with the fact that he was an actor, or that he didn't make a living. I had a job. I could deal with all that. But I couldn't deal with the cheating."

Camille tried to smile. "And here I always thought you just didn't go for the lifestyle."

Polly inhaled and exhaled heavily through her nose. "You always put your father on such a pedestal."

"It must be a relief to get him off it."

"No."

"You never could stand how much I . . ." Loved him, Camille thought. Loved him more than you.

"You idolize him. Have devoted your life to this acting profession that I'm afraid you've done just to please him . . . win his love . . . which really was impossible to win because he was always running away from anything that mattered."

"I'm his daughter, not his wife. He didn't cheat on me."

"But he did disappoint both of us. He failed both of us."

"It's not that I think you're lying," Camille said getting up from the table, "but I can't—"

"You were so young when it was all happening. Of course I wasn't going to tell you then. By the time you were in your teens, the way you adored him, it seemed cruel to tell you. And then he died. . . . It just never seemed right. 'Oh, by the way, your father was a liar and a cheat.' "

Camille flinched.

"Sorry, I shouldn't have said that."

"I guess it's true."

"Well . . . anyway . . . you saw me as the evil one," Polly went on, "and he could do no wrong. Maybe it was better that way. More comforting for you. But god knows I wanted to tell you. It could get pretty infuriating knowing what he did and how you chose to blame me."

Polly ended on that bitter note.

"Well," Camille said, "if you think I'm going to apologize . . ."

"No . . ."

"I didn't know."

"How could you? But you aren't a child anymore. You're thirty-four years old. And you've been disappointed so many times by men . . . the theater. . . . Maybe it's time you let your-self see the world for what it really is . . . a hard, difficult place—"

"I know how hard and difficult it is." Camille heard herself. She sounded ugly. Snide and full of spite. "The real question is, how could you mislead me all these years? I feel so stupid! Like a stupid idiot!" She stood and felt like turning over the table, sending the cups and dishes crashing to the floor. "It really makes me feel a lot better about my entire fucking life!"

"I'm sorry." Polly looked as if she was expecting to be slapped. Was her mother afraid of her?

"I guess I should've told you the truth a long time ago," Polly said.

"Is it the truth, or just your version?"

"You want to look at some old letters?"

"You can burn his old letters! What difference does it make? He's gone! There is no truth anymore! The only truth is that my entire life has been a lie!" It sounded so melodramatic; she heard her father chiding her. *Sarah Heartburn, don't make such a big deal out of nothing. Your mother exaggerates. The only special girl in my life was . . .*

"I shouldn't have told you." Polly put her hands over her mouth. "I didn't mean to hurt you. I thought you wanted to know. I thought it might help."

"I'm going out." She didn't know where.

"Will you be back for lunch? Dinner? We can order pizza. We'll get mushroom and onion from Olive's, okay?"

"I'll be eating out tonight."

She had to get out of that kitchen. Maybe she'd cut the visit short. Now she just wanted to get back to New York and her own apartment. Even though nothing was waiting for her there.

"Please. I'll make you some lasagna. With spinach. Just the way you like."

"You think I'm going to give you the pleasure of feeding me?" That was a good exit line. So she left.

* * *

But on the street, she felt unbearably alone. There was nothing to do but get on a trolley and go downtown. It was infuriating that she'd been lied to for so long, but now that she'd lost the lie she wanted it back. She looked out the window as the trolley passed down Market Street. Every time she came back the city was different. More cutesy. What was wrong with people? Putting up all these façades trying to insist that the world was a benevolent place. At least New York City tenements acknowledged misery every step of the way.

Downtown was better. She got off on Powell Street grateful for the bums and the tourists and the crowds of shoppers.

She wondered which department store Jimmy Stewart and Kim Novak had gone to in *Vertigo*. Did it still exist? Was it the old I. Magnin's? City of Paris was gone, and so was The Emporium. Macy's was still there, but Macy's had become so boring. She found her way to the Swedish Bakery—one of the few cafés left from her childhood—and had a tuna sandwich on a roll. While she ate and sipped Diet Coke, she wondered how her father had felt when he moved to New York. Sorry to leave them behind? Glad to have his freedom?

She thought of Wanda. Wanda had stayed with that husband for years blind to the fact that he gave her nothing in return. Wasn't that what she herself had been doing? Being faithful to her acting? Why? For what?

She took a sip of her Diet Coke and felt a surge of energy. Maybe she really had wasted her life trying to please her father, all for a deluded fantasy. He wasn't a handsome, romantic figure; he was a jerk. This acting thing? A farce. Why not let a man support her and have a baby and just fuck it all?

She took the last bite of her sandwich. Maybe it was too late. Maybe she'd ruined her chance with Daniel. And he was her last chance. And she was destined to be an ugly, lonely old maid.

Camille threw her paper plate in the garbage and walked around the corner to a See's candy store. Her father used to buy her boxes of See's candies when he came to see her. He knew all her favorites. Marzipan, ginger, almond clusters. Everything in the store was painted a glistening enamel white. The walls, the shelves, the cabinets. The black woman in a white apron behind the counter put chocolates in a glossy white box for another customer. The only sound was the rustling of the paper cups the candies were nestled in. Then it was her turn. She wasn't sure what her mother liked, so she bought a pre-boxed one-pound assortment of nuts and crèmes. Then there was nothing to do but go home.

Polly was in the living room watching a rerun of *Law and Order*. It happened to be an episode with an actress Camille knew. She had two lines. This was a beautiful actress who'd been made up so her face looked plain, who'd been stuffed into an unflattering policewoman's uniform.

Camille remained standing. She gripped the box of candy in her hand. "I've decided to quit the theater."

That sounded wrong. Too melodramatic.

"Because of your father?" Polly asked.

"Because of me."

"Well . . ." Polly glanced toward her and then looked back at the screen, "I can't say that I blame you. It's a very tough life."

Camille sat down next to Polly. She could tell her mother didn't really believe her. Well, why should she? It wasn't the first time she'd "quit." But this time, she meant it.

"What do you think you'll do instead?"

"I don't know." It seemed better not to mention Daniel in case he'd already written her off. She remembered the box of candy and handed it to her mother. "These are for you."

Polly took the box. "Oh." She seemed surprised and flattered. "That's very sweet. I was worried you might be angry with me. Thank you, honey."

"You're welcome." She *was* angry but didn't want to dwell on it right then. Peace seemed more important.

Polly opened the box, took an almond cluster, and offered the chocolates to Camille. She took a molasses chip even though it always got stuck in her teeth. They both turned back to the television set and chewed. A commercial came on. There was only about fifteen minutes left of the show. She'd missed that scene with her friend.

Chapter Nineteen

She didn't cut the trip short after all. As a matter of fact, Camille dreaded going home. It was relaxing to go to movies, walk around, shop on her mother's credit card. When she did get back to New York on the Friday before Labor Day weekend, it was depressing. The city was still empty. She was afraid to call Daniel. And there was a letter from Sheila in the stack of mail that had accumulated at the post office.

Camille Darling,

Guess what. I'm moving to Canada of all places! Got a job teaching at the University of British Columbia and forcing myself to face the reality that I never will be using Grandmama's darling apartment. Cut to chase: this is my last check. What does this mean for you? Well, darling, I don't know. I'm afraid they'll want to kick you out when they realize you're not me. But maybe not. In any case, they'll probably bump the rent way up because of the rent control laws, so on and so forth. I would love to bequeath the apartment to you, but I'm afraid it's ultimately up to the landlord and since he's a money-grubbing asshole . . . well . . . good luck! Hope it works out!

Love,
Sheila

Camille got dinner at the Yaffa Café, a kitschy place with posters of Marilyn, Elvis, and Scarlett O'Hara on the wall. An abusive waiter made her sit at the worst table by the door even though there were empty tables (for four) in the back. Her hamburger was dry. She went home. The air was thick with humidity. Tree branches were swaying and the sky was darkening; a thunderstorm was coming. She couldn't face Daniel. Didn't want to call anyone. Most likely no one was around. Just as she got inside, it started to pour. She holed up in her apartment watching TV wondering if the old woman on the floor above was doing the exact same thing. Couldn't call Daniel. Couldn't sleep. Ended up taking a valium at three in the morning and then waking at one in the afternoon.

She went to the 2nd Ave. Deli and read the *Times*. It was a pleasant way to pass the hour. But when she was done with her third cup of coffee, the day loomed. She still didn't call Daniel. Didn't want to have some big important talk with him.

She decided to go to the flea market on Twenty-fourth Street. And then maybe she'd walk up to the Guggenheim Museum. She'd read in the *Times* that there was a Wayne Thiebaud exhibit. His pop-arty paintings of pastries were so cheerful and comforting. His San Francisco street scenes always made her feel at home.

She headed north. Peered into the windows of the beautiful brownstones in Gramercy Park. The very decorated, cozy living rooms were for secure people, married people, content people. But not for her.

The flea market turned out to be depressing too. Hardly any vendors were out and everything just seemed like junk. *Was* junk. Only a pink princess phone from the sixties tempted her, but who has the patience to dial anymore? And they were asking sixty dollars for it! She walked on.

Midtown was strangely empty. Everyone was out of town. Enjoying the country. She followed Park Avenue up past Grand Central. She could take a train. Get out of the city too.

See some brand-new scenery. Nothing was stopping her. But walking around aimlessly on roads in some strange town would really be depressing. Bad idea.

She cut over to Fifth Avenue and passed the windows of Saks, Bergdorf's and Tiffany's, then walked along the border of Central Park. At least there was some life here. Hot dog vendors, mothers pushing strollers, elderly men in hats. She found herself in front of the Guggenheim.

But she was exhausted and wanted a cup of coffee. She could go to the Patisserie Margot. She remembered it as pleasant and inviting. But the museum was closing in an hour. What should she do. Food? Art? Food? Art?

The food won out over the art. She headed toward the bakery. But first she circled past Daniel's white brick high-rise. She didn't go inside—had no intention of doing that. Just a wish for proximity. To see how proximity would make her feel.

It made her feel anxious.

She checked for messages on her cell phone and at home. There were none.

She reached the bakery and was glad to find it open. She hadn't paid much attention to it that day she'd popped in with Daniel, but now she took in every detail. It was small and had little round marble-top tables very close (too close) together, but it didn't matter because there were no other customers. She bought a croissant and a cup of coffee and sat by the window with a good view of the people passing on the street.

She sunk into the chair glad it wasn't air-conditioned inside because she had no sweater. Her feet hurt more than she'd realized. And she was starving. She peeled the top off a small plastic container of strawberry jam, tore the nub off the end of her croissant, and slathered it with the jam. She would have to try not to eat too quickly. Croissants never lasted long enough. And it was pleasant in this place. The woman behind the counter had her hair in a French braid. Camille liked French braids.

A man in chino shorts, loafers, and a pink polo shirt walked in. When the door shut, a rush of warm air hit her in the face. The man peered at the display case and then asked for a cherry Danish. The woman said they didn't make cherry Danish, but they did have prune or apple. He didn't want either of those. He left. Warm air hit her in the face again.

She peeled a layer off her croissant. And then another, regretting how quickly she was chewing it all down. But as the caffeine hit her brain, she almost felt happy and optimistic. About what? It had to be the coffee. She watched the woman behind the counter pretend to look busy wrapping napkins around silverware like they were each a little gift. She would've liked that job. It probably didn't pay well, but still, there had to be something comforting about standing behind pastries all day. Maybe she would look for a job like that. Really, it was all she needed. She felt so tired of those tedious vocal drills.

Camille went to the counter and asked for a refill on her coffee. The woman said they didn't give refills for free; she would have to pay for a second cup. Camille gave her another $1.75 and the woman gave her a new cup of coffee. She was sorry she had nothing to read. She should've grabbed a *Village Voice* from a box on the street but hadn't thought to; now it was too late. So she sat back down and sipped her coffee and looked out the window.

That's when she saw Daniel. He was wearing blue jeans and a blue T-shirt, just to stir up her regrets. And he was walking down the sidewalk facing her direction, and there was a very good chance he would see her sitting there! She sat up straight, ready to look surprised and like a happy person.

But as he got closer, she saw that it wasn't Daniel. She slumped back down in her seat. As a matter of fact, the man was in his sixties and had a pot belly. How could she have confused him for Daniel?

She exhaled. Had she walked all the way uptown and stationed herself here just to see him?

No. That was idiotic. Ridiculous. She was sorry now she

hadn't gone into the museum. The paintings would've been distracting. But all she'd managed to do was consume a fattening croissant that left her craving a second fattening croissant.

She threw out her paper plate and the empty cup of coffee in a stainless steel bullet-shaped garbage container by the door. The chrome flap was shiny and clean and sharply reflected the entire café.

She didn't want to go back home. What would she do when she got there? But she couldn't think of where else to go. A movie alone? No. It was getting dark. By the time she got home, the only thing left to do would be to get in bed and watch TV. Well, that didn't sound so bad.

She took the subway downtown. Back home, her eye immediately went to the answering machine. It was not flashing. Her existence mattered to no one.

She sat down on her sofa. Looked at the phone. Yes. She should really call Daniel. What did she have to lose? She decided to have a cup of tea.

She put some water on. Skimmed an article in the *Voice* about how AIDS research was being neglected because all the money was being funneled to the fight on terrorism. It was an incredibly detailed and boring article. Astonishing how many porn ads were in the back. Were there really so many men out there who responded to these ads?

By the time she was done with the paper, she felt angry he hadn't called. Why was it up to her? She read over the movie listings. She knew why it was up to her.

Maybe she would get his machine. He answered on the second ring.

"Daniel?"

"Camille?"

"Hi."

"Hi."

"How was Arizona?

"Hot. How was San Francisco?"

"Cold."

"Really?"

"And my mother never has any heat on in the house."

"Well. I'm glad you got home safely."

Scary how his voice reassured her. "I was up in your neighborhood today, at the Guggenheim."

"They have something good there?"

"Wayne Thiebaud. You know. The guy who paints the pastries?" (She'd been eating a pastry, so it wasn't completely unlinked.) They were both silent for a moment. "So would you like to get together?" she asked. Another silence.

"Okay."

"There's a movie I'd like to see on the Upper West Side. At the Thalia. It's one of my favorites. But it's just playing tonight."

"Is it about a psychiatrist?"

"No. An actress. But I think you'll like it."

Chapter Twenty

Day for Night was an old Truffaut film. Camille had seen it three times before; Daniel never had. It was a film about the filming of a movie. There were no psychiatrists in it.

After it began, she regretted her choice. Unlike *Frances*, it showed the joy of acting. She was not in the mood to romanticize the profession. And then she remembered the plot point where Jacqueline Bisset (the actress who plays the lead actress in the movie within the movie) sleeps with her leading man Jean-Pierre Léaud even though she seems to be happily married. Oh well, it was just a movie. And the husband was extremely understanding at the end, as he led the emotionally delicate Jacqueline back to their home in England to repair their marriage.

After the movie, they filed out of the small theater along with everyone else. That's when she spotted them.

"Oh my god," she said under her breath. "It's Eric Hughes and Mimi Tyler." She nodded toward the couple. They were a few people ahead of them.

"So it is."

They were both dressed down in jeans and T-shirts and baseball caps, obviously trying to blend in. Yet they still seemed to broadcast an aura. "I saw him recently at a restaurant. Isn't that funny?"

"You must have the same taste."

Eric and Mimi turned down Broadway. Camille and Daniel walked behind them. She tried not to be preoccupied with the fact that they were ten feet in front of her and proceeded to talk about the movie, like she would have. "I don't think the actress really would've slept with that actor. She was in love with her husband and there was no sign she found him attractive. Truffaut just did that to advance the plot."

"I don't know," Daniel said. "She needed to convince the actor not to quit the movie."

"I think that's a little beyond the call of duty."

"The show must go on . . ."

Eric and Mimi turned off Broadway. "Let's follow them."

"Why?"

"Because." She liked the idea of doing something silly with Daniel.

Eric and Mimi headed down West End Avenue, a few blocks later turned right again, then turned down Riverside Drive.

"They must live around here."

"We're too close," Daniel said. "They're going to notice us."

"No they aren't. We have every right to walk on this street. Maybe we live here too."

Riverside Drive was one of the few Manhattan streets that curved. Tall trees overhung the two-lane road. On one side were beautiful old pre-war buildings; on the other was a cobblestone sidewalk lined with benches facing into Riverside Park. The Hudson River was past the trees, in the darkness. It was a lovely secret pocket of the city. Take away the cars and streetlights, and it could've been the turn of the century.

Eric and Mimi stopped in front of a tall slim building. Black iron numbers announced the address over the entrance: 111 Riverside Drive. A doorman held open the door as they passed inside. Camille and Daniel kept on going. She broke out into a run.

"Hey!" Daniel called after her.

"Hey!" she yelled back, laughing.

She was still laughing at the corner as Daniel caught up with her. She put her arms around him and kissed him. Like they were in a movie. Making out on Riverside Drive. What could be more romantic? At least until someone yelled an obscenity from a passing car. "Let's go," Daniel said, and he flagged a cab.

"I missed you," she said, snuggling up to him in the back seat. He put his arm around her. "Me too." They kissed again. Kissed all the way back to the East Side. Were still kissing when the cab turned down Lexington and stopped in front of Daniel's building. He paid the driver and didn't even ask if she was coming up.

They walked arm and arm into his lobby, kissed some more in his elevator, stumbled into his apartment, and went straight for the bed. Everything was going to be okay, she could see it. She was home free.

But then he rolled off her, onto his back.

She didn't perceive the signal. Thought he just wanted her on top. So she crouched over him, her knees on each side of his hips, her elbows stationed on both sides of his head, her hair falling against his cheeks. She dipped her head down and pressed her lips to his lips, let her chest relax onto his chest, and let her knees slide down the length of his body so she was all spread out on top of him. They kissed some more, and she started rubbing up and down on him, wanting him inside, but he lay there, passive, not putting his arms around her, not rolling over, not covering her with his own body, not even, it would seem, having an erection.

"We shouldn't do this," he said.

"What's wrong?"

He slid out from under her and sat on the edge of the bed looking away from her.

"Am I moving too fast for you?" she said. Sarcastic. Sort of.

But he was serious. "I just don't . . ." His voice trailed off.

"What?"

"I'm very attracted to you, obviously." He stared down at the wood parquet floor. "But you should go." He got up.

"What?"

He went out to the living room. She followed him.

"I'm sorry," he said.

What to say? *It's okay.* (It wasn't.) *It doesn't matter.* (It does.) *I'm fine.* (I'm not.) So she said nothing, slipped her sandals on, and braced herself for going back out into the night.

He followed her to the door. She smiled tightly. He seemed distressed but offered her nothing. He just opened the door for her.

"Well, then. Good night," she said, stepping out into the hall, trying to appear as if she wasn't completely humiliated.

He walked her to the elevator. The door slid open. She turned around and asked him, "Why am I going home?"

She knew the answer, of course.

He sighed. She heard the elevator doors close behind her. She looked at him. He put his finger on the button, opening them back up again. He said, in a very contained voice, "I promised myself."

"What?"

The doors closed behind her again. This time he let them. Spoke in a stage whisper, as if all the neighbors were standing with their ears up to their doors. "I'm very confused," he said, "about you and me."

"Because?"

He looked down the hall, then back to her. "I think you know the problem. We don't want the same thing."

"You know what I want?"

He sighed. "We can't have this conversation out here."

She followed him back into his apartment.

He asked her if she wanted anything, a glass of water. "No thanks." She sat down on his couch and waited while he went into the kitchen. She heard him getting a glass and turning on the faucet. She took in the wall unit with the large flat-screened television, shelves of medical and psychology text-books, a small sculpture on a metal stand that looked like a cement figure of a woman flying through the air. The framed Rothko print behind the couch. Was she fighting for the privilege to live among these things, these things not chosen by her, not even her taste? It beckoned with a foggy promise of comfort and security that would deaden her senses, dull the pain and disappointments of her life, but help her feel safe.

He came back out with the water and sunk into the black leather chair that was sideways to the couch; he set the water down on the glass coffee table between them and stared at it. "This is hard to say. And I'm sorry, because it sounds so . . . I don't know. Premeditated. But I'm thirty-eight years old."

"So?"

"You know my work. Long hours and I get preoccupied and busy and it's easy for me to neglect other parts of my life. But I did always want to have a family. And I invested so many years with Nancy and then it fell apart and—I know this sounds calculated—but I'm looking for a woman who wants to get married and have kids. You know that. And that's not what you want. So I just don't feel like it's right . . . fair . . . to either of us . . . to get involved. Like I said, I'm very attracted to you, but . . ."

He fell silent. This was a long speech for him.

"But having children, a family," she heard herself say, "is important to me too."

"Is it?"

Did she mean it? Or was she trying to convince herself by saying the words out loud. Saying what needed to be said in order to take refuge in this apartment.

But hadn't she known, since she called him and invited him to the movie, that she would bring them to this point of saying these words? It scared her, seemed reckless, but she couldn't stop herself. "I want to have children."

"That's not what you said the other week."

"I was in fantasyland. Because of the play."

"Yeah. But still . . . There will be another play. And you'll feel that way again."

Camille knew what she needed to say. *Acting is believing,* they liked to say, and she could make herself believe anything for a while. "What's the point of living a life if you don't experience having a child? That's more important, in some basic way, than anything."

"Do you really feel that?"

"Yes." And she did, right at that moment. "I want to have a full life. And that includes being a mother." She looked him in the face. So her eyes could convince him of her sincerity.

"I don't know. . . ." He shook his head and avoided her gaze.

"You think I'm lying?"

"I think maybe you don't know what you want. You're disappointed with your career. You see me as a way out."

"Or a way in."

"But it would never satisfy you."

Camille went to the window and looked out to the buildings across the street. She remembered this view from before. The television was on again in an apartment on the ninth floor. A *Seinfeld* rerun.

"I'm sick of my life," she heard herself say. "I hate the theater. I can't believe I wasted so much time chasing something that doesn't even exist." She leaned her forehead on the cold glass and peered down at the tops of cars and buses streaming down the avenue. It seemed so odd that it was just a thin sheet of glass that kept her from plummeting to the ground.

"If someone offered you a part in a Broadway show right now," he said, "you'd take it in a second."

She said, as if to a not very bright child, "Well, that's not going to happen, is it." Closed her eyes. Heard a siren in the distance.

"But you'll get cast in something. Sooner or later. And . . . I hate how this sounds. . . . But I don't think I would want the mother of my children to be out at night performing all the time."

And running around in her underwear? And kissing other men?

"And that wouldn't be fair to you," he went on. "And I would never want to discourage you from being an actress or hold you back in any way."

Don't be so goddamned reasonable.

"So," he said, "I feel this is doomed."

"It's not as if actresses don't have children." *Friends* was now on across the street. She was so much better than Courteney Cox; you had to wonder who she'd slept with to get that part.

"But I work very long hours," he said. "And you know as well as I do . . . Actors have a hard time making their marriages work. You're always out at night. Or you're out of town, doing summer stock and that sort of thing."

The last time Camille had gone out of town for work was three years ago for a production of *You Can't Take It with You* in northern Maine. It was dreadful. They'd put her up in a cabin with no plumbing and the theater was infested with flies. "It does present certain challenges. But people work it out."

"I don't know," he said. "It just doesn't seem . . ."

It was maddening that he was making this argument against marrying her based on perceptions that didn't even apply to her because she wasn't successful enough. And even though it involved respecting her work and her ambition and she basically agreed with everything he was saying, it was offensive hearing someone else limit her options like this! She didn't want her options limited. Not by him or anyone else.

"Fine." She got her purse and went out to the hallway again. The elevator was slow in coming. It had gone up to the sixteenth floor. They both looked up at the numbers as it slowly made its way back down to the tenth, each number taking its turn being illuminated.

Finally, the doors slid open. No one was on it. She didn't get on, and the doors started to close. She pressed the button to open them up again. "Daniel," she said, her back to him. She looked inside the empty elevator. It had ugly fake wood-grain paneling and a gold handrail. "I'm thirty-five, not twenty-nine." Her finger on the button. "Time is running out for me. And I just said that, about not wanting a baby, because I wanted to believe it, that night, because I wasn't sure if you liked me and sometimes I just tell myself it doesn't matter to me because I'm not sure if it's ever going to happen. . . ."

She took her finger off the button and turned around. They looked squarely at each other. His arched little eyebrows questioned her. Was this sincere? Or for effect? It occurred to her that it might be profoundly true. Something she hadn't been able to admit even to herself.

Or maybe it wasn't.

The elevator was closing behind her. He put his finger on the button to open it up again. Had she been a fool to admit her age? Maybe she was sealing her fate. Her value had just plummeted as a potential baby maker. Now he was about to dismiss her.

"You're good," he said. "I almost believe you."

"I know how I can convince you."

"How?"

"Have you ever taken a diaphragm out?"

"When I was a resident."

She raised her eyebrows.

He raised his.

She had him on this one. Every good actress knows a prop will make a moment real.

She heard the elevator doors closing behind her. This time, he let them go.

Chapter Twenty-one

She was starring in her own wedding. In addition to the lead, she was producing, directing, casting, everything. Well, not everything. She had to share some of the directing responsibilities. With the fetus. The fetus had a big say in the timing of the whole production. Yes, her clever use of a prop led to an immediate pregnancy. She didn't even entertain the idea of an abortion. As a matter of fact, once she got over the initial shock she felt proud of herself for getting pregnant. She was impressed by how easily it happened. Maybe she was a very fertile woman. Maybe she was meant to be a mother. This acting stuff, it had been a nice amusement. A good way to spend her time. A fun way to meet people. But why had she taken it so seriously? Why had she allowed it to take over her entire life?

But she was not intending to "show" on the day of her wedding. So they got married in her fourth month. And since it was so rushed and she felt overwhelming fatigue during the first three months, she could only get it together to plan a relatively small wedding. They rented out The Screening Room, a hip movie theater slash restaurant downtown. The ceremony would be in the dining room, which was designed to look like a forties movie palace. Camille felt it was an omen when she found it; the place was perfect.

And at least she got to choose her own costume. It was a

beauty with no sleeves, sleek lines, a plunging neck. Vera Wang. Way too expensive. But Camille would not compromise. If she wasn't going to be a famous actress accepting her Academy Award, at least she was going to look gorgeous on her wedding day.

Daniel was the ideal male lead. He let Camille make all the decisions. Just learned his lines, made his entrance, and let her look good.

His father flew in from Arizona. A very elegant man with a salt and pepper beard. He made Daniel seem talkative in comparison. Camille felt very intimidated around him. "I hope you will be very happy together," he said, and she felt sure he was implying that she wasn't good enough for his son and would inevitably disappoint him one day.

Polly was so obviously delighted by the whole occasion it almost made Camille want to call it off. But the worst part for Camille was that she didn't have her father to walk her down the aisle. So she didn't walk down an aisle, just took her place with Daniel at the front. A lump was in the back of her throat the whole time the rabbi (a friend of Camille's who was also a director) spoke.

And then there was the awkwardness with Lisa, who was there with Wally. They hadn't spoken since Camille had insulted her for giving up and getting married! Lisa didn't even know she was pregnant. Her own wedding was months away. Camille had "beaten her to the finish line."

But she couldn't *not* invite her. And Lisa probably came because she couldn't *not* come. Camille felt nervous that they would have an exchange of bitter words, but Lisa just came up to her after the vows and said, "Congratulations." She and Wally didn't even stay for the dancing.

They went to Rome for their honeymoon. Camille had wanted to go there since she saw *Roman Holiday* with Audrey Hepburn and Gregory Peck. Audrey was a disillusioned princess who escapes the drudgery of her duties in Rome. She meets Gregory Peck, a newspaper journalist. Neither of them tell who they really are. They fall in love, but she makes herself return to life in the palace. When she finds out who he really was, she realizes he could've exposed her but chose not to, and loves him even more. But they don't get to be together. Gregory Peck was so handsome it made her head spin. Rome was nice too.

Camille said good-bye to Miss Dinsmore and hello to Mrs. Kessler. She was now an "Upper East Side housewife." She now had her own uniformed doorman. While Daniel was at work, which was a lot, she walked up and down Madison Avenue. Went to the Guggenheim or the Whitney or the Metropolitan Museum of Art. Bought maternity clothes. Ordered a crib. Had her hair done at Bergdorf's, her legs and bikini line waxed at Elizabeth Arden. She hired a personal trainer to help keep her figure and went to a masseuse every week. She wasn't really comfortable with this new role; she wasn't used to having so many people service her needs. But the novelty of the situation kept her occupied. She had never spent this much money in her life.

Not that Daniel actually made that much money. His staff position at Bellevue and the private patients he saw in the evenings and on weekends brought in about $125,000 a year. Not a huge amount for New York City, but enough for a couple to live very comfortably. Plus he had stocks and bonds and a father who was ready to help with a mortgage whenever they were ready to find a larger apartment.

Life was refreshingly straightforward for the first time she could remember. No striving for something she could not have. Just existing. Being pregnant. This was all she had to do. By this simple act, she was useful. Strangers smiled at her. She didn't have to justify her existence or impress anyone. She didn't even mind how her body changed. Daniel was so delighted with her, kissing her tummy all the time. She made him happy and making him happy was making her happy.

It wasn't until the third trimester that she started to dislike her appearance. The whole beached whale thing. Didn't her stomach protrude farther than the other women in the Lamaze class? Her midwife tried to reassure her. But how was this baby actually going to come out of her body?

By the third trimester, sex was the last thing on her mind.

Daniel was understanding. He knew how much her appearance meant to her. He was content to lie in bed with her and snuggle and make do with the occasional hand job. She just wasn't interested in anything else going into or out of that opening of her body. That was all. It didn't mean anything. She knew that she would want it again, after the baby was born. She wasn't worried.

During her last week of pregnancy, she lived off doughnuts and bagels.

"Isn't it funny," she said to Daniel one night when she was sitting on the bed finishing up a sesame bagel with cream cheese. A bag of Dunkin Donuts was waiting patiently. "All I want to eat are round foods with holes in the middle."

"You're identifying with your food," he said.

"What, I'm a holy person?"

"You're a vagina. An opening. A hole that has been filled."

"Whatever," she said, reaching for a glazed.

If Scarlett O'Hara could give birth, then I can too. She didn't want to think too hard about the fact that Scarlett was a fictional character. Vivien Leigh was real, and she had Laurence Olivier's baby. But then she had a nervous breakdown. But this was not the time to think about that. She was on her back in a small sterile hospital room and Daniel by her side and a nurse walking in and out and another contraction was going to come and she was scared out of her wits. JUST CUT IT OUT OF ME; I DON'T CARE IF I'M SCARRED FOR LIFE! Did Elizabeth Taylor have one? Baby, not breakdown. She must have had children. But who were they? Who was Vivien Leigh's child, for that matter? What happened to these people? FOR GOD'S SAKE! Another contraction was coming.

PLEASE GOD! Anything but another CONTRACTION! Contraction really was the wrong word. It was such a calm, understated word for what was going on; it should've been explosion or volcanic eruption or implosion or VOLCANICIMPLOSION, as in, she's having another VOLCANICIMPLOSION! And she really was not joking, but no one was taking her seriously when she pleaded: "I can't do this! Cut it out of me! Now! PLEASE OH GOD!"

At least, she thought, as the contraction eased and Daniel wiped the sweat off her brow, she wasn't the child of a famous actor. Those people were only footnotes to their parents' lives. They never lived in their own right. At least I'm not one of them. Though at that moment she would've traded with anyone. "Maybe I should have an epidural," she said, more than once, "epidural . . . epilady . . . epicenter . . . in the middle of my body . . . oh God, I'm having another VOLCANICIMPLOSION, give me drugs, give me anything, put me out, I'M BEGGING YOU!"

Labor lasted through the night. When the baby finally came out, it felt like a fish. A big, slippery eight pound, two ouncer gushing through the remnants of her vagina. The midwife announced it was a boy. Offered Daniel some sort of appliance to cut the cord. There was a snip. A rush of activity as three nurses did what they did.

"A boy?"

There had to be some mistake. Her body could not create a penis. There was no way a penis could come out of her body. It was much more likely that it was a girl with an abnormally large clitoris and everyone was confused.

She looked at Daniel. "A boy?"

He nodded. Looked pleased. Yes. Men wanted boys. She felt relief. She had done her job. Like Jane Séymour who finally delivered a son to Henry VIII after so many women had failed. (Let's not think about the fact that Jane died two weeks after giving birth.) She didn't have to accomplish anything else on this earth.

Though she would've liked a girl. Butterflies and flowers were preferable to cars and trucks any day.

"Would you like to hold him?" a nurse asked.

No, later, she was about to say, but curiosity won out. Daniel handed her this little thing wrapped in a blanket. It wasn't crying. *He,* that is, *he.* *He* seemed very calm, considering he'd just made his entrance. Calm and stoic. He already had character. And it wasn't hers. Polly loved telling her how she'd cried for hours after she was born.

"He has your nature," she said.

"You think?"

His eyeballs went from side to side like twin pendulums. As if he was scanning in this new world around him. He had a perfect round little face. And Daniel's little eyebrows in miniature. Camille gazed down at him. "Hello," she said. "It's nice to meet you."

At the sound of her voice, he seemed to focus on her. For a moment. Then he yawned a big yawn and let his eyelids fall closed.

And Camille was utterly seduced.

Part Two

Chapter Twenty-two

Let him starve.

Matthew's wail woke her from a deep, delicious sleep. For the third time that night. That was her thought.

Let him starve.

She snuggled under her blanket. What was his problem? He'd been alive for a week. Couldn't he go two hours without food? Was this a lack of moral fiber? Gluttony?

"Go back to sleep! I'm begging you! Because there's no way I'm getting out of bed!" The crying continued. "I have my own needs! And you aren't going to starve to death if you don't eat every fucking two hours!"

"You want me to get him?" Daniel asked evenly from his side of the bed.

"Why should both our nights be ruined?" She got out from under the nice warm cover as gingerly as she could (it felt like a bomb had exploded in her vagina) and walked, bare feet on cold floor, to Matthew in the living room.

He was face up in the center of his crib. His tiny fists clenched; his whole body shaking with tension. You'd think he'd been abandoned naked and hungry on a snowy mountaintop instead of tucked in all warm and cozy under his light blue down quilt with the bunny embroidered in.

She unpeeled the blanket. Picked up his chicken-bone body under the armpits. He sure could get a lot of volume out of those tiny lungs. At one week old, he already had indignation down pat.

"You are overacting."

She lowered herself (gingerly) into the sofa cushion and put him on her lap. His screeches made her fumble (this was not yet routine and it was four in the morning) as she unbuttoned the front flap of her nightgown. She produced the main attraction—her right breast—cupped it with the palm of her left hand and braced. It was that first suck that really brought pain, like a jolt of electricity searing her nipple.

He was so busy crying, Matthew couldn't even perceive it was right in front of his mouth. Which was funny, sort of, considering how massive it was.

Funny. But freaky, too.

Her breast was about the same size as his head! She would've laughed like a maniac if she wasn't about to kill herself.

Camille rose (gingerly), put him on her shoulder and paced to his screams. It was a good horror movie idea: The Attack of the Killer Breasts. She imagined a poster with a breast the size of a grown man's head after some implant surgeon couldn't stop himself from making it bigger and bigger and bigger. *These knockers lure horny men then smother them with a single suck.*

Oh, god. She wanted to collapse into a heap on the floor. She sat (gingerly) on the couch and positioned him in front of her breast again. He was still unaware that the object of his desire was right there for the taking. All his attention was on venting his outrage at the world.

"Matthew, my breast is right in front of your face! Okay?"

This had no effect. She brushed her nipple to his lips. He wailed on, his mouth a wide-open megaphone for his cries.

What did he want? Had she taken too long? Did he expect her to station herself on the floor next to his crib? Well, yes, of course he did. Like a servant, she was supposed to be at his beck and call.

"I have a life too, you know." But her declaration (plea?) was drowned out by his cries.

Because she didn't have a life. (Her eyes tearing up now.) She only existed to get the milk from her breast to his stomach, then get his shit from his butt to the diaper pail. Which at that moment was stinking up the living room, but what did it matter, they never had guests. Not that she had friends anymore that might've been potential guests.

She took a deep breath. Exhaled.

I can do this, she told herself. It won't be forever. *I am not going to crack up.*

Maybe he'd had a bad dream. Did infants dream? She didn't dream. Not these days. Or if she did dream, it was only of his mouth. His mouth screaming, his mouth pumping air, his mouth searching for her, for her breast, for the milk he could get out of it.

I won't cry, she thought. Someone had to stay calm here. "Relax. Matthew. Come on. Relax. Nothing horrible is happening."

Except for the fact that all she wanted to do was throw him out the window.

Bad thought. *Bad thought.* Did not think that thought. She held her nipple near his mouth again. Milk was now leaking out like drips from a faucet. He had to smell it. He had to know it was right there in front of his face! But he cried on. She laughed hysterically. Where was Daniel with the straitjacket? Because this goddamn fucking baby was crying for no discernible reason at all! Or maybe this wasn't about hunger. He had gas, or a hernia, or was suffering from some unbearable obscure pain that was leading to certain death while she was sitting here wishing he'd never been born.

She did not think that. *Did not think that.* He was the most precious thing in her life; of course he was. She reminded herself that Matthew was new at this too. But he didn't even *know* he was new at it, or that *he* was new or that there could be a *concept* like new, and it wouldn't be like this moment for him forever!

She stood up and paced with him over her shoulder jiggling

him. "Everything is going to be all right, Matthew. Nothing bad is happening. Everything is fine."

Finally, if from nothing else but fatigue, Matthew started to quiet down.

She sat down (gingerly) on the couch again, brought out her humongous breast again, and offered the nipple. Please eat, please eat, please eat. With some annoyed grunts and snorts (his nose was runny with snot now and he had to clear an air path) he latched on.

She cringed at the zing of pain as he gave her nipple a serious suck. Winced. Reminded herself to breathe in . . . out . . . in . . . out. The pain lessoned and the milk let down and she relaxed (gingerly) back into the sofa cushion letting herself slip into a daze. Once he got going, it didn't hurt that much. Thank god. Peace. Silence. Her breast. His mouth. The center of the universe.

What had she done?

Chapter Twenty-three

"Thank you for coming."

"Of course I came."

Her mother never travelled to New York to see her perform; it took a baby to get her there. Not that Camille was ungrateful. More than ever before, she really needed Polly.

"I'm totally incompetent."

"Are you kidding? You're doing great."

"I'm not cut out for this. It was a huge mistake."

"Don't be ridiculous. You're wonderful. I'm so impressed."

"Would you mind getting me some tea?" Camille asked.

"Sure."

Polly went to the kitchen. Oh, to have someone wait on her! She was ready to ask her mother to move in.

Polly returned with an orange.

"That looks good." The nursing made her thirsty all the time.

"Would you like me to peel it for you?"

"Would you?"

"Of course."

"Thank you."

Her mother dug out the rind with her nail. "I know it isn't easy. But you look great."

"My hemorrhoid is flaring, my vagina is ripped to shreds, my nipples are killing me, I have a hangnail, and a pimple grew right on the bottom of my nostril last night. I should just dump myself in a garbage pail and die."

Polly handed her another slice. Camille bit into it and felt the sweet spray of juice on her tongue and the sides of her mouth. Nothing had ever tasted so good.

"The first three months are the hardest. It will get easier, I promise."

"Do you really? Because I can't stand this much longer. I'm not kidding. I really am going insane."

She felt like crying (she was now always on the verge of tears) but her mother laughed, handed her another slice of orange, and took one for herself. "Just get past the first three months."

"Do you remember what it was like with me?" She asked with trepidation, unsure whether Polly would make her feel better or worse.

"It was horrible. I couldn't wait to get out of the house."

"Gee. Thanks." Worse.

"I remember I didn't start to feel better until I made friends with some other moms. I know you feel cut off from your old crowd. You really should join a mother's group or something."

"It sounds so boring."

"You need to compare notes. Complain to each other."

"Did you complain when I was a baby?"

"Of course."

Camille knew that her complaints were worse than all the other mothers' complaints. Other mothers would never have thoughts about throwing their babies out the window. "Did you feel like your entire life had been taken away from you?"

"Of course. Nothing is ever the same again."

Camille had never even considered what motherhood had been like for Polly. Or if she had, it was only to idealize those precious years her father had still been with them. "You first met Dad when he was in a play, right? You were in the audience?"

"I was in the play."

"No you weren't."

"I think I know how I met your father! It was a lousy, stupid comedy about this man who lived with his mother in Petaluma raising chickens. Written by a mutual friend. I just had a small part and your father had the lead. I still have the program somewhere; I'll show you next time you come out."

"So why did you stop acting? Because of me?" Camille couldn't believe her mother had ever actually allowed herself the pleasure of going on stage.

"Oh, no, I stopped way before you were born. I guess I wasn't confident enough to think of myself that way. You know, John was 'the actor.' When I fell in love with him, I knew I'd need to do something practical to hang on to him. So I went back to school, got certified . . ."

"And resented him?"

"Not really. I do like to teach."

"So . . ." Camille hesitated. This felt intrusive, but she was still having trouble grasping the truth in her head. "When did Dad start cheating? When I was a baby?"

"As far as I know, it wasn't until you were about four or five."

"And it was more than one woman."

"Like a compulsion. He kept promising he'd stop. But he didn't. Or couldn't."

"I have a hard time getting it through my head. I believed for so long that he came to New York because you wouldn't come with him. You couldn't understand his 'need to act.'" She couldn't believe that here she was, referring to his ambitions with sarcasm.

"The marriage was over years before he moved to New York. He followed a director here. . . ."

"Who?"

"Oh, I don't remember. He was doing some new play. . . ."

"Where?" She wanted every detail. Why? What difference did it make?

"I have no idea. The Public Theater, maybe? I don't know.

Your father thought he would get cast, but it didn't work out. Nothing much did. Though he did get that small part in *Tootsie*. But he loved it here. We hardly ever saw him after that. Well, you know that. Then he had the heart attack. Boom."

Camille looked at Matthew. So innocent. "How could you leave your wife and child?"

"The thing that really made him feel alive was being out there. On stage. That high. He couldn't resist. You know how that is."

"I hate him."

"Don't say that."

"It's just . . . so . . . selfish."

"And let me tell you . . ." Polly laughed, though it obviously wasn't a pleasant memory. "I was jealous. He was out at night all the time having a ball and I'd be stuck at home. . . ."

"With me."

"Well. Not with you. With *the baby*."

Polly chuckled, as if that was funny. Camille didn't chuckle.

"I found a sitter as soon as I could. Even though I couldn't afford to. It was that or slit my wrists. The last thing I wanted to do after teaching all day was cater to your needs."

"What about Daddy?"

"He was no help. Even when he wasn't cast in anything, he was hanging out at the bar with the others. Always claimed that's when the real casting got done. Being a mother is dull and lonely. But, hey. Someone has to do it."

"Thanks."

"Come on. Don't be offended. I'm empathizing."

"Yeah. Well, I know what you mean. Daniel is always at the hospital, meetings, seeing patients, working on his papers . . ."

"You gotta get yourself out of the apartment. Did you find a baby-sitter yet?"

"I'm not looking."

"Trying to prove you're a better mother than I was?"

"Thank you, Dr. Freud."

The kettle started hissing in the kitchen.

The noise from the kettle disturbed Matthew, and he started to cry.

"Look," Polly said, rising from the couch, "I did my best. That's all you can do. Don't be so hard on yourself." Polly went to the kitchen to make the tea. Camille glared at Matthew and mentally willed him back to sleep. The kettle stopped hissing. He faded back. Maybe her glare did it.

Chapter Twenty-four

Daniel liked his routines.

For breakfast every morning, he had two pieces of whole wheat toast with some whipped butter and—not on every bite, but intermittently—a bit of jam. Blackberry or raspberry. He didn't like strawberry. He felt it was too sweet.

With his toast every morning, he drank one cup of coffee that he made from grinding Starbuck's Italian Roast beans. When he finished that cup he would have a half-cup more. He usually microwaved a half-cup of milk for one minute and added that, though sometimes when he was feeling impatient he just added the milk cold.

He left for work at 7:25 every morning and took the bus downtown. He was back around 7:00 in the evening.

Dinner. He liked a glass of red wine, some kind of meat, and a vegetable or salad. Then he wanted coffee (2-percent milk, no sugar) and dessert. This could just be grocery store cookies, but he was happier with something from the bakery. Rainbow cookies were one of his favorites.

Sometimes Camille enjoyed taking care of him and she embraced the fifties housewife role with gusto. For the first time in her life, she was a success as far as society was concerned. To the extent she could go along with it, she felt satisfied.

To the extent she could not go along with it, she considered sticking her head in the oven.

After dinner, Daniel played with Matthew some, but there wasn't really too much they could do together yet. The boy had a distinct preference for his mother. So Daniel would often migrate to his desk and the paper he was now working on: "The Psychiatrist as Know-It-All in American Film."

Daniel liked to make love in the evenings. Never in the morning. And he only liked to do it once. Then he fell asleep.

But since Matthew was born, they hadn't made love at all.

The morning Polly was leaving, Camille paced with Matthew, who was in a very cranky mood. He wailed if she tried to put him down. Wouldn't let Polly hold him. And cried every time she sat down with him. The only way he was happy was if she stood up holding him. As if it could really matter to him if she was standing or not!

Polly packed. Camille considered asking her to stay longer, but she knew she couldn't. It was so amazing. She actually wanted her annoying mother around! She felt as if she was being left alone on a tropical island. Tom Hanks in *Castaway*. But instead of a ball named Wilson, she had Matthew.

"It's very sweet," Polly was saying. "Daniel loves having a family. The way he looks at you. He loves you so much. You can see that the minute he walks in the door."

"Yes. The problem is, he's usually walking out the door."

"I'm sure he would be very supportive if you decided to go back into acting."

"I'm not so sure about that. Anyway, I don't want to. Why do I need to do anything more than this? Why make my life even harder? It's not like you ever really wanted me to act, so why are you even encouraging it?" Maybe it was just as well her mother was leaving.

"It's not that I didn't want you to do it, I just thought it was hard on you. But now you have a safety net, other things in your life, it's not the 'be all and end all.' "

"Mom. You of all people know I spent too much of my life beating my head on that wall."

"It was obvious, even when you were little . . . nothing was going to stop you. And John always encouraged you. I'll never forget his face when he saw you play Dorothy in sixth grade. . . ."

"I still have those red sequin shoes! After the show, he took me out for hot fudge sundaes at Ghirardelli Square. Then we took a cable car downtown. He let me pick out a new dress at Macy's. . . ."

"He was so proud of you. You were a natural."

Camille sighed and looked out the window to the building across the street. Matthew looked too. What good was being a natural if no one would hire you? The truth was, her father had corrupted her with his own frustrated dreams. Thank god she'd managed to extricate herself.

Matthew had calmed down, so Camille tried again to sit. He started to cry again. She stood up. He stopped crying. She started to sit again, just to test him. He started to cry again. She stood up. He stopped.

"You were so incredibly tenacious," Polly said.

That use of past tense annoyed her. Even if she was glad she'd extricated herself. "You mean foolish."

"No! You knew what you wanted and you didn't give up."

"But now I have."

"You may go back to it some day."

"No."

"You don't know."

"I'm glad to be out. I can't believe I stayed with it for so long."

"What about your vocal coaching?"

"We don't need the money. What's the point?"

Matthew was calm again, so she tried sitting. If she didn't sit, she thought she might faint. She sat. He started to cry again. She stood back up and now *she* started to cry. "Why is he doing this? Is he trying to punish me?"

Polly took him. He started to cry even louder. "Get yourself a baby-sitter."

"Let me feed him. At least he'll let me sit, and it'll shut him up."

She took Matthew back, sat down, and lifted her shirt. It still hurt a little when he started to suck but not as bad as the first week. Polly watched. "Lots of women have all sorts of trouble getting into the breast-feeding, but you have a real knack for it."

"Yeah, right," Camille smirked. "I've finally found a talent for something useful. Wet nurse. Too bad I was born in the wrong century." But she liked hearing her mother say it. Considering how many negative, evil thoughts she was thinking, she really couldn't hear enough praise. "Does having a child mean a lifetime of being interrupted out of your own life?"

"Until he goes away to college."

Camille looked down at him. Kissed the top of his soft little head. "He is cute, isn't he?" she asked for what seemed like the millionth time.

"Adorable."

She gazed at him with pride. Even if he had ruined her life, she could take pleasure in his perfection.

She was quickly discovering that she hated playgrounds. They dotted Central Park like a bad case of acne. It didn't matter which one she went to. So dull. But what else could you do with a baby? Push his stroller up and down Madison Avenue looking at clothes there was no need to wear even if you could pay those outrageous prices? It wasn't like they socialized. Daniel hated parties. They had gone to some psychiatric functions when she was pregnant, like the analytic convention at the Waldorf. Those people were the worst dressers. The women all wore shapeless dresses accessorized with beaded necklaces from Guatemala and were badly in need of make-overs. Hadn't they ever heard of Max Factor? The gym?

The doctors' wives were, in their own way, worse. Every conversation was a contest over clothes, apartments, renovations. Finding the right help, finding the right private school for the kids, finding the right therapist for the kids. Names dropped like pigeon shit. How is Woody's lawsuit going? Did you hear Bloomberg bought an apartment on Fifth? My son is in the same class as Sarah Jessica Parker's son!

But the most dreadful conversations at these parties were about the theater. Everyone seemed to have a subscription to the Roundabout or Manhattan Theatre Club—Off Broadway nonprofits that had never cast her in anything. These people discussed the actors as if they knew how to judge a performance. Disgusting. (None of them had any idea she'd been an actress. She'd forbidden Daniel to tell.)

She did have her figure back already, thanks to compulsive exercising during pregnancy. Too bad there was nothing she could do about the stretch marks. Which she couldn't quite look at. Too distressing. Her days of wearing two pieces were officially over.

After her mother was gone, Camille felt loneliness bleed with alarming speed into despair. She took Matthew to the café at the Barnes and Noble on Eighty-sixth Street thinking it would at least get her out into the adult world and maybe cheer her up. But he shrieked so much, she couldn't even get him to take her breast. She had to give up drinking her latte. Everyone glared at her as she maneuvered his stroller onto the escalator while trying to balance the cup of coffee that sploshed right through the lid onto her jeans.

Then she took him to the Metropolitan Museum of Art on Fifth Avenue. Her father had once written to her about the display of knights in shining armor and how amazing it was to see those props straight out of King Arthur and the Knights of the Round Table—yet they were for real!

She'd gone straight to the museum after moving to New York, as if she would find him standing in front of a suit of metal contemplating the days of chivalry and sword fights. Now here she was, living a few blocks away, and she hadn't yet gone in. Today was the day.

She maneuvered Matthew's stroller up the stairs to the entrance, then went straight to the back of the first floor. There they were. Human-shaped cages perpetually waiting for battle. So incredible anyone had actually worn them. They weren't just inventions out of fairy tales.

It still made her sad that he never saw her in *Camelot*. Never heard her sing "What Do the Simple Folk Do?" Everyone had said she was wonderful, even complimented her singing. She circled the procession of armored horses in the middle of the room and wondered. When her father had been here, had he missed her as much as she'd missed him? As much as she, back in California, had treasured the thought of him? No, of course not. He was relishing his freedom. The freedom she missed so much right now. Oh, yes. He'd escaped from the shackles of family and responsibility. So he could have fun. She stopped in front of a particularly tall, hulking man of iron. Stared into the darkness behind the helmet's visor.

She did hate him.

Matthew started to get impatient. This baby had no sense of history! She rolled him out to the Ancient Playground and sat with him on a bench under the trees and watched the older children play. Camille was still generally avoiding other mothers but one sat down next to her and started up a conversation (monologue) about how she was looking forward to going back to work at her PR agency. She ended with the claim that her baby had "slept through the night since the day she was born."

Matthew had never slept through the night. Not once since he was born, not one single time, not ever. He had not, as a matter of fact, slept longer than three hours in a row yet.

"I think there's something wrong with babies that sleep through the night," Camille said. "They don't have the self-esteem to make their needs known."

"Well. That is one way of looking at it." The woman looked the other way.

That shut her up.

That evening, Daniel got home late. She sat with him while he ate lamb chops and string beans.

"Some excitement at the hospital today."

"Do tell." She did like to hear about his patients. Getting the lowdown on a secret world she wasn't supposed to know about.

"An autopenisectomy."

"Tell me that's not what I think it is."

"A guy took a big pair of scissors and cut it off."

"Why?!"

"I don't know yet. He's not saying too much."

"Can they . . . reconnect it?"

"They should be able to. It's his head—well, maybe I should say his 'mind'—I'm worried about. We'll see."

"To actually cut it off. God."

"And how was your day?"

"Let's see. Matthew had ten poops today."

"Really? Is that normal?"

"Actually I read that's a good sign. It means he's getting lots of nourishment. Of course, we're going through the diapers like crazy. Not to mention the laundry, because they're so watery, which is normal too—I checked—but it keeps seeping out and staining his clothes. Can you believe my life has come to this? Reporting on the texture of my child's shit?"

"You're helping our son grow. That's important!"

"I knew you'd say that, but the truth is, you'd never trade places."

"Hey, we don't get an autopenisectomy every day."

"Are you done?" She got up to clear his dish.

"You know what you need?"

"What?" She was really hoping he might come up with a

good piece of advice. That was, theoretically, a fringe benefit to being married to a psychiatrist.

"You need to have sex."

"That's your advice?" She'd never seen such a blatant example of projection in her life. "You've got to be kidding."

"After we make love, you'll feel good about yourself again." Camille smiled politely.

"Maybe tonight," Daniel said.

"Maybe," she said. Or maybe not.

Midnight. She sat on the sofa and stared at the wall unit. Matthew's little mouth worked away at her breast. Daniel's penis waited for her in the bedroom.

Autopenisectomy! That would solve their problems. Or maybe she should cut her breast off. Okay, no. Leave the body parts alone. She was simply not in the mood. That's all. Matthew was almost falling back asleep, so she jiggled him a little to get him to keep eating. *What to Expect the First Year* said it was important to empty out each breast at a feeding. They'd also claimed that you could hope for a longer stretch of sleep if you tanked up your baby. She hadn't given up hope.

Eventually, Matthew's jaw went slack. She burped him and gently, very gently, set him down in his crib and went to the bedroom. Sleep beckoned. Sleep sleep sleep sleep sleep. It felt so good to be free of his little mouth. The weight of his body. Have her body back to herself, if only for an hour or two.

Daniel emerged from the bathroom naked. *Don't* make any comments about cutting penises off. He ambled up to her.

"I miss you," he said.

"I miss you too."

He put his arms around her. She tensed up. He nuzzled his mouth into the crook of her neck. She moved her head away.

"It would be nice to reacquaint ourselves, don't you think?"

His arms strapped her in from behind. She longed to yank free.

"Yes. It's been too long. I'm just so tired all the time."

"I know."

His lips on the back of her head, his cock on the crack of her butt like a hot dog on a bun.

"Matthew, you know, it's like he's consuming me."

"I'm willing to share until I can get you back to myself."

"I don't think there's enough to go around right now." She extricated herself from his embrace and forced herself to kiss him on the cheek in as chaste a way as possible. "I'm sorry. . . ."

"Don't apologize."

"I feel bad."

"It's okay. I understand. It's for a good cause."

He put on his pajama bottoms.

"I'm sure I'll be back in action soon."

"I'm sure you will too."

In bed they kissed briefly on the lips and said their good nights. Camille turned her back to Daniel, and he snuggled up next to her and put his arm around her. She let him.

Matthew woke at two A.M. And then again at four. So much for tanking up. She no longer bothered with the nursing night-gown; the buttons just got in the way. Just pulled up her T-shirt. Matthew latched on with no problem. Her nipples were no longer sore. They'd become huge bulbous rubbery appliances. He sucked away. She stared at the wall unit. After he was done, she put him back in his crib. She knew these early morning hours intimately, now. The quiet of the dawn. The corner newsstand that stayed open twenty-four hours. The cabs cruising to nowhere. The newspaper hitting the door.

They were both up at six for yet another feeding when Daniel's alarm went off. Camille made his coffee and toast.

"I hope today goes a little better for you," he said before leaving.

"Maybe he'll only have nine poops."

"Why don't you look into hiring a nanny?"

"Why should we pay someone to do my job?"

"So you can have some free time?"

They'd had this conversation before. "Please don't."

"You're doing a wonderful job." He kissed her on the forehead. "Maybe we could get someone to come in on the weekend. Just so we can spend some time alone together. We haven't seen a movie in months. I miss watching movies with you."

"We could watch a movie when he's napping."

"That's not the same."

"But we could. We don't need a baby-sitter to watch a movie. You're always working. That's why we don't watch movies together anymore."

"So we'll make a date to rent a video, okay?"

"Okay."

But don't think that means I'll have sex with you.

He kissed Matthew on the cheek.

When she turned on *Regis and Kelly* at nine, Matthew fell back asleep. She turned off the TV and tried to sleep too, but her brain just went in swirls when she shut her eyes. So she turned the TV back on and watched them interview a young actress who had just gotten her "big break" in a new series about women lawyers.

That actress. Did she really think anyone cared about her stupid show? Dressed up like a mannequin, mouthing stupid drivel written by hacks. Her show would be canceled within ten weeks and she'd be out of work anyway, depressed and forgotten.

Ambition. Thank god she'd gotten ambition out of her soul. Was this the relief a victim feels when her rapist has been put behind bars?

Camille looked down at Matthew. His innocent brown eyes stared back at her with, could it be, adoration? Yes. He had rescued her from all that. Her hero. Her master. Her slave driver.

Chapter Twenty-five

Camille sat in the waiting room and resolved that today she was going to bring it up. Ask her midwife Emily Austen for help. The sex. Or lack of it. She knew Daniel was running out of patience.

She gazed down at Matthew, asleep in his carriage. He had such a perfect little face. She could admire it as much as she could admire her own. His delicate little cherry lips and perfectly formed little nose and ears with their delicate little folds.

She wished he was awake. Not so they could interact. She spent enough time being his one-woman entertainment committee. But it was a waste for him to nap now, in the waiting room, when she would've been able to nap along with him at home.

A bulletin board displayed photos sent in by proud moms of past babies delivered. (See? Many babies do survive our deliveries!) None of the babies were, of course, as cute as Matthew. She knew all the other mothers thought they were. But they were wrong.

"Camille Kessler?" Camille wheeled the carriage back into the examining room and passed two pregnant women. She'd already given birth while they were still gripped with the fear of the unknown horrors that lay ahead. *Been there done that.*

She'd avoided the dreaded Caesarean and produced the re-quired baby. For once in her life, she had delivered.

This was only her second office visit to the midwife since Matthew was born four—"seemed like eternity" yet "passed in a flash"—weeks ago. It was still a bit strange to be there with him outside of her. She passed the bathroom where she'd always had to pee into a cup and steered the carriage into the office of her midwife with the lovely name. Daniel had wanted her to use a doctor, but she had insisted on a midwife for the pure word of it. Midwife. It linked her with the past, with women through the ages. Shakespearean women used mid-wives, Moliere, Strindberg . . . She wanted one for herself.

"Camille, how are you?"

"Exhausted."

"And so you should be. Let me see him. Oh! He is so adorable. What a handsome little baby." She was of course oblig-ated to admire every baby that passed through these doors. But Camille felt certain this woman's admiration for Matthew was real. She lay down on the examining table and spread her legs.

"How are you feeling?"

Camille's thighs framed Emily Austen's face in a V shape.

"I'm having some tension at home."

"Your husband's feeling neglected, right?"

"Yes! He wants to make love. And I'm really not that inter-ested."

"Of course."

"So should I do it anyway? Just to . . . you know . . ." *Get him off my back.* "I feel like I should satisfy him. He's so frus-trated."

"All you should be doing now is helping your baby eat and sleep. That's all. I don't want you to even think about having sex for at least two more weeks."

Camille's spirits rose. "Really?"

"Yes. You had a lot of tearing around the perineum and those stitches still have to heal."

Camille felt like a mental patient whose been given a two-week pass to live it up in the city before returning to the sanitarium. "But he's pestering me already, because the sex wasn't so good when I was pregnant either. He's, like, I have to say, really hard up."

"Were you having problems with your sex life before you got pregnant?"

"No." Was she?

"Then don't worry about it."

"But—"

"He'll live. You shouldn't be pressured into doing anything before you're ready. Matthew is the one who gets all your attention for now."

"So . . . two more weeks?"

"My dear. Don't have sex until you're ready. I don't care how many weeks it takes."

This was just what Camille wanted to hear. "Thanks. I feel better."

"Just get yourself through the first three months."

"And you think my sex drive will actually return then?"

"Breast-feeding makes your vagina less lubricated, plus you're getting a lot of the physical intimacy you might've wanted with your husband from your baby."

"Don't tell him that."

"He knows."

"That's part of the problem."

"Don't worry about it. This is a very special time. But that doesn't mean it's easy."

That night while getting ready for bed, Camille told Daniel about the moratorium Emily Austen had imposed (granted?). She was a good enough actress to sound disappointed to be delivering this news. "So we really shouldn't even think about sex for another month."

"Wow. That's a long time."

"I know."

"But it's an arbitrary rule. She'll never have to know."

"It's not for her benefit."

"Well it's certainly not for mine!" He gave her a wounded puppy-dog look. "It's been so long. Don't you miss making love with me?"

"Yes. Of course I do. But I'm still healing. And she's concerned about my stitches. Evidently I got pretty torn up in the delivery." She took some satisfaction playing the ripped-vagina card. "And you of all people know that it's important to give people time to heal."

She prayed he wouldn't suggest something along the lines of a blow job.

"I'm sorry," he said. "I must sound pretty insensitive."

"I know this is hard for you."

"But I can be patient."

"And you have been patient."

"And I will remain patient."

"And you will be rewarded for your patience."

As they got under the covers, Daniel gave her a chaste good-night kiss. "Your life certainly is different now. That takes a lot of getting used to."

"Yes." She knew he was trying to be understanding and it made her tense.

"Do you think part of your," he paused to search for the right word, "moodiness . . . is because you miss acting?"

"Don't worry." She suddenly felt very grouchy. "I don't miss the theater. Okay? The midwife said I just need time to heal. So can we please not make more of this than it is?"

"Fine." She could hear the annoyance in his voice. He'd been trying to address her unhappiness, she knew, and she'd reacted with hostility. But she couldn't address it, she was too tired, and she had to get some sleep. She turned to her side and shut her eyes. "I'm going to sleep." As soon as she began to drift off, Matthew started screaming to be fed.

* * *

Daniel emerged from the bedroom. It was morning. Camille was already up, feeding Matthew on the sofa. "You should start looking for a larger apartment," he said, as if he'd been thinking about it all night. "Matthew is going to need his own room one of these days."

"I know. But real estate agents can be so obnoxious."

"It's better than hanging out at the playground, isn't it? You can look around and then have me come see the ones you like."

"How much can we spend?"

"See what you can get for a million. And we'll go from there."

"Really? Can we afford that?"

"If I sell some stocks . . . and my father helps with the down payment . . . we should be able to swing it."

Matthew paused from his meal and gave her a smile. Smiling was his new talent. She leaned over and kissed his forehead. *A million dollars.* She switched him to her left breast. This would be interesting.

Camille discovered that she liked apartment hunting. It was a fully sanctified-by-the-community opportunity to intrude on a stranger's privacy, see what horrible art they put on their walls, and disapprove of the scum on their bathroom tiles.

The ones she disdained the most exhibited no individuality whatsoever. They had the requisite gourmet kitchens so over-equipped with Wolf stoves and Sub-Zero refrigerators you'd think the owners were catering parties, not ordering in every night. The same designer seemed to have convinced every apartment dweller in the city to install granite countertops (with backsplashes!), custom cabinetry, and tastefully bland furniture from Ethan Allen. (Individuality expressed as conformity?) The biggest decision these people seemed to be able to make was whether to get their furniture in cherry, maple, or oak.

Naomi Kline was the perfect agent for her. They'd made contact when Camille called about an ad in the *Times* that mentioned an apartment with a "Juliet balcony." Camille was intrigued. She could do the *rose by any other name* speech to Daniel (or anyone who would listen) down on the sidewalk.

"That's a lovely apartment," Naomi said on the phone, "with a wood-burning fireplace. Would you like to see it?"

"What exactly is a Juliet balcony?" She pictured the imposingly high stone balcony in Zeffirelli's *Romeo and Juliet*. But this was an apartment building, not a castle.

"Basically, it's a ledge with a railing and enough room to lean. Not very useful, but nice to be able to say you have one."

Here, Camille thought, is someone I can trust.

Born and raised on the Upper East Side, Naomi was in her late forties, had a decent figure; short brown hair with bangs; and a big, generous, toothy smile. She had a daughter in high school, her husband was a stockbroker, and she was only selling real estate because she couldn't figure out what else to do with her life. She toyed with the idea of going back to school and getting her MSW, but she couldn't face taking the GRE.

"Maybe I shouldn't tell you so much about myself," she said their first day out, "but what kind of freak wants to be a real estate agent when she grows up?"

"It's fun to look at apartments."

"I do love to help people get settled. It's a compulsive 'Mom' thing. We're going to find the perfect apartment for you."

Camille knew it was Naomi's spiel, but it seduced her in just the same.

It was Naomi who swayed Camille to look in Carnegie Hill, the northernmost section of the East Side before it turned into Harlem. "It's the most desirable place to live in Manhattan," she claimed. "More families. More relaxed. Quiet and leafy, beautiful brownstones, very few high-rises, gorgeous mansions, the best museums in the world. And *scads* of people in publishing, theater, the arts . . . Kevin Kline, Paul Newman, the list goes on and on." Even *Naomi* lived in Carnegie Hill. She knew where to get your hair done (Amore de Hair), where to take yoga (Open Skies), the best Italian food (Vico), the best scones (Sarabeth's), best clothes for mom (Nancy & Co.), best French label clothes for baby (Jacadi).

Did Camille have a choice? Not really. She didn't feel like she fit in on the Upper East Side, but Daniel wasn't interested in moving downtown; Carnegie Hill it was. In any case, once they started looking at places, she didn't really care about finding an apartment. She finally had someone to hang out with during her long hours with Matthew. The trick was to keep her interested without letting her close a sale.

"I think you're going to like this one," Naomi said one Tuesday morning as they entered the lobby of a building on Park Avenue and Ninety-third Street. (The apartment with the Juliet balcony had turned out to be too small.) Naomi turned to the doorman and gave him her business card. "We're here to see apartment 5D."

The doorman, a chunky young man who looked like he was sleeping on his feet, got them the key from a cabinet in the vestibule. "Nice lobby," Camille said. The creamy white carvings that laced the periphery of the ceiling reminded her of a wedding cake.

"Isn't it gorgeous?" Naomi pushed the button for the elevator. "Did he sleep well last night?" She was much more up on her life (Matthew) than Daniel.

"He was up at two, and I fed him, and he went back; then he was up again at four, and I refused to feed him again and he cried for like thirty minutes." There was a desperate need to report these idiotic details to anyone who would listen.

"What did you do?"

They stepped onto the elevator. "I gave in. And then he was up again at six and then . . ."

Naomi looked at her.

"He never went back to sleep."

"No."

"Yes."

"Poor thing."

Camille didn't mention how Daniel had slept through the night while she nobly carried on. Sometimes she felt like a single mother. Of course, he was up at 6:00 and going all day so she really couldn't complain.

"Did you keep Mommy up all night?" Naomi asked Matthew as they stepped off the elevator. "You have to let Mommy sleep or Mommy gets very tired."

"And cranky," Camille added, as if it would do any good. Matthew just smiled and basked in their attention. It sure was nice to have Naomi to talk to, even if she was just indulging her because she wanted to make a sale.

"He's so delicious." Naomi put the key in the lock. Camille wasn't comfortable with the idea of her child as a meal. "Look at those cheeks," Naomi went on. "I just want to eat you up!"

Matthew looked at Naomi with, Camille felt sure, distrust. As if he knew that Naomi had ulterior financial motives and was not just into hanging out with his mother for fun, attractive and amusing as she was.

Camille did relish that moment of anticipation as Naomi opened the door. As if she was a game-show contestant and her prize was being revealed. A contestant, though, with the power on her side. If she didn't want it, she could turn it down in the hopes that the next offering would be better.

They strolled through the rooms. Naomi pointed out how the previous owners had taken care to preserve all the old details like wainscoting and glass cabinet doors. But it made Camille feel claustrophobic. The dining room looked out on an air shaft, which was typical enough for these New York apartments, and the living room looked smack into the building across the way, and since it was on the fifth floor there really was no light, and who needed to spend over a million dollars to live like that?

They took the elevator back down and returned the key to the doorman.

On the bus ride home, Camille thought about how Naomi didn't seem to mind spending so much time showing her places. She was rarely the one to say they should push on, even when she had to be able to sense that Camille wasn't seriously interested but only having fun with the fantasy of living in the apartment with park views, or the building with the parking garage in the building or a gym on the ground floor. . . .

"It's nice," Camille often found herself saying. "But . . ."

Too small, too dark, too expensive . . . or the trusty and reliable standby: any new listings? Seemed like she could find something wrong with anything they could afford. Naomi said everyone felt that way, even if they had millions of dollars to spend. "Everyone always wants what's just beyond their reach."

But it wasn't only that. Camille could imagine driving her shiny new SUV into her own garage and tossing the keys to the solicitous parking attendant. She could imagine waking up in the morning, putting on her sweats, and riding down the elevator to her fully-equipped gym. She could imagine riding the elevator up to her penthouse and stepping onto the terrace for 360-degree views of Central Park, midtown, and the East River. The only thing she couldn't imagine was picking one way of seeing herself.

Chapter Twenty-six

It was Matthew's six-week birthday. The sex moratorium was over. Would Daniel remember?

It was a typical boring day. Wake up, change diaper, breast-feed, make Daniel's toast and coffee, buy her own coffee and a muffin, walk to playground, walk to grocery store, go home, change diaper, breast-feed, watch *All My Children*, *One Life to Live*, empty the dishwasher if cleaning woman was there to show her you weren't a complete lazy slob, eat snack for self, take nap while baby napped, breast-feed, change diaper, sing sweet lullaby, cry, breast-feed, change diaper, cry some more . . .

It was as if she was sitting in an endless bad play with no intermission and she was in a seat in the middle of a row in the orchestra with no way out. Knowing that Daniel was going to want to make love at the end of this particular day just put her in an especially bad mood.

Some women, she knew, found the whole motherhood thing a very sexual experience. She'd read all about it in some depressing book by some overachieving doctor who had given birth to one child while breast-feeding another while giving a pap smear to a patient while blowing her husband while writing her best-seller about how to be a great mother. Well fuck her.

The high point of her day (drumroll please) was Matthew's afternoon nap. Matthew's afternoon nap (the words made her want to dance a jig!). She could hardly wait for him to fall asleep. This had to be how an addict craved drugs.

Maybe, she thought, after Matthew drifted off and she got under the covers of her nice warm bed for her own nap, Daniel would forget this was Matthew's six-week birthday. Or maybe he'll be so tired (didn't he have some sort of budget meeting scheduled for today?) that the subject wouldn't come up and she wouldn't have to reject him so she wouldn't have to feel guilty. . . .

Daniel came home at the usual time with a bouquet of flowers and a fruit tart from Patisserie Margot. During dinner, he told her about a new patient who believed he was Jesus Christ. "He felt he wasn't obligated to carry health insurance." And he volunteered to watch Matthew while she took a shower. Then he made some calls while she fed Matthew, and took his own turn in the bathroom while she put Matthew down to sleep. While he showered, Camille sat on the edge of their bed flipping through a Victoria's Secret catalog noting that none of these women had stretch marks. When the water stopped, she buried it in the garbage. Daniel opened the door while still drying himself with a towel.

He got behind her and massaged her shoulders. "How are you feeling tonight?"

"You know . . . it's so great that we've reached the six-week milestone, and it's really wonderful that we can go back to making love because I miss you so much." She looked up at him and tried to appear frustrated. "But Matthew hardly napped today and I'm just . . . so . . . tired!"

"Oh. Okay." He looked hurt. She felt bad. Was he fighting off the impulse to rape and pillage? "Maybe tomorrow night?"

"That sounds nice."

He leaned toward her and said in a slightly naughty tone, "I'll be looking forward to it," and kissed her on the cheek.

Camille produced a naughty smile also. "Me too." He kept his eyes on her—she continued to smile naughtily—all the way back into the bathroom. He shut the door. She stopped smiling.

How long would she be able to hold him off? She turned on the TV and got under her thick white goose-down comforter and stretched out on the bed. This was all she wanted. A chance to relax by herself. As she settled back against a pile of pillows, she flipped channels with the remote and settled on Larry King. He was interviewing Nicole Kidman, who was telling him everything but what everyone really wanted to know: what really went on between her and Tom Cruise. Obviously she'd only agreed to the interview with the guarantee that her relationship with Tom was off limits.

Who could blame her? Camille could just imagine, if she went on Larry King, how he'd lean over with his bow tie and go for the dirt.

"So, Camille, tell us. Why aren't you interested in sex anymore?"

And she would say, "You know, Larry. I'm afraid I don't know how to answer that question."

"Aren't you in love with your husband?"

"To the extent that I believe in the concept of romance, yes."

"Aren't you attracted to him?"

"Objectively speaking my husband is as attractive as he ever was."

"But subjectively?"

"Subjectively . . . I'm not attracted, like that, at this time in my life, to anyone. The only person I really feel attracted to is my baby. Not, of course, that I want to have sex with him."

"Of course not."

"But I do like to gaze into his adorable face."

"Yes?"

"And kiss his sweet little cheeks."

"Go on . . ."

"And embrace his soft, warm body to my breasts . . ."

"Do you think that may have something to do with your lack of sexual interest in your own husband?"

"It's true that my husband's cheeks are not nearly as kiss-able as my baby's cheeks."

"Of course."

"And that applies to both pairs of cheeks." That was meant to be a joke, but Larry didn't smile. Maybe that wasn't appropriate for national television.

"Can you think of any other reasons you prefer your baby to your husband?"

"He has hair on his back. My husband, not the baby."

"You don't like that?"

"I don't go for the furry-animal type in general."

"Anything else?"

"I hate to admit this but . . . his penis is not nearly as cute as my son's."

"Hmmm."

"Not that I think of my baby's penis in a sexual way."

"Of course not."

"It's just . . ." She could see Larry was trying not to be judgmental. "It's so little. It reminds me of those little cocktail wieners my mother used to serve at parties. . . ."

"I thought there's nothing women like better than a big, strong, erect penis, Camille. We'll take this up after the break."

Larry looked to the camera. "Camille Kessler, ladies and gentlemen, on the front lines of motherhood. Don't go away; we'll be right back."

Chapter Twenty-seven

"So," Emily Austen said after she was done with the examination, "how's it going with you and your husband?"

Camille wasn't surprised she brought it up. Emily had undoubtedly made a notation about her in her chart. Frigid bitch? Selfish wife? Failure as a woman? *Everything is great. During foreplay my husband loves suckling milk from my breasts. He even eats me out sometimes while my baby is nursing. I feel so much more in touch with myself as a woman.* "I still have no sex drive."

"Uh-huh."

"Am I a freak?"

"Are you kidding? I hear this all the time."

"This book I read said some women feel *more* sexy after they've had a baby...."

"And some women don't. There are lots of reasons you could be feeling this way. Some of them physical, some mental. If you want, we could do some tests."

"Such as?"

"You may have had some injury to the pudendal nerve during labor. This could cause some pain or lack of sensation."

"But I wouldn't even know if there's lack of sensation. I don't want to have sex in the first place."

"We could test your testosterone levels...."

"I'm not going to take hormones." She'd read about women growing moustaches.

"Of course the most likely explanation is you're having a case of the good old postpartum blues."

"But Matthew is two months old. Shouldn't it be easing off by now?"

"Not necessarily. There are things you can do to give yourself a lift. Are you using a baby-sitter?"

"There's no reason. Daniel is always working. We never go out."

"So you can go out by yourself."

"I don't have anywhere to go."

"A restaurant? Shopping?"

"Why?"

"You need to have some time away from the baby. Give yourself a break."

Postpartum depression was such a cliché. She was not going to stoop to it. "Thanks, Emily, but you're really worrying too much. I'm fine," she said and stood up, wheeled Matthew out, and dreaded having to get through another day.

"Camille? Is that you?"

She turned and knew who it was before she saw her face.

This was awful. They hadn't spoken since Lisa's wedding. Camille had been eight months pregnant with Matthew. They'd never really made up—just attended each other's weddings as if still friends and then never spoke again.

"Lisa! Hi!"

"Camille! What are you doing in this part of town?"

"I was just seeing the midwife for my checkup. You look great."

"Thanks. So do you."

Camille noticed she didn't even look at Matthew. "So how are you?"

"I'm okay. How are you?"

Camille felt a craving to get together with her for lunch, just the two of them. But it would be awkward, she knew. Lisa was probably trying to get pregnant. How could she complain about being a mom—all she really wanted to do—without coming off as callous and superficial. "How are you?"

"Great, thanks. So we should get together sometime."

"I'd love to," Camille said. "How's the theater world?"

"I have no idea. I'm totally out of it, thank god."

"Me too, thank god."

"Well," Lisa said, "give me a call."

"I will."

"Good to see you."

"You too."

Lisa headed downtown. And Camille headed up.

Chapter Twenty-eight

"Hello and good morning to y'all!"

Cindy, the cute and bubbly twenty-year-old blonde fresh from Texas, was the Gymboree class leader. She greeted each mom and nanny as they arrived and sat on the periphery of a huge nylon multi-colored parachute.

Cindy chatted away with a young woman with a belly ring (a nanny?) next to her as they all waited—one baby to a lap—for class to begin. Listening in, Camille learned that Cindy had come to New York to act. Hah! Better get rid of that accent.

Camille looked around the circle. Did the others feel as demoralized as she did? It was hard to tell. Most of them appeared to be nannies; they looked bored and trapped. The mothers had to be the ones with self-satisfied grins. It made Camille sick. She wanted to yell: *You aren't anything special! Women have babies all the time, and there's nothing wrong with being childless! You're all just a bunch of baby-machine lemmings!* They were all most certainly under the illusion that their own offspring were the most handsome/brilliant future presidents and beauty queens of the nation. Except the mother of that bald, fat baby who drooled. That mother looked depressed. Thank god Matthew didn't drool. And he really was the most handsome baby.

She wondered if the other moms weren't having sex with their husbands either.

But she stayed quiet and kept a polite smile on her face. Maybe they were all having hot and steamy sex while their babies slept through the night and, by the way, their babies didn't take pacifiers and their shit didn't smell either.

Okay. She really had to get past this or she would never make a friend. After all, that was the real reason for being here. Matthew was too young to appreciate the selection of music much less sing along.

One woman interested her. She had straight black hair with a Betty Boop bob cut and ruby red sweetheart lips. The alert baby in her lap was about six months old.

Finally, Cindy started the class. First she led them in a few verses of "The Wheels on the Bus." Camille's voice—trained for musical theater—was wasted on the song that went "round and round" so many times she thought she would lose her mind. She glanced at Betty Boop. Had she just rolled her eyes?

After a few more songs, Cindy had them remove the parachute and put the babies on the floor inside the circle. The babies looked like appetizers ready to be speared by giant toothpicks. Cindy had them whoosh the parachute in the air over the babies. A couple of them started to cry, like they were on bad LSD trips. Matthew just looked up in the air with a sort of "What the fuck?" expression.

When it was over, Camille considered approaching Betty Boop. But one of the others was already asking her to the park. "I'd love to!" she said. Camille put Matthew into his stroller. Other mothers were lingering, bonding, heading off together. This was the moment to make contact. But she couldn't do it. She just couldn't count herself as one of them.

Matthew was napping. Camille was at the computer poking around on the *New York Times* real estate section on the web.

She scrolled through the listings. Problem was, she'd seen everything there was to see in Carnegie Hill and most of the Upper East Side, and she was having trouble coming up with excuses not to buy. Though Naomi was hiding it well, she had to be chomping at the bit for a sale.

She decided to check out the West Side. That would give her a whole new bevy of apartments. She clicked the box for two bedrooms, clicked the box for up to a million dollars, and went down the list. Her eyes landed on a listing for 111 Riverside Drive. That address sounded familiar. There was a photo of the building façade.

Yes.

That was the building Eric Hughes and Mimi Tyler had gone into that night.

Why not?

Camille called Naomi. "Can you show me a place on the West Side?"

"You want to look there now?"

"I've been looking online. There's a very nice place on Riverside Drive."

"So far west?"

"Would you mind?"

Yes, this was the building she remembered. Did Eric and Mimi actually live here? An elderly doorman opened the heavy front door and let her in. "Hi," she said, "I'm here to see apartment 3C. My agent is meeting me. I'm a little early."

"Would you like to wait in the lobby?"

"Yes, thanks."

The man was stooped and had thick glasses and gray hair. If he'd gotten on a bus she would've given him her seat. It seemed wrong that he was expected to stand every day at his job. Was he expected to actually, like, fight off criminals?

She was about to ask him who was selling the apartment. Could it be Eric and Mimi? She didn't want him to think she was there just to get a glimpse of them. She doubted, in any case, they would live on such a low floor.

Matthew started to complain. She rolled the stroller over the marble floor to a wooden bench against the wall. Parked him facing her. "Who is the cutest boy in the world?" He smiled, bounced in the seat.

"How old is he?" the doorman asked.

"Twelve weeks and four days."

Why couldn't she just say three months? She kept track like a prisoner in jail. Marked off each day like an accomplishment, just for having survived.

Matthew bounced his legs with impatience. She looked toward the door and regretted arriving early. As if Eric Hughes would be hanging out in the lobby. She considered picking up Matthew, but he was getting heavier all the time. He made a wail of protest and strained against the buckle. "Naomi will be here soon," she said, as if that would calm him for more than one quarter of a second. He started to cry, so she gave in, undid his buckle, picked him up, and took him to the doorway. Her arms were sick of holding him all the time.

A young woman was passing by. Walking down the sidewalk by herself. Her arms swinging. Wearing sneakers and shorts. So unencumbered. God. To have such freedom! That girl could go wherever she wanted! Camille couldn't believe she'd reached the point of being jealous of someone just for being able to walk down the street by herself.

Naomi arrived. "Hi," she said to the doorman, "I'm Naomi Kline." She gave him her business card. "Toni Lipton left us the keys to 3C." She turned to Camille and pulled on Matthew's foot. "Hello beautiful boy," Naomi said. "Your mommy picked a beautiful building."

"Hi."

"Art nouveau. Limestone façade. Built in 1904. Isn't it gorgeous?"

"Beautiful," Camille agreed.

The doorman handed Naomi the key. They had to wait for the elevator. It was slowly making its way down from a high floor. Eric and Mimi's floor? Naomi sighed. "So my daughter just called from school. She was working on a paper till one in the morning last night and then forgot to take it."

"Bummer."

The elevator door opened. A chubby woman with two little dogs got off. Naomi pushed three. "So she wants me to bring it to her. I said no, and she hung up on me. Now I feel guilty."

"She hung up on you. *She* should feel guilty."

The elevator reached the third floor quickly and they stepped into the hallway. There were framed Matisse prints on the wall. Naomi put the key in the door. "I have a good feeling about this one," she said. As Naomi turned the lock, Camille prepared to cross the threshold of the apartment as if making her entrance on stage. Who was she? (Housewife) What was her motivation? (Find a home for her family.) Naomi pushed opened the door, and they entered the vestibule.

She enjoyed the delicious moment of silence charged with anticipation. What kind of set had the crew built? How much money had they put in? Was she the right character for this set?

Naomi was her audience. Watching her take it all in. "Nice," Camille said. It did have potential. But it was shabby. The owners—most certainly not Eric and Mimi—had done nothing to keep it up. The paint on the ceilings was peeling. The faded floral pattern on the sofa was dirty and frayed. The wood floors were scratched and dull.

"This apartment," Naomi said as she went to the windows, "has winter views."

"Winter views?"

"When the trees lose their leaves, you see the river. The rest of the year you have a beautiful view of the park."

Camille joined her at one of the two huge windows that faced west. The trees in Riverside Park were lush with leaves, but she could imagine how, in the winter, there would indeed be a view of the stretch of river that separated Manhattan from the rest of the United States.

She looked down to the street below. There was a constant stream of traffic and a bus went up this street, so it wasn't ideal. But the thick-paned glass seemed to cut out most of the noise.

Naomi pointed out the hardwood floors, the wainscoting, the high ceilings. "It could look gorgeous with a little work. . . ."

"Do you know anything about the owners?"

"An elderly couple. Moving to Florida."

Camille took Matthew out of the stroller and carried him from room to room. The apartment really wasn't bad. It had enough space. Winter views could be nice. Too bad it made Daniel's commute longer. But he would appreciate the benefits of living right across the street from the park. And at $900,000, it was under their cap. The only remaining question: Did Eric and Mimi actually live in the building? Not that it would decide anything. But it would be fun to know.

"Everyone on the lower floors must feel inferior to the people on the upper floors. They must have fantastic views."

"Oh, yes. And . . ."

"What?"

"I don't know if I should mention it. But I'm just going to tell you. There is another two bedroom for sale in this building—16C. I didn't mention it because it's out of your price range."

"I bet it has great river views."

"Full frontal fantastic sweeping views up and down. You can see all the way to central New Jersey. I'm not trying to frustrate you. I just want you to know that it's the exact same layout, same line, but since it's on the high floor and it's had extensive renovations, it costs $400,000 more."

"We can't afford that."

Naomi smiled. "You want to take a look? Just for fun?"

She could tell Naomi was into it.

"I don't suppose it would hurt to take a peek. Could we go now?"

"The doorman might have the keys."

"But you know we can't afford it."

"Just for fun. Right Matthew?" Matthew smiled, not knowing he was getting snookered into looking at another apartment. "I think he wants to see it."

"Okay. Let's go."

Camille immediately felt her spirits rise as they took the elevator down to the doorman. One more apartment to look at. Something else to covet. Another chance to run into Eric Hughes. Maybe this one was *his* apartment. And he would be there, and . . .

This was ridiculous. She was really letting her imagination get away from her.

Naomi asked the doorman if it would be possible to look at 16C. He gave her the key. Camille lifted her chin as if she could in fact afford a $1.3-million-dollar apartment.

"The owner is in show business," Naomi said as they waited for the elevator. Camille's heart blipped. "You might've heard of him."

"Who?"

"Eric Hughes."

"You're kidding."

"You like him?"

"He's very good."

"Hasn't done much lately. Toni, the agent with these listings, says he has a house in London and a mansion in Beverly Hills. Uses this as a pied-à-terre. He's directing something for Broadway right now."

"Directing?"

"I think so. And his wife . . . What's her name?"

"Mimi Tyler. She was in that romantic comedy with him. The one that flopped."

"I think they're getting divorced. Actors should never marry actors. It never works out."

Naomi didn't know Camille used to act. "They never learn, those actors."

The hallway was the exact same as the hallway on the third floor, except it was freshly painted a very light blue and there was nothing on the walls.

Naomi had some trouble getting the key to turn, but then she pushed open the door.

This was gonna be good. You couldn't pay admission for the chance to take this tour.

Though the layout was exactly the same as the apartment they'd just been in, this was a set that upstaged any player. The room was done in gleaming deco furniture. She expected Fred Astaire and Ginger Rogers to come waltzing by any moment. What looked like (could it be?) an original Picasso hung on the wood-paneled wall. An ebony Steinway piano anchored the far corner of the room. She could imagine Eric getting together with his successful friends singing show tunes and then retiring to the other end of the room where a huge built-in television screen (the kind she'd seen in sports bars) was surrounded by a wall of curved shelves crammed with hardbacks, antiquarian books, and curios.

The three went to the window like they were approaching Oz. From this high up, the river cut a wide blue aisle that stretched from the George Washington Bridge down to the Statue of Liberty.

"Gorgeous"

"Beautiful."

Even Matthew was impressed. He stared out the window. "Look at the boats," Camille said. Boys were supposed to like boats, right? "See the pretty boats?" But his face was pointed up at the expanse of blue sky. His chin had literally dropped. Had he ever noticed there was a sky in Manhattan?

She wanted this. How could she settle for the third floor now?

Naomi led her around. The master bedroom had the same view. A huge king-size bed was angled to look out across the river. She looked at the top of his bureau. That's when she saw the framed photo. It was a snapshot, really. Eric and Mimi, glossy and tanned, arm in arm, smiling.

"There they are," she said.

"She's too skinny, but he's handsome."

"Very," Camille said. Even his crow's-feet were sexy.

"He looks nervous in the picture."

"You think?"

"She's so much younger. What do you think he is, early forties?

"Must be."

"His career is plateauing. He's ready to start a family. Meanwhile, her career is taking off. I bet you that's what happened; she wouldn't produce anything to go into that second bedroom."

"Maybe." Camille shifted Matthew to her other arm.

"It's hard, isn't it," Naomi said. "After you see this, to want the other. Maybe we shouldn't have come."

"No. I'm glad I got to see it."

"3C really is a very lovely apartment."

While checking out the bathroom, Camille checked herself out in the mirror. At least motherhood hadn't aged her face. Daniel liked to say she looked more beautiful than ever, but was he just horny? Matthew cooed at his own image. "Do you think he's living here alone?" Camille asked. The marble vanity top had nothing on it except some men's deodorant and a razor.

"I don't know."

"Because I don't see any makeup."

Naomi's cell phone rang.

"Leah?" It was Naomi's daughter. "No! Because I'm with a client. I can't believe it makes that much of a difference to your teacher. Then put her on the phone and I'll tell her you finished it last night. . . ."

"Go ahead," Camille said, "take it to her. We don't have any more apartments today anyway."

Naomi rolled her eyes. "Fine. I'll bring it. But you owe me." She hung up.

"She needs you. It's sweet."

"I suppose. It goes so fast. Before you know it, little Matthew will be going off to college. And you'll be an empty nester."

"You're depressing me."

"Look on the bright side. You'll be able to trade in for a one bedroom with views like this one."

"It would be amazing. . . ."

"Maybe you should talk to Daniel. Figure out if there's any way you can afford it," Naomi said, heading toward the door.

"Seems doubtful." Camille wished that Eric Hughes wasn't moving out of the building. That would make 3C more interesting. It would be fun to see him on the elevator. "Do you mind if Matthew and I stay here a few minutes longer?"

"Here?"

"It's time for his lunch, and if I feed him now, we'll be able to head straight to the playground and I won't have to nurse him on the park bench."

"I don't have a problem with it personally, but I'm really not supposed to . . ."

"I'm also thinking that maybe," Camille added, switching Matthew back to her other hip, "we really should consider this apartment. It is so fantastic."

"Really?"

"And I feel like, if I have the chance to sit here for a few minutes alone . . . you know . . . it's like trying a dress on in a store. You have to wait for the saleswoman to leave the dressing room so you can really see what the outfit looks like."

"I know what you mean. . . ."

"And I'm starting to think maybe this is the one. And Daniel and I will just have to find some way to make it possible."

"I would let you stay, really, but I have to return the key to the doorman. . . ."

"I'll lock up and give it to him."

"Well . . . Okay. What's the harm, right? Just keep it short."

"Just long enough to tank up Matthew. I promise."

Naomi pressed the key in Camille's free hand.

Chapter Twenty-nine

"Don't tell," she said to Matthew as soon as they were alone. "I'm being very bad."

Camille took him straight back into the bedroom and opened the top dresser drawer. Black socks and white jockeys. The next drawer down was folded T-shirts. The next one down, folded button-down shirts. Prada. Yves Saint Laurent. Ralph Lauren. There was another bureau. She opened the top drawer. Empty. She opened one closet door. It was crammed with suits and jackets. She opened the other closet door. A walk-in. Empty.

"Well, Matthew. I'm afraid Mimi is out of here. Not a teddy to be found. And I'm not talking about teddy bears either." She kissed him on his nose. He laughed. But the laugh turned into a grouchy wail.

"We're going, we're going," she said.

The bookshelf. He had the classics. *Moby Dick*. *War and Peace*. *The Red and the Black*. *Pride and Prejudice*. Ibsen, O'Neill, Strindberg. All of Chekhov's plays and story collections. And, of course, all of Shakespeare. Beautiful old hardback editions. Except for one paperback. *Men Are from Mars, Women Are from Venus*. "Looks like Mr. Hughes didn't read his John Gray carefully enough."

Matthew wasn't amused. He grunted with impatience. She

knew he was hungry. Her breasts were feeling full. "Okay, lunch time."

He started to wail.

"Okay, okay," she sank down into the huge, cushiony sofa, lifted her black tank top, and unhooked the flap of her nursing bra. Matthew started to eat hungrily. Her gaze went to the window. Light and sky. She started to feel sleepy. She had to fight to keep her lids open. But after about ten minutes of guzzling, it was Matthew who fell asleep. She took him off her nipple. His mouth remained open, as if the nipple was still in it. A tear drop of milk dribbled down the side of his chin. She felt a wave of love for him and set him down gently in his stroller. He took a deep breath, shuttered a little as he exhaled, and seemed to fall more deeply into sleep.

It was so tempting to lie down on Eric Hughes's couch. Just to lie down and take a sweet little nap on his cushiony couch. He was probably off filming somewhere and would never know—

There was the sound of a key in the door. A good thing she'd left the door unlocked, she thought. It gave her the extra moment, while the person with the key locked the door (thinking they were unlocking it), to hook up her bra and pull down her top.

Eric Hughes entered his apartment.

"Hello," he said pleasantly.

"Hello."

"This is my flat, isn't it?"

"I don't know. Did you get off on the right floor?"

He put a brown leather satchel on the desk by the window. "The décor does look familiar. But I can't say that you do."

"That's not what you said last night." *Did I just say that?* But he was so good-looking. Blue eyes. Brown (carefully arranged) rumpled hair. Dimples. The charming way the corners of his mouth turned down.

"Ah. Well. Not that you aren't very attractive, of course." His eyes took in Matthew sleeping in his stroller.

"I'll bet you say that to all your potential buyers," she said.

"Only the women."

Camille smiled modestly. "I must say. This place is a real eye-opener."

"If you throw in the baby," Eric Hughes said, "I'll take $50,000 off the asking price."

"You're in the market for a baby?"

"Especially the sleeping kind."

"Nyquil is the secret."

"I'll have to remember that."

"So I must apologize."

"That's quite all right. I love coming home to strange women in my apartment. Really."

"My agent was just showing me around. She was in a hurry. And I was down in the lobby when I realized we'd left his rubber squeaky bear up here." She took it from the stroller bag (exhibit A) and returned it. "My agent had to rush to another appointment, so she let me come up and retrieve it."

"I see."

"I didn't want him to wake up and find it gone."

"God forbid."

"I do hope you don't mind."

"I would be a monster if I did, wouldn't I?"

"Well, yes," she said. "You would."

She smiled. He smiled back. She wondered if he assumed that everyone knew who he was.

"So," he said, raising his eyebrows, "are you interested?"

"The apartment is quite marvelous."

"And I'm a fool for letting it go."

"Is there something wrong with it," she asked, "that you aren't divulging?"

"Apart from the fact that a tap dancer lives directly above? Just the memories. My wife and I are getting a divorce."

"I see. I'm sorry. That must be hard."

"Wait until the tabloids start in."

"My agent mentioned you're trying your hand at directing a play."

"Yes. I must be a masochist. We're still casting, actually. Mimi was supposed to be in it. We're looking for someone to take her place."

"Really."

Which play? She was dying to know. She could do any role Mimi Tyler did. If she'd still been acting. Ah well! It was time to excuse herself for intruding. Though, as a potential buyer, she could afford to be a bit pushy. "So are you going to be acting in this play?"

"Just directing. I don't know why. It's one headache after another."

"I'm sorry she left you in the lurch."

"It's just as well, really. She hasn't been properly trained for the stage and has no idea how to take direction."

"Well," Camille said diplomatically, "she is good at what she does."

"Yes. Close-ups and nude scenes, neither of which we could utilize for the play. But she's proving hard to replace. I can't tell you how many bad actresses I've suffered through today."

"I'm sorry. That must be so unpleasant." Should she tell him she was an actress? Would it turn him off? Best not to. As if it mattered.

"Before you go," he said, "I would like to ask . . ."

"Yes?" She tried not to appear too eager as she looked at him. Maybe he had a sense that she could act. Saw, just by looking at her, that she happened to be perfect for the part.

"And I hope you don't think I'm prying . . . but do you think you might be bringing your husband around?"

"My husband?"

"You aren't married?"

"Oh." Camille looked at Matthew. "Not . . . especially."

"I assumed. Silly me."

Camille put her hands behind her back, slipped her wedding ring off, and put it in her hip pocket.

"The baby . . ."

"You're the nanny?"

"No, actually, this is my sister's baby."

"Oh."

"I'm just looking after him while she's in the hospital."

"Nothing too serious I hope?"

"She'll be fine. It's just . . . you know . . . she's in a coma."

"How horrible."

"Yes. She fell. Out a window. A man was chasing her. With a knife. Jealous. Luckily the ambulance got her to the hospital quickly or . . ."

"My God. How many floors?"

She hesitated. "Ten?"

"She fell ten floors?"

Camille laughed. "I thought you meant the hospital."

He laughed. "Well, I'm glad you have a sense of humor about it."

"Yes. Well. Thank god, they fully expect her to come out of it." She'd obviously been watching too many soap operas.

"I hope she does. So, then, you're looking for yourself? Alone?"

"Myself alone. Yes." Before he got it into his head to ask her how she had enough money to afford this place, Camille smiled. "Well. It was very nice meeting you."

"I don't believe I got your name."

"Camille."

He took in his breath, as if in shock. "As in *The Lady of the Camellias?* The beautiful prostitute who is able to leave behind her bitterness and cynicism and love again."

"And the man who looked beyond her station in life and was able to love her back."

"But they couldn't be together."

"Society wouldn't allow it."

"Tragic."

His theatricality was overblown and pretentious. She loved it. Not to mention how goddamned sexy he was.

"So." He held out his hand. She held out her own, to shake, but he brought it to his lips and kissed her on the knuckle. "Mademoiselle. Charmed."

She forced herself to ignore a twinge of desire. She forced herself not to look at him wistfully, not to linger, not to let him see how much she wanted to pounce on that brown leather satchel, pull out the script that was undoubtedly inside, and get a look at it. After all, she was (as far as he knew) a potential buyer of his apartment. If anything, he was the one who needed to kiss up to her.

"I hope you'll come back for a second look," he said. "You should see it in the evening with the moonlight reflecting off the Hudson."

"Sounds lovely." Was he inviting her to come around again on her own? Real estate agents didn't usually show apartments in the evening.

She could've sworn he looked at her with regret as she wheeled the stroller out the door. She wished she hadn't worn her blue jeans and running shoes today. As if she ever wore anything else these days. Oh well. Perhaps after a long, hard day of auditioning actresses, Eric Hughes was lonely for a down-to-earth sort of woman. Who was not in the theater. Who could love him for himself, not as someone who could make or break her career as an actress. A career that (let's face it) was just a self-indulgent excuse to go around pretending to be someone you're not.

"I hope your sister recovers soon," he said.

"I have absolute faith that she'll wake up when she's ready to."

As she reached West End Avenue, Camille paused to put her wedding ring back on and realized she still had the key to Eric's apartment.

Oh well. She could give it to Naomi, no big deal.

Though it would be nice to get a look at that script. That was sitting on his coffee table. Hmmm. If she could get herself in there, study the scene, and then somehow arrange to have an audition . . .

But no. That was ridiculous. Crazy. She wouldn't do something like that.

But then, it just so happened, she passed a hardware store with a sign saying they made keys. It could come in handy. Not that she would ever use it. But just for the hell of it . . . why not?

Chapter Thirty

She closed the dishwasher. One thing was for sure. She couldn't risk meeting Eric Hughes again, so she really had to rule out both apartments.

She wet a sponge and wiped the counter. At least her temporary insanity consisted of a little harmless fun, not leaving her baby unattended in a bathtub or anything.

She looked up from the counter. It was very quiet out in the living room. She'd left Matthew with Daniel. Hadn't she?

She went to peek in the doorway. There they were at the changing table. Daniel was gingerly peeling open a dirty diaper and Matthew was cooing with contentment. She went back to the kitchen. Still, she'd have to figure out what to do about the fact that Naomi was expecting to show Daniel apartment 3C on the weekend.

She threw the sponge into the sink. The kitchen was clean enough. Time to relax. This would all work out somehow. She'd just have to figure out a reason why he wasn't interested.

But part of her wanted to return to the scene of her crime. Speak to Eric Hughes again. She wanted . . .

What did she want?

"Honey," Daniel called from the living room, "Matthew has a rash. Do you know where the Desitin is?"

"The bathroom. I'll get it."

She found the tub of ointment on the ledge of the toilet. The most annoying thing was, she had never gotten this far (a whole conversation) with anyone as powerful as Eric Hughes in her old days (years) as a struggling actress.

Matthew was splayed out naked on the changing table. She unscrewed the top.

"Here."

"Thanks."

She hated the smell of Desitin. When it got on clothing, you could never get it off. But it seemed to work like magic on rashes—asphyxiating them, she always imagined. She watched as Daniel carefully dipped his index finger into the dense white cream and dabbed it onto the red-blotched crease of skin between Matthew's legs and genitals. Daniel had a gentle touch. Camille stiffened at the intimacy of it.

"Poor thing," she said, though Matthew didn't seem to be suffering and did seem to be enjoying his father's application of the cream. "Maybe I left a wet diaper on too long." Matthew was paying the price for her flirtation.

"Don't blame yourself. All babies get rashes."

Daniel got out a fresh diaper and slid it under Matthew's bottom. Yes, he enjoyed doing these little things. But when you're gone most of the day, it's much easier to take pleasure in the novelty, she thought.

Camille stretched out on the sofa. In any case, there was not going to be any more flirtation with Eric Hughes, so there would be no more price to pay.

"So," Daniel said, picking Matthew up off the changing table, "did you look at any apartments today?"

Matthew held his arms out to Camille.

"Let Daddy hold you," she said, not wanting to get up off the couch or feel his weight in her arms. He leaned out to her.

"He wants you."

"Won't you let your daddy hold you?" she pleaded.

She really didn't want to hold him; it was so nice to have her arms free.

"Daddy wants to hold you for a little bit," Daniel said. But Matthew whined and leaned out farther.

"Matthew, I've been holding you all day. Give me a break!"

He sniveled. Cross. The little dictator. "He sure does love his mommy," Daniel said. "Of course, you taste better than I do. And your skin is a lot softer."

She gave up. Matthew nestled into her lap and immediately smiled up at her. Oh, hell. The way his body merged into hers, she couldn't stay annoyed.

And she did feel a certain satisfaction that he rejected Daniel for her.

"So did you see anything?" Daniel sat down next to her, put his arm around her.

"Well, yes, actually, we did." She wanted to provide evidence that she'd done something innocent and productive that day. "But it was on the West Side. Riverside Drive."

"It's nice over there."

"But it would be silly to go that far west."

"I am a little tired of the East Side. Maybe a change would be good."

"It was only on the third floor, so it didn't have a view of the river, just the trees."

"Trees are good. How was the building?"

"Excellent."

"Does it have enough space?"

"Yes."

"And you like it?"

"Yes."

"So I'm sure I'll like it too."

She felt annoyed. Why did he have to be so reasonable? He trusted her too much.

Or maybe he just didn't care, because all he wanted to think about was his patients, so he would move anywhere she wanted as long as he didn't have to make the effort to look.

"If you want," she heard herself say, "I'll set it up with Naomi."

"Good." He kissed her on the forehead. "Thank you for handling this."

"You're welcome. So how was work? Any progress with your autopenisectomy?"

"A little. Got him talking about his daughter."

"Don't tell me he abused her."

"No. Just thought about it. Noticed himself having an erection around her. Made him feel really guilty."

"And that's why he did it?"

"Well, it's more complicated than that. Among other things, he's very religious. . . . But obviously there are many people who have those kind of thoughts who don't feel the need to actually cut off their penises. . . ."

"There would be a lot of eunuchs around."

"People could save themselves a lot of grief by realizing that thinking a 'bad' thought isn't the same as acting on it."

"That's right." And she hadn't acted on her bad thoughts. Had she?

After Matthew was asleep, Camille took refuge in the shower. She cupped her breasts under her arms and let the warm water wash over them. What if they ran into Eric Hughes at the apartment? How would she handle that? She adjusted the temperature of the water, letting it run warmer. It wasn't like she wanted to have an affair with him. How could such a thing take place? She was a happily married mother. With no apparent sex drive. Her physical attraction to Eric Hughes? That had nothing to do with him as an individual. The water was too warm. She turned up the cold. It was simply a by-product of what he represented. Meaningless as a reflex. Now the spray was too hard, so she adjusted them both down.

Not that she was going to try to get him to give her that part. The very thought of telling Eric Hughes she was (used to be) an actress was humiliating. And why should he do anything for her anyway? He just wanted her to buy his "flat." That was probably the only reason he'd turned on the charm at all.

No. Camille squeezed some thickening shampoo onto the crown of her head. That couldn't be true. He really had seemed to be interested in her.

She massaged her scalp with the tips of her fingers. They did have common interests. And he had to be feeling a little lonely. And she'd been starved for good company recently. Maybe they could just be friends. There was nothing wrong with that.

She leaned her head back and rinsed the shampoo out of her hair and smiled. Friends! She might as well admit it. She wanted to have an affair with Eric Hughes. To become his mistress and let him cast her in everything he did!

I'm a horrible person, she thought to herself (with a smile, because this was such an impossible scenario and, as Daniel had said, what was the harm in fantasizing about it?). After giving herself a final rinse, she stepped out of the shower and wrapped a towel around her shivering body. Daniel was probably on the other side of that door wanting sex with her. She could go out there right now, all naked and dripping, and make him happy.

She put on an oversized T-shirt and quickly got under the covers and turned off her lamp. Daniel appeared at the doorway.

"Are you sleepy?" he asked.

"Yes. And he'll be waking me up soon enough."

"Okay," Daniel said, coming to kiss her good night. "I'm going to do some reading. I love you," he said.

"I love you too." She closed her eyes. He'd given up on her rather easily. Was he getting used to no sex? Oh well. That was fine. She closed her eyes and pictured herself sitting next to Eric on his white couch. Thought of the way he'd kissed the back of her hand. How he knew all about literature. The theater. Everything she loved. After a while she noticed her hands were clenched and her pulse was racing and her breathing was shallow, as if her body was on some kind of alert. Impossible to fall asleep. Eventually Daniel came to bed. His soft snores started within minutes. But she could not relax. She decided to give up; if she drifted off now it would be hell to wake up for Matthew. So she decided to try to stay awake.

And she fell asleep.

In her dream, she realized (as if for the first time) that she still had the key to Eric Hughes's apartment. And she realized she had to return it to the doorman right away or Naomi would be in trouble. So she took a walk through Central Park to the West Side. But she got all turned around and ended up near a lake she didn't recognize. There was a fancy restaurant with white tablecloths and a pink-and-green neon clock on the wall. She thought how strange it was for such a nice restaurant to be in the middle of the park and she never even knew it. Everyone was having a really nice time. But she couldn't stay; she had to get to the West Side and return that key, so she kept walking down path after path, but no path seemed to lead out of the park. The paths kept twisting and turning and never getting anywhere . . . somewhere . . . anywhere . . . Matthew was crying. The sound seemed to come from under water. And she had to fight to resurface, so she could get to the air, to Matthew, and his cries for help. She opened her eyes. Looked at the clock. Three A.M. He was bellowing. How long had she slept through his cries? Maybe not long. Daniel was fast asleep. How could he sleep through this screaming? "Coming!" she called out from the bed. She could project her voice but not her body. Couldn't move. It was so nice and warm in the bed. Her body felt like it was melded between two soft, warm marshmallows.

But the crying, of course, didn't stop.

"Be right there!"

Still, she didn't move. She felt so at one with the quilt and the mattress, it was as if she didn't even have a body.

"Don't you think you should go to him?" Daniel mumbled.

She groaned and forced herself out from under the quilt. The air in the room was cold. "I'm coming!" She walked on the hard wood to the carpeted living room. Never mind that she'd spent the entire day and evening with him. There he was, eager for her again.

She lifted him out of the crib without saying anything and took him to the couch.

He didn't give her a glance before going for her breast.

Chapter Thirty-one

Saturday afternoon, Matthew, Daniel, and Camille took a cab across town to meet Naomi at 111 Riverside Drive. Camille had already made it clear to Naomi that she'd "discussed it with Daniel" and there was no way they could afford 16C. She just prayed the subject wouldn't come up again.

There was yet a different doorman from before—a young man with a bad complexion. Camille wondered how someone so young could tolerate a job that involved standing in a doorway all day. Though at least he could stand outside in nice weather and look at the park.

"The lobby was redone last year," Naomi was saying. "Excellent co-op. The people who live here are all professionals; it's really an East Sider kind of building. The financials are excellent. . . ."

Naomi pushed the button for the elevator. It was descending from a high floor. Camille stopped breathing. Oh, god. He could be on it.

She'd attempted to disguise herself with large sunglasses and a scarf around her head à la Audrey Hepburn. Daniel stood behind Matthew in the stroller. She stood behind both of them and tried to fade into the background.

Of course, Eric Hughes would not remember her like she remembered him. He'd probably forgotten that she existed. If he did think of her, it was only as a buyer. Even so, her entire body clenched tight as the elevator descended lower and lower to the lobby. Finally, the doors opened on a tall bald man wearing a gray V-neck and brown corduroy pants. They let him pass and Camille followed the others.

Apartment 3C looked shabbier than she remembered it, probably because she'd been so busy picturing 16C. The stove was old and the kitchen floor was ugly rust-colored linoleum, and the bathroom cabinets were cheap white formica.

"It needs some sprucing up," Daniel said. "But you'll enjoy doing the place over, right?" He looked at Camille, his eyebrows raised in approval. She didn't know what to say.

Naomi jumped on Camille's silence. "It's perfect! Funny how that works. You just walk into an apartment and you know: this is the one."

Camille had a sick feeling in the pit of her stomach. "The kitchen floor is ugly. And the stove is old," was all she could bring herself to say.

"I'll take another look." Daniel went into the kitchen.

Naomi pounced. "I heard 16C was swamped with people yesterday. It's sure to get snapped up. We could take him up to see it."

"It really is beyond our range."

"Let me point out to you, my dear, that the higher floors with the river views cost more, but they also appreciate more. Investment-wise it's very smart—"

Daniel returned. "We could redo the kitchen."

"I hate to renovate," Camille said, "when we can barely afford to buy the place."

"We'll be so much in debt," he chuckled, "what's another few thousand?"

"It makes me nervous."

"It's becoming real for you," Naomi said, "now that you've found the right one. Listen. No place is going to be in perfect condition. And everyone wants to give it a personal stamp."

"That's true," Daniel said.

"You can always wait a couple years and then enjoy making

improvements gradually," Naomi went on. "That's part of the fun of having an apartment. It becomes your little project."

"We would need to paint right away," Camille pointed out. "You can see it's peeling off the ceilings. . . ."

Naomi gave Camille a look. *Are you crazy?* She had to be wondering why they suddenly seemed at cross-purposes. "Everyone paints when they move into a new place. It's like changing the sheets."

"Well," Daniel said. "I think we should make an offer right away."

Camille gave him a look. "I think we should talk about this."

"What's to talk about? You like it. I like it. Even Matthew likes it."

They all looked at Matthew. He smiled and bounced his legs.

"So it's settled!" Naomi said. "I know you three will be very happy here. I'd suggest you make an offer ten percent less than the asking."

"Daniel, we really need to talk."

"I thought you liked this one!"

"I do, but . . ."

"I think she's just sorry to end her search," Naomi said. "We've been having such a good time! So talk, get used to the idea; I know it's scary. Then give me a call. But we should move quickly. These apartments on Riverside Drive go very fast."

"It's so far from your work."

Daniel pushed Matthew's stroller down the path to the playground. Camille wasn't going to relax until they got out of the neighborhood, but it was safe to assume Eric Hughes would not be anywhere near a sandbox.

"But I like the idea of moving over here. You were right. I'm sick of the East Side. It's too conservative."

"It's boring over here too."

"But it's a family neighborhood. That's a good kind of boring."

"Maybe we should be looking in Gramercy Park. It's so much closer to the hospital." And her old neighborhood. And her old friends . . .

"You know what I think? I think the real reason you won't commit to this apartment is because you're too afraid of sealing your fate. You can't really accept who you've become."

"What?"

"As long as you live in my apartment, you can pretend you're visiting my life. But buying this place together and moving here together will mean you've become, we've become . . . *us*."

"That's ridiculous." Maybe he was right.

"And you will have become a conventional, middle-class housewife. What you probably think of as ordinary."

"Is that what you think I am? Ordinary?"

"No, I said that's what *you* think you'll become."

"No. You said *I will become* a conventional, middle-class housewife."

"Camille. There are lots of people who would feel lucky to live in this apartment, who wouldn't find it ordinary at all."

"So now you're saying I'm an ungrateful bitch." How much of this conversation had to do with the fact that they hadn't had sex in months, she wondered.

"No."

"Yes you are!" She was yelling now, and she couldn't stop herself. "You think I don't appreciate what we have. That I'm just going around feeling deprived. Well that's not what's happening here, it really isn't!"

"Okay. Calm down. All I'm saying is . . . I like this apartment. I like this neighborhood. And I don't think we're going to find anything better. At least not that we can afford."

"Fine," she said sharply. "Then it's settled. Whatever you say."

"You were the one who brought me here. Why are you being like this?"

She tried to relax. Her behavior had to seem odd. She *was* a bitch. At the very least she should just take him home and give him a blow job during Matthew's afternoon nap. "I'm sorry. I'm just . . . tired." Now she felt like crying. Oh God. She was a mess. "Ignore me. You're right. I'm sorry. It's a wonderful apartment."

"I think so too." Daniel kissed her on the cheek. Matthew started squirming against his buckle, whining for her breast. What could she do? There was no way out.

Chapter Thirty-two

Sunday morning Daniel went to the hospital for a staff meeting. "We're talking admitting policy, so it could end up taking all day." Camille had nothing to do. So why not head back over to the West Side? It wasn't like she was going to speak to Eric Hughes. Or even let him see her. She just thought it would be nice to sit on the bench under the trees across the street from his building and imagine what it would be like to live there. In 3C, of course. Take in a little atmosphere. Fantasize a little. In the name of research.

So why not arrive at 11:15, a little before his open house was beginning? And watch him exchange pleasantries with the doorman, then head up the street, bowing his head to the wind that never seemed to stop breezing up Riverside Drive.

And, having seen him leave, why not follow him over to Broadway and see where he went. It wasn't like she and Matthew had anything else to do. On the contrary, a long lonely day loomed.

Then he bought a newspaper and went into the Starbucks on Eighty-first Street. She could use a cup of coffee. Maybe it would perk her up a little. A cup of coffee, as a matter of fact, sounded very nice.

She took her place in the back of the line. Eric Hughes was at the front of the line. People were doing a good job of not appearing to notice him. Or maybe they really didn't. He was dressed to blend in. Sweats, a T-shirt, sunglasses, and a base-ball cap. He paid for his cappuccino. Turned to look for a table. That's when he saw her. She smiled neutrally, in case he didn't remember her. He smiled back.

"Camille."

"Hello. How are you?"

"Exiled from my own apartment."

"Why?"

"My real estate agent has insisted on conducting an open house."

"You wouldn't want to be there with all those strangers tromping through."

"True enough." He looked around for an empty table. There was only one stool by a counter against the window.

"Looks like that's my spot," he said.

"Better grab it while you can."

"I think I will." He looked at her like he was unsure what to do with her.

"I'm heading to the playground," she said, to let him off the hook.

"How lovely. It's a beautiful day. On the way, you and your nephew should take another look at my apartment. They say it's going to sell very quickly."

She noticed he looked distressed. "You're having second thoughts?"

"Oh, no. I'm determined to sell. It's just, they say there might be a bidding war and the idea makes me a bit queasy. I am a pacifist at heart."

She laughed. "I'm sure there won't be any bloodshed."

"If there is," he said as he went to sit down, "let's just hope it doesn't stain the Oriental rugs."

After she waited for her coffee, Camille let herself look over to where he was sitting. He was watching her. He nodded and smiled. She nodded and smiled. Her entire body wanted to stay. But there was nowhere to put her body (and the stroller holding Matthew's body). So she wheeled him out to the sidewalk pushing the stroller with one hand and holding her coffee in the other trying not to let it spill onto her white cotton capris. She sighed. "Well, Matthew," she said. "What shall we do now?"

He looked at her blankly.

She decided to head back to the bench on Riverside Drive. And, after downing a cup, she could see no reason not to take a look at 16C.

The real estate agent, Toni Lipton, mauled her with enthusiasm when she entered. "Hello! Welcome! Come in! Please sign in. Here's a floor plan."

Camille wrote Samantha Jones on the sign-in sheet and put the floor plan in the stroller bag.

"What a darling baby," Toni said. "He looks just like you."

"Thank you." She was tempted to say he was adopted. It annoyed her how obvious it was that Toni was just trying to butter her up. But he did look a lot like her, and she did enjoy hearing it.

"I don't know if you're aware, Samantha, but this apartment is owned by Mimi Tyler and Eric Hughes."

"And why are they selling?"

"The marriage . . . you know how it goes . . . kaput."

"It's tough in that business."

"Very. So let me show you around. Obviously the views are incredible."

"Incredible."

"And let me tell you, they spared no expense." Toni gave her the deluxe guided tour that Naomi had not been primed to deliver. "The paneling on the walls is makore wood; of course the artwork won't stay, but the French deco wall sconces will. As will the custom-made cabinetry and built-ins—let me show you the pullout trays in this coffee table. Don't you love it? For snacking while watching the sixty-inch television."

The script was not on the coffee table anymore.

"Let me show you the master bedroom."

Camille followed her in. Another couple was already in there discussing the square footage in thick Long Island accents. She pushed Matthew's stroller carefully so she wouldn't crash into anything valuable. It seemed like she was seeing the apartment for the first time. So much she hadn't noticed before.

"More views, of course; the room is gigantic, incredible closet space. In here we have his-and-her dressing rooms . . ."

The satchel was on his desk, she noticed, and that had to be the script next to it.

"The bathroom is to die for. Slate porcelain tile floors, polished plaster and glass tiles, a shower with multiple showerheads, body sprays, and a waterfall spout. And the whirlpool tub has a view of the George Washington Bridge."

"Amazing," Camille said. Even Matthew was listening attentively from his stroller.

"And in here we have the second bedroom. Small but charming." It looked out on an air shaft. "Very cozy and quiet. And another bathroom in the hall . . ." Toni led her back out to the living room for the final coup de grace. "In addition to radiant heated floors, the apartment is outfitted with motorized window shades, a humidifying system, computer-programmed lighting, and deluxe communications wiring. Please feel free to look around. Take as long as you want. If you have any questions . . ."

"Thank you."

The middle-aged couple emerged from the bedroom. Camille thought she would have to buy the apartment just to keep them from having it.

"It's gorgeous," the woman said. "Absolutely fantastic!"

As they all continued to gush, Camille strolled back into the bedroom. It would be so simple to slip that script right into Matthew's stroller bag.

But she couldn't. She wouldn't. She just wanted a look. A little look, just to satisfy her curiosity. She reached out, and was just about to open the cover, when Toni walked in. So Camille—to give the impression she was just trying to get a better look out the window—put her hand on top of the script (as if she didn't notice it was there) and leaned farther forward and made a show of craning her neck. "It's really an amazing view."

"To die for. The building is in excellent shape and the maintenance is quite reasonable."

"I'm sure."

"Do you have any questions?"

"I was actually looking for something with a bit more square footage. But I'll certainly give it some thought." Camille started wheeling Matthew toward the front door.

"The second bedroom is perfect for the little one."

"Yes," Camille said. "Thank you so much."

"It's a wonderful building," Toni continued. "They just put in new windows; the maintenance staff is excellent; there's a playroom in the basement; you have full-time doormen. Did I show you the kitchen? Come. You have to see the fabulous kitchen."

Camille let her corral her and Matthew to the kitchen. "We have English limestone floors and Italian cabinets by Varenna, recessed lighting, marble countertops . . ."

Camille noticed there was a calendar mounted on the side of the stainless steel fridge. Another couple (fresh meat) came in. Toni pounced. "Welcome! Come in!"

She glanced (casually) at the calendar and saw an entry for that coming Tuesday where he had made a note: Washington, D.C., Arena Stage, Amtrak noon. Channel Inn Hotel.

"Please sign in and take a floor plan. . . ."

"Oh," the young woman said as Camille wheeled Matthew out the door, "just look at those gorgeous views!"

Chapter Thirty-three

Camille took the call from Naomi while she watched *All My Children*.

"So I submitted your bid for 111."

"Okay."

"You don't sound very happy."

"It's just . . . I'll miss looking."

"Well, it's not over yet. I just heard back from the broker. Evidently some other people are interested."

"If they accept our bid, what happens next?"

"You put ten percent down. Get approved for a mortgage. Get approved by the board and you're in."

"Oh. Well. Good."

"Don't get too excited."

"I am excited. Really." They hung up. Camille turned back to the soap. Watched the two sisters Bianca and Kendall bickering in their eternal quest for the love of their mother Erica. The love they would never receive because Erica is too emotionally stunted. Eventually Bianca (supposedly gay, but could they keep that story line up forever?) and Kendall will have grown children of their own. Depressing thought: Susan Lucci will make occasional guest appearances in a wheelchair.

Matthew started to grunt with impatience. She held a blanket in front of her face. Then took it away. "Peek-a-boo!"

He laughed. She held up the blanket again. Took it down again. He looked at her with astonishment.

"Peek-a-boo."

He laughed again. Funniest thing he'd ever seen. Couldn't get enough of it. She did it again.

"Peek-a-boo!"

He laughed again. Now what? If she couldn't look at apartments, how would she get through the day?

This was ridiculous. She should be happy. As Daniel said, she was lucky to have the chance to live in 3C. She had a loving husband and an adorable son. How dare she be unhappy?

"Peek-a-boo!"

So what if today was the day Eric was going to Washington, D.C.? To see a play she'd like to be in. To go to a party she'd like to attend. To flirt with an actress she'd like to be. He was, in fact, on the train right now. And here she was with Matthew— "peek-a-boo!"—watching a soap opera with the day stretching out ahead of her. There had to be something interesting they could do together, but what?

Gymboree. "Would you like to go to Gymboree?" She would force herself to strike up a conversation with someone. Make a friend. Maybe the Betty Boop woman would be there. Or maybe not.

"Peek-a-boo!"

Betty Boop was not there. During class Camille told herself to ask someone, anyone, if they knew of an available baby-sitter.

But she didn't ask. Just could not join in on the after-class chatter. When everyone was filing out, she paused near the door to the street to read the bulletin board. A number of people had posted notices for nannies. She found the concept of "nanny" pretentious and annoying. No one she knew growing up in San Francisco had a nanny. Mary Poppins was a nanny. Fran Drescher was a nanny. She just wanted a baby-sitter. Was that too much to ask?

She didn't love the idea of using a stranger off a bulletin board. But there was one notice that caught her eye. Written in shaky pencil handwriting: *Welling to watch your childrens at home.* She wondered if the wording meant at the sitter's home or the parents' home. It was signed Berthe. Camille wrote down the number.

Wearing Matthew in a snuggly, Camille straightened the living room. She had the dishwasher going. A load of laundry drying. A chicken cooking in the oven. Daniel would be home any minute.

Eric Hughes was getting dressed for the theater now. Or perhaps he was already down in the hotel bar having drinks with the people who ran the Arena Stage. And they were trying to convince him to do a play there. And he was trying to decide if he could fit it in between projects. . . .

That script could very well be sitting on his desk. And the key to his apartment was in her purse. But could she do anything about it?

Biography was on and they were doing Natalie Wood, nee Natasha Nikolaevna Zacharenko. Camille loved Natalie Wood. Not so much for her acting, but more because she was an intelligent-looking brunette. They tried to make her up to be glamorous, but she wasn't, really. Her features were too small and regular. Lovely, yes, but not glamorous.

As the program got to the part about Natalie's death by drowning, Camille sat down on the couch and let Matthew have dinner. It was so sad. But there was something satisfying about watching a movie star get punished for being one of the chosen few.

Daniel opened the front door. "Hi."

"Hi."

Not that Natalie Wood deserved to drown.

Daniel came to kiss Camille on the cheek.

And not that it stopped anyone from wanting to be one of the chosen few.

"I see Matthew is having a nice meal at the Café Between the Breasts."

"The waiter is just about to clear the dishes," she said. "Maybe you'd like to play with him a little after he's paid his check."

"I'd be happy to. After I take my shower."

Camille nodded.

If Daniel took Matthew, she could go out for a bit. After all, he had encouraged her to take some time for herself.

Not that she would go across town, sneak past the doorman, and go into Eric Hughes's apartment while he was in Washington, D.C. just to get a look at that script. That would be crazy.

And, in any case, it would be too hard to sneak by the doorman. They guarded those buildings like Buckingham Palace. So there was no way to get in even though she did have the key. The key, really, was worthless.

Then it occurred to her that even if the key was worthless, she still might be able to get in.

No. This was absurd. She wasn't going all the way over there for that script.

Though she could take a cab both ways and return in time for Matthew's next feeding.

But really it was totally ridiculous.

But what was the harm?

"You know, it's such a beautiful evening. And I really need to get . . . nursing bras. Because, you know, my breasts, they're getting a little smaller since Matthew was born—I think I'm down to an E cup believe it or not—but I'm not sure and I really should try them on and it's so hard to do that with Matthew there, and they're having a sale that ends today on the kind I can never find anywhere else and they're open late tonight until eight o'clock, so would you mind if I raced over before they close?"

"Oh. Well . . . is there any food?"

"There's a chicken in the oven. It'll be ready in ten minutes. You just take it out and . . . that's all you have to do! And there's cole slaw. And some macaroni from the deli. Here, I'll get it out of the fridge. And there are some Fig Newtons . . . or I could pick up something special for dessert if you'd like, though that would take extra time . . ."

"That's okay," he said, surprised at this course of events. "Have you eaten? Should I wait till you get back?"

"No need. I'm not hungry."

She went to her closet and fished out a black wool tailored jacket from Ann Taylor. Just the sort of thing a real estate agent would wear. But not the matching skirt. It would look too conspicuous if Daniel bothered to notice.

She gave Matthew a kiss, handed him to Daniel, then kissed Daniel. "Thanks. I really appreciate it. Since he just ate, you shouldn't have any problem, but if he gets cranky you can give him some water. . . ."

"We'll be fine. I guess. We'll be fine, right Matthew?"

Matthew looked at him like they'd just met on a blind date and was ready to call it a night. Before she could change her mind, Camille opened the front door and went to the elevator. Daniel followed her out with Matthew in his arms. "I'll be back really soon," she said, trying to maintain a tone of casualness. "Less than an hour. I promise."

The freedom of being totally unencumbered by baby or stroller as she walked down the street made her feel as if she could float into the sky. Remember this feeling, she said to herself. Call Berthe.

She hailed a cab on Seventy-ninth Street and Fifth Avenue and the driver followed the winding road through Central Park. She couldn't get over how odd it was to be out by herself. Like a kid playing hooky. The closer she got to the West Side, the more nervous she got. There would be a different doorman on now, for the night shift, not the nice elderly gentleman. So he wouldn't recognize her. Still, the theme music to *Mission: Impossible* played in her brain. Duh duh, duh duh duh duh, duh duh duh duh . . . She was one of *Charlie's Angels,*

Lucy Liu perhaps—she was the most reliable one—or maybe Kate Jackson from the old series. Certainly not Farrah. Or Drew. Or Cameron. Anyway, blonde or brunette, the Angels always succeeded in their mission.

They emerged on the West Side. Central Park West. Columbus, Amsterdam, Broadway, West End. She swore they hit every red light to Riverside. She paid the driver $7.50 with the tip and approached the doorman. This one was a Hispanic man with a moustache, short hair, and broad shoulders. Handsome enough to be a movie star.

She opened her purse, pulled out Naomi's business card and gave it to him.

"Hi, I have a couple coming to see 3C but I'm a little early. I think I'll wait upstairs."

He glanced at the card and then looked her in the face. Camille smiled, attempting calm. She could've pretended that she'd arranged to see 16C. But she was worried he'd be more vigilant because it was owned by celebrities. The glitch in her plan would be if the doorman knew Naomi well enough to recognize her.

"Well . . ." the doorman said, taking another look at the business card and then at her, "if you want, I'll send them up when they arrive."

"That would be great. Thanks."

The doorman gave her an elegant little nod. Camille headed for the elevator. She was brilliant.

Now. What would Lucy do? She had to be careful. Was there a hidden camera in the elevator? She took the elevator to the third floor. Then took the stairs. By the time she reached the sixteenth floor, her heart was pounding and she was out of breath. She got the key from the inside zippered pocket of her purse. She knocked on Eric Hughes's door, just in case. No one answered.

And so, once again, she found herself in 16C. She went straight to the desk in his bedroom. Yes! The script was there. She took it to the sofa in the living room and opened the cover. It was like lifting the lid on a new box of candy. She flipped to the title page.

A jolt of shock. The play was titled *The Seagull: Malibu.* Could it be? She flipped through. Ugh. Eric Hughes had taken her favorite Chekhov play and modernized it, so it didn't take place in czarist Russia but in modern-day Malibu, California.

At first, Camille felt confused. Had Mimi been going to play Nina? She was really too old. But then again, if you were the wife of the director, maybe that didn't matter. Mimi certainly wouldn't want to be the mother, Arkadina. Camille started to get excited, thinking maybe this was one more chance in her life to play Nina! Maybe Eric had cast an older mother to suit Mimi's age and now she could be slotted right in!

Then she saw a monologue flagged with a Post-it note and some scribblings in the margin. It was a monologue for the part of Marsha. (Masha in the original.) So that was the part, not Nina. And that made sense. Eric had given Mimi a smaller, less important role. Because, as he had said, she was not trained for the theater. And that's probably why she quit, too. She was too much of a prima donna to play such a small part.

But Masha got to say the famous Chekhov line: "I am in mourning for my life."

Camille would take that part in a second. And the fact that it was a smaller role made it even more likely that—

No. She couldn't allow herself to even form the sentence.

She put the script in her black canvas bag, locked up the apartment, went back down the stairwell to the third floor, pushed the button for the elevator, and rode down to the lobby. She said to the doorman on her way out, "My client just called. He's running late. I'm going to get a cup of coffee and be right back."

He nodded.

She walked to a Staples on Broadway. Gave the script to the young woman behind the counter. Ran down the street to a

Filene's and bought the largest, cheapest bra she could find off the rack. Stopped at the Starbucks on the corner, bought a cup of decaf, picked up the copy of the script, and walked back to Riverside Drive.

The doorman nodded and smiled to her as she went in. (They were old buddies now.) She took the elevator to the third floor, walked up to sixteen and put the original script back on Eric's desk. Lucy Liu—make that Charlie—would've been proud.

But she wasn't done yet. She had to blow a little time so the doorman wouldn't be suspicious. It wasn't long before she found herself at Eric Hughes's answering machine. The little red light was flashing.

Why not?

Well, for one thing, if she played his messages the light would stop flashing. But it wouldn't incriminate her, only the machine. She pressed the button through the cloth of her jacket so she wouldn't even leave a print.

The first message was from his lawyer with a question about releasing Mimi Tyler from her commitment to *The Seagull: Malibu*. The second was from his stockbroker about some bonds that were coming due. The third was from Mimi.

"Eric. I just want to confirm our lunch date next Friday. Please don't cancel this time. There's no reason to make this difficult. Has anyone made an offer on the apartment yet? I'll see you on Friday at one o'clock at Ouest. And please don't be late, I'm flying out to L.A. that evening."

Camille smiled to herself. Thank you Mimi.

When she left the building, Camille commiserated with the doorman over the fact that her clients had canceled on her. "It's so rude."

"As if your time is worth nothing," he said with sympathy.

"They just don't care."

He shrugged. "What can you do?"

"It comes with the territory."

"Have a good evening."

"Good night."

In the cab, she could feel her breasts firming up. Matthew would be ready for his meal as soon as she got back. Everything was timing out perfectly.

"Did you find what you needed?" Daniel asked from the sofa. Matthew was on the rug practicing holding up his head.

"Yes!" she said, immediately hiding the script up on the high shelf in the hall closet.

"You were out a long time."

"It's beautiful out. How was Matthew?"

"A little cranky. But I gave him a nice bath and that made him happy."

"Did your daddy give you a bath?" She picked up Matthew and kissed him on the cheek. Daniel kissed her on the cheek.

"Mmmm, you smell so good," she said to Matthew as she sat down with him in her lap and lifted her shirt. "Any interesting patients today?"

"Just the usual assortment . . . One new patient is sort of interesting." Daniel settled into the easy chair. "She's originally from Boston. Went to Yale as an undergraduate. Johns Hopkins Medical School. Became a pediatrician. Got very depressed. Lost her practice. Ended up living with her mother. Now she thinks she's Marilyn Monroe."

"Is she sexy?"

"Not particularly. Too bad no one on the ward thinks he's Joe DiMaggio. We could fix them up."

"You're such a romantic." She suddenly felt warmth for Daniel. He really was good to her. It was nice to be home with her little family. What could be more peaceful?

Chapter Thirty-four

There was no chance to read the script until Matthew's nap the next afternoon. It took him an unusually long time to eat, and then she had to hold him for another ten minutes before he would go into the crib without waking. Finally, he was out.

She took a deep breath and sat still to enjoy the moment.

Sun came in the window. The city seemed quiet. The apartment was cozy. Two luscious hours to herself.

She put on some coffee, got herself two butter cookies, and went to the closet for the script. Then she sat down and read it straight through in a little over an hour.

It was really, she had to admit to herself, sort of disgusting. He'd taken the classic, well-loved play about theater people and modernized it to become about Hollywood and the movie-making business. It did transpose easily enough into the current climate of self-absorbed, celebrity-crazed people chronically yearning for impossible levels of success. (Such as herself?) And she could see how that would appeal to Eric, since he'd been seduced in by the world of Hollywood with dubious results. (Two critically praised flops in three years.) And it certainly was trendy.

Chekhov would be revolted.

And, possibly, amused.

But none of that really mattered. It would be heaven to perform the part of Marsha, or almost any part for that matter, on Broadway. Broadway! Somehow (she finally allowed herself to think outright) she was going to have to find a way to get Eric Hughes to cast her.

Camille read Marsha's monologue through a few more times. She would start to memorize it that night. Right now, she had to sleep. There was still a good hour left before Matthew would wake up. She stretched out on the couch and closed her eyes. She really needed a nap.

Matthew started whimpering.

No. No, please no. Please? Go back to sleep?

His whimpering turned into crying. "Go back to sleep!" she pleaded. This only made him cry louder. She sighed. Got out of bed. Walked to his crib. Stood over him. Glared. Didn't pick him up. He continued to wail.

"What are we going to do?"

She didn't pick him up. She hated him.

"We have the whole afternoon to get through. Don't you know that? And I really want to sleep!"

He wailed on. Finally, she lifted him and started to cry too. She hated hating him. She walked aimlessly with him through the apartment, both of them crying. He wanted to eat. She knew he wanted to eat, and she was withholding her milk as some kind of punishment. But for what? Existing? Appetite? The fact that he needed her?

"I'm sending you to a wet nurse," she said. "I don't care! I'll see you again when you're five. I can't do this."

She took him to the couch, sat down with him, pulled her shirt up and stuck her nipple in his mouth. Anything to shut him up. He sucked her dry. Sapped her power. Drew the energy out of her.

I'm in mourning for my life, she thought. *Mourning for my life!*

When he was finished, she stood his little feet on her thighs. He smiled. So innocent. So oblivious to everything he made her feel. She hugged her to him and brushed the wetness off her cheek with his cheek. Oh, god. She was a hideous person.

* * *

That night she told Daniel about Berthe. "She gave her cousin as a reference. So I spoke to the cousin on her cell phone. She's a nanny for a family just a few blocks away. And she gave me her employer's number and I called them, and the woman, a lawyer—as uptight as they come, so you know she has standards—said that Berthe's cousin was wonderful and had worked with them for six years, and she was *sure* that any relative of hers was trustworthy. Berthe's English isn't too good, but my Spanish isn't bad."

"I don't speak any Spanish."

"And don't you wish you did? This could be a great way for Matthew to become bilingual."

Early forties, stout, round face, short curly hair, big smile. Berthe wore jeans and sneakers and a New York Yankees T-shirt with the name Justice on the back.

Her eyes lit up as soon as she saw Matthew.

"Do you have experience with children?"

Berthe laughed. "I have ten grandchildren." She held out her hands for Matthew. "Please?"

Camille gave him to her. She thought he would never allow this stranger to touch him, but he went willingly enough.

"What a beautiful boy!" she said in English. "Beautiful, beautiful boy!"

Camille waited for Matthew to realize she'd given him away to a stranger and he could be sold into slavery later that afternoon.

"I love babies," Berthe said.

Any moment Matthew would realize his mother was abandoning him and should be thrown into prison for neglect.

He smiled. He laughed. Seemed to enjoy perching on the hip of this soft and cheerful woman. The unfaithful cad.

"You go now," Berthe said. "We have fun."

"Now?"

Camille hadn't been intending to leave Matthew yet. This was just supposed to be the interview.

"Say bye-bye to mommy," Berthe said, waving good bye to Camille. "Bye-bye."

Matthew smiled.

"Well. Okay." Camille got out a piece of paper and started writing down phone numbers. "I have a cell phone. So if there are any problems just call me. And here's my husband's number, just in case it goes out of service for some reason, and here's Matthew's pediatrician's number, and my mother's number in San Francisco just in case. . . ."

"We be fine. . . ."

"Okay. If you're sure. Are you sure?"

They hadn't even discussed pay. Days off. Health insurance. Did she do laundry?

"Bye-bye, Mommy," Berthe said.

She got the script from the closet. Matthew was smiling and happy now, but once she was out the door that would all change. Berthe would plop him on the rug in front of the TV and he would be condemned to cry his head off in a urine-soaked diaper while Berthe watched *General Hospital* and made long distance calls to her relatives in distant lands.

"Bye," Camille said, forcing herself to sound casual. She explained to Berthe that if he got cranky, she could give him a bottle with some water in it because he didn't take formula, and she would be back within an hour. Did the woman understand a word? Who knew?

She proceeded to walk out the door and lock it.

Then she stood on the other side of the door listening.

Berthe was still saying something to him in Spanish about Mommy being pretty.

Every bone in her body wanted to open up that door again and clench Matthew to her chest and send Berthe home.

But her brain said *get the hell out of here*.

So she took her breasts to her favorite café on Eighty-fifth

Street, where she ordered a piece of carrot cake and a café latte. She told herself not to feel guilty. Everything would be fine. She could be home in ten minutes, if needed.

She opened the script in front of her and worked on memorizing the monologue. For one delicious hour Camille completely forgot about the fact that she had a baby.

Then she ran home. She was starting to leak. Matthew must be hysterical.

When she walked in the door, Berthe was still sitting on the couch talking to Matthew. He didn't even notice her walk in. Camille gave her a twenty and thanked her and grabbed him. Her nipples were hot and sore. She started feeding him before Berthe even got out the door.

She decided she'd better get into the habit of pumping milk. She would need to get used to doing this if she was going to leave Matthew with Berthe for any extended time. Unless she started him on formula. But since that would be a double betrayal (fake caregiver *and* fake milk) she felt it was the least she could do.

She pumped her milk by hand, squeezing her breasts like a farmer massaging a cow's teats, in just the right spot with just the right motion that made the milk squirt out of her nipple in thin white streams. She found that, with practice, she could hit a target five or six feet away.

Cool.

Chapter Thirty-five

"Hello, Lisa? It's Camille."

"Camille. Hello."

"Hi. It's been a while."

"Yes. It has."

Awkward silence. Maybe this was a bad idea.

"I'd really like to get together."

"You would?"

Lisa sounded wary but interested.

"Can I take you out to lunch?" Camille asked. "I miss you." She really did miss Lisa. And she'd been a jerk for keeping a distance. "I don't suppose you're free this Friday?"

"Well . . . yeah . . . I guess I can do that. Where should we meet?"

"If you don't mind coming uptown, the West Side would be a halfway point. There's a restaurant I've been wanting to try. Ouest. Sort of a French comfort food kind of place . . ."

"I suppose it might be nice to have an excuse to get above Twenty-third Street."

"Great. I'll make a reservation. One o'clock?"

"Perfect."

After they hung up, Camille felt optimistic. Even if her plan to accidentally run into Eric Hughes while he was having lunch there with Mimi didn't work out, this was a good idea. It would be interesting to see Lisa again.

She tanked up Matthew before she left. With the reserve of pumped milk, she figured he wouldn't go hungry even if she got hit by a bus and they couldn't be reunited until that evening. He produced a resounding belch just as the doorbell rang.

She handed him over to Berthe's exclamations of "Beautiful baby! I miss you!" and took advantage of the luxury of being able to take a shower without rushing. After drying off she took a peek into the living room. Berthe was singing the ABC song to Matthew. Camille hated the ABC song.

She changed into her favorite empire-waisted black-lace dress with a thin purple ribbon threaded through the plunging neckline, and emerged from the bedroom feeling a little too dressed up for a mom going out for a carefree afternoon. Not that it mattered. Matthew had seemed to forget that she existed. Berthe was tickling his toes and he was laughing away.

It was insulting, really. After all she'd done for him!

Berthe said, "Doesn't Mommy look pretty?"

But Matthew didn't even look at Mommy. He was much more interested in the gold cross that hung from Berthe's neck.

"Should I say good-bye to him?" Camille asked in a sort of panic. "Or maybe I should just leave. Maybe the separation anxiety will be less traumatic that way. You know how babies have no sense of time." Camille knew her English was beyond Berthe's abilities, but she couldn't stop herself. "Maybe if I just disappear and reappear later he'll think I went into the other room, so it would be better if he doesn't see me walk out the front door. . . ."

Berthe nodded and smiled and said "Bye-bye" as she waved to Camille.

Camille said nothing out loud so Matthew wouldn't notice her leaving. She closed the door. Took off her ring. Put it in her change purse. Doomed. Most certainly destined to be punished for her sins.

The waitress, who wore a manly black vest and maroon necktie, set their dishes of lamb shank (Camille) and quail (Lisa) on the table. Since it was the middle of the day in a residential neighborhood, the restaurant was not very crowded. But still, with Eric Hughes and Mimi Tyler sitting in the curved red leather banquette by the window, the place felt lively.

"I can't believe we end up in a restaurant *again* with Eric Hughes," Lisa said. "I mean, what are the odds of that?"

"Isn't it wild? I've been in his apartment, you know."

"What, you're his cleaning woman?"

"Very funny."

If Lisa could tease her like that, maybe they'd be able to get back to how they'd been.

"Daniel and I are looking for a larger place. And his apartment is on the market."

"Must be nice."

"Riverside Drive, sixteenth floor, fantastic river views."

"How lovely. You gonna buy it?"

"I don't know. It's so expensive."

"You should think about buying a loft. The space, the light . . . I hear there are some fabulous spaces in Tribeca. I was thinking of looking around there myself."

Lisa didn't mention she was pregnant, but certainly they must be trying.

"How is Wally?"

"Great."

"That's great."

"How is Daniel?"

"Good. Busy. As usual."

She snuck a look at Eric. He was facing in her general direction. She hadn't planned past this point. She would have to improvise. It would be too humiliating to walk up to him. But if he was on his way out and still hadn't noticed her, maybe she could do something subtle, like stick her foot in the aisle and trip him.

Lisa had asked nothing about Matthew. She must still resent her for saying marriage and motherhood was a sellout. Or maybe she was having trouble getting pregnant. So Camille didn't bother telling her how cute he was. Or complain about how he still hadn't slept through the night. And how she was exhausted all the time. And felt like she had no life even though she was supposed to feel "fulfilled" now. It was obvious, by the time the food came, they were not going to be able to simply jump back in to being best buddies.

The lamb, though a little too salty, cut like butter. Camille savored the juicy bits of meat and even allowed herself a generous amount of the oniony wine sauce as Lisa admitted she was thinking of going back into acting.

"Really?"

"I need something to distract me."

"Wow. That's great." *She must be desperate.*

"I resisted for a while. And then I just realized that I really miss it."

"That's really great." She stole another look at Eric, whose conversation with Mimi seemed to be serious. "Are you still planning on kids?"

"Of course. We're trying. In the meanwhile . . . I figure why not. At least now I don't have to worry about supporting myself."

"True."

"Do you miss it?" Lisa asked.

"No. Not at all." At least Eric and Mimi didn't seem to be reconciling. Their body language was very stiff and they sat far back in their chairs. "I'm so relieved to be out of that business. . . ."

"Yeah. Well. That's one of the encouraging things. There's a lot less competition the older you get because people drop out. So I figure I can try to crack a whole new age range. I hear there's a lot of demand for 'mom types,' especially for commercials."

"You would make a great mom type," Camille said, keenly aware that neither of them had yet acknowledged Matthew's existence. Though in a sense, everything seemed like a sideways reference to the fact that she had a baby and Lisa didn't, or maybe that was only in her imagination.

The waitress with the necktie returned. "Would you ladies like some dessert?" *Ladies?!* Camille realized that she had become a "lady who lunched." God. That was horrifying.

"Do you want dessert?" she asked Lisa.

"I don't think so."

"No?" The waitress tilted her head and smiled as if to say she would not take it as a personal rejection. "I'll just bring your check, then."

"I'm so glad that you called. This was such a good idea." Lisa sounded so polite. "The Upper West Side isn't known for its food, but this is a nice place."

Indeed. The softly lit restaurant was beautiful, with wood paneled walls, a double-height ceiling, white tablecloths. Camille wondered why Eric and Mimi chose such a pleasant place to discuss unpleasant subjects like equity contracts and real estate and divorce . . .

"So I'm going to have some new head shots made," Lisa said. "Market myself as a suburban mom. Pledge. Pampers . . ."

"Paxil . . ."

Lisa failed to see the humor.

Eric and Mimi got up to leave.

Camille gave her hair a quick fluff, sat up straight, and tried not to smile too obviously as he walked up the aisle in her direction. If he didn't see her, well, maybe she would just have to say something. She couldn't just let him go, could she?

But she didn't have to say anything. Because he did see her. And he did a double take. And then he smiled, and he stopped in front of their table, and then he said it. Her name.

"Camille."

"Hello." It pleased her, the way he said it. As if he actually had some affection for her, which was ridiculous, she knew, but that was the way it sounded. "How are you?"

"Very well, thank you. This," Eric said to Mimi Tyler, "is Camille, *La Dame aux Camillias*. She's thinking of buying our flat."

"How nice. Does she know there's an offer on the table?"

"No." Camille pretended that worried her. "I didn't know."

"Well there is. If you really want it, you'll have to act quickly."

"My friend Lisa was trying to convince me to buy a loft in Tribeca."

"Was she really?" Eric said. "Then let's take your friend Lisa to see it and let her tell you it's not the most fantastic property in Manhattan."

"Eric . . ." Mimi said, as Lisa and Camille exchanged pleased looks, "is this really necessary? We have a buyer."

"My dear, let me handle this. Before you know it, we'll have a bidding war and you'll be calling me a financial genius real estate mogul."

Mimi smiled fake-graciously at Camille. "Please excuse him. He knows nothing about practical matters."

Camille didn't hesitate. "I think it's a brilliant idea."

Camille and Lisa stood next to each other in front of the Ouest bathroom mirror frantically redoing their makeup. They had a minute while Eric was putting Mimi into a cab.

"You didn't tell me you *knew* him."

"I met him once. That's all. When I was looking at the apartment."

"It seemed like more than that."

Camille applied lipstick. "Really?" (Dare she believe Lisa had observed a real connection?)

"I thought you said his place was too expensive."

"It is. But he doesn't have to know that."

"So you aren't really serious."

"It's impossible."

Lisa turned to face Camille. "Oh my God! Camille! You're stalking Eric Hughes!"

"No! What a thing to say!"

"Did you know he'd be at this restaurant?"

"Of course not. That was a total coincidence. How could I know such a thing?"

"You tell me."

Well. She could see how this could be *construed* as something like stalking, but she certainly hadn't done enough to justify, for example, a headline in a tabloid newspaper. This was just a little harmless fun for a bored-out-of-her-skull mother. It was cleverly manipulating a situation so that it might pay off in some way down the line. But it certainly wasn't "stalking."

"By the way . . ." Camille said, "if he says anything about my sister and her baby, just play along."

"Your sister?"

"Oh. And if it comes up in any way, shape, or form, just so you know, I'm not married. Okay? Come on. Let's not keep him waiting."

"Well," Lisa said. "The views are just gorgeous. Maybe *I* should buy this apartment."

Camille glared at Lisa. She was enjoying this way too much. And, disconcertingly, Lisa could afford it. Camille wondered how she could get rid of her. Her inner timer—her breasts swelling up with milk—was going off.

"We could have a three-way," Eric said. The two women looked at him. "Bidding war, I mean, of course."

Camille and Lisa smiled as if that was amusing. Were stars allowed to make inappropriate dirty jokes?

"So how much are they offering?" Lisa asked.

"The other buyers? I don't believe I'm supposed to divulge that information."

"Lisa. Didn't you say you had an appointment to get to?"

"No . . . I have nothing. . . ."

"Did you see the second bedroom?" Eric asked. "It doesn't have the views, but it's marvelously quiet. I've been using it for yoga in the mornings."

"Let's take a look," Lisa said.

Lisa started in with him to the second bedroom, and Camille stayed back, muttering something about needing another look at the kitchen.

She went back to the refrigerator to see if there were any interesting notes. (There weren't.) The answering machine had no messages. His appointment pad was not on his desktop, and she considered sliding open the top drawer and just taking a peek. Did she dare? Yes, she did. For her art, for the theater, for the script, for the part, for something to do that didn't involve babies—but it was most certainly *not stalking*—she looked and found two tickets to *The Producers*. She committed the date (two weeks away on a Saturday night) and the seat location to memory. Row 5, seats 104 and 106.

Sensing moisture, Camille looked down at her chest. Two wet spots were forming where her nipples pressed against the front of her dress. Well, she would just have to make a dash for it, even if it meant leaving Lisa to Eric. What could she do?

"You two?" she called out. "I just got a call on my cell phone . . . my nephew . . . I hope you don't mind if I make a dash for it!"

Lisa and Eric emerged from the back end of the apartment but she was already heading out the front door so they couldn't see the front of her dress, "I'm sorry to run like this. Eric, I'll have my agent call yours; Lisa it was wonderful to see you, darling, ta ta!"

Eric and Lisa barely had time to say good-bye before she was trotting down the stairwell. Maybe her quick disappearance would seem odd, but she could not let him see the front of her dress. Her life, it seemed, depended on it.

Chapter Thirty-six

As soon as she was out on the street, Camille was overcome with a sense of imminent disaster. She would arrive home to find Matthew dead on the living room floor. Or drowned in the bathtub. Or basting in the oven.

She took a cab back and sprinted through the lobby. The elevator slowly made its way up to her floor. She dashed down the hall, fumbled with her keys, and pushed open the door.

Berthe was sitting with him on her lap singing the ABC song. Matthew was gurgling with happiness. She wondered if they'd been doing this sort of thing the entire time she was gone, or if Berthe had been anticipating her return and it was just for show.

She looked for burn marks or puncture wounds.

But far from being abused, he was more buffed and polished than she'd ever seen him. Berthe had put him in new clean clothes: a pair of little twill pants and a button-down white shirt. She'd also given him a bath and combed his hair with a part down the side. He looked like a tiny little man.

The tiny little man turned to her and smiled.

"Matthew," she said. "Look how handsome!"

He smiled even wider and kicked his feet.

"Did he nap?" she asked Berthe.

"One hour," she said. "And he drank all his bottle just now."

"Good."

The front of her dress now had two damp spots the size of silver dollars. She'd have to pump.

"Well thank you so much, Berthe."

"Thank you. I come back tomorrow?"

"Yes. Tomorrow. Same time."

"Good." She paid her in cash. Fifteen an hour. "I will see you tomorrow."

"Thank you."

Holding Matthew, Camille walked her to the door. Berthe kissed Matthew on the cheek one more time, as if it was really hard for her to leave him. "Beautiful boy," she said. "I love you! I love you!"

"Thanks again. Bye," Camille said, and shut the door behind her. She looked at Matthew. The couch. The window. Immediately had a tremendous feeling of letdown. The rest of the boring afternoon held no promise. She wondered if she should've kept Berthe longer. She felt completely incapable of filling the time. He'd had his nap. Now what?

She turned on the TV. Dr. Phil was talking about self-motivation. Daniel hated Dr. Phil. If it was that easy to change your behavior, Daniel liked to say, then everyone would change his behavior.

But still, there was something so inspiring when you listened to the big Southern man who looked like he could've been a football player. Dr. Phil, the boot-camp sergeant of feelings. You felt inspired, like you could change yourself by pure force of will.

Camille sat on the couch with Matthew on her lap and listened to him really give it to a husband who had cheated on his wife. She resolved that she would be a better person. Work harder to take care of her husband and child. Quash these wayward feelings. But first, she wanted to get that monologue memorized. An ad came on. She went to get her pump.

* * *

That evening, while they ate spaghetti and Matthew sat on the table in a rock-a-roo, she told Daniel about her successful afternoon.

"He loved the baby-sitter. He didn't even miss me. It was a little insulting, really."

"A little jealousy will be good for you."

"You're probably right. I should've done this a long time ago."

"So where did you go?"

"Oh, I just walked around. Did some window shopping . . ."

"Did you buy any windows?"

"Very funny."

Camille got up and took the dishes to the kitchen. When she came back, Daniel put his arms around her. "I'm glad you're finally getting some free time."

"Thanks." Matthew was squirming to get out of the rock-a-roo. "Matthew wants to get out." She broke from Daniel's embrace to pick him up.

"Do you notice," he said, "you seem to be getting all your physical gratification from your son?"

He made it sound so creepy. "Because I hold him and feed him?"

"Sometimes I just feel like you'd rather cuddle with him than with me."

She handed Matthew to Daniel. "I know you're frustrated. I'll try to get more rest in the day. And maybe, with Berthe coming, my spirits will improve."

"I'm glad you found someone."

She got a sponge from the kitchen and wiped down the table. "Maybe I'll even go out and get some kind of job."

"Maybe you should consider the idea of getting some therapy."

"Therapy?"

"I think you might find it helpful."

Camille scrubbed at a scab of dried food. "I really don't

think that's what I need." One more person she'd have to lie to.

She locked herself in the bathroom to express more milk, even though there already was that bottle in the fridge. Milk now meant freedom.

After she'd filled a four-ounce bottle and put it in the freezer for safekeeping, Camille went back into the bedroom. There was Daniel, propped against the pillows reading the *Journal of Nervous and Mental Disease*. So absorbed in his work. So unsuspecting—not that he had anything to be suspicious of.

He looked up. "Do you like my new reading glasses?"

"Yes." She hadn't even noticed.

"It was hard to pick out the frames. I should've had you come."

"They're very nice. They look just like your old frames."

"The rims are thinner. I had to get a stronger prescription. It's depressing."

"Awww," she said in sympathy. He went back to his journal. It was true that she hadn't been paying much attention to him. And it had been a very long time since they'd had sex. But that didn't mean she needed to go to some therapist. She got into bed and said—in her seductive voice that promised a little more—"Would you like a back rub?"

"Really?"

"Yes."

"That would be nice." He closed the journal. "I was worried I made you angry before."

"No, you're right. I have been neglecting you."

Daniel looked astonished, but like he'd better not say anything or it might turn his luck.

And so she gave him a back rub. Which turned into a hand job. Which turned into a blow job. What the hell. He deserved it.

While she made him happy, she made her plans.

The problem was, she thought, while licking his penis (long

time no see) from shaft to tip, tip to shaft: how to get a ticket to *The Producers* in two weeks. It was sold out up to February of the following year.

Bigger problem: even if she could get into the theater, how would she go to a play on a Saturday night without Daniel?

She started to speed up. Daniel moaned with pleasure.

And would she feel comfortable running into Eric Hughes on a Saturday night all by her lonesome self? She wasn't going to bring Lisa along, that was for sure.

Her jaw was starting to get stiff, so she decided to switch to her hand. Daniel was so turned on he probably wouldn't notice. She started squeezing and releasing in a pumping action that she recognized was not all that different from the way she pumped her own breasts for milk.

She could go with Naomi. As a way of thanking her for her time. But there was still the problem of getting a ticket.

Daniel snuck a look at her. She switched back to some lip action, and he closed his eyes, in heaven again.

That's when she had an excellent idea.

An excellent idea that solved all her problems at once. Why hadn't she thought of it in the first place?

When she'd first moved to New York oh so many years ago, she used to sneak into Broadway plays during intermission when everyone tended to spill out onto the sidewalk to get some air or smoke a cigarette.

"Oooohhhh . . ."

She was definitely earning points here.

Then you just filtered back into the theater with everyone else, being one of the last in so you could nab an empty seat.

Giving her jaw another quick break, she held the shaft of his penis with her hand and gave his testicles some swirly licks. This drove him wild. Of course, in the case of *The Producers*, there probably wouldn't be an empty seat. But she might not need to do the filtering-back-in part.

She went back to sucking. She was starting to suspect he was enjoying this so much, he would never come.

"OOOOHhhhh . . ." he said, getting there. Not much longer. Up and down, in and out, light and loose, the end was near.

She only needed to be able to wander in and cruise near Eric Hughes's seat and appear to be a member of the audience. He wouldn't even have to know she was there by herself. If it came up, she could say someone offered her the seat at the last second and so of course she nabbed it because when she'd seen it long ago with Nathan Lane and Matthew Broderick she'd been stuck with a bad ticket in the rear of the orchestra.

"OOOOHHHHHHHHH!" Daniel was on the brink. She went faster and faster, increasing the pressure. Was he never going to come?

Then, when the lights went down for the second act, she would escape, like Cinderella at midnight.

"Arggghhhhhhhaaaaaaoooooohhhh!"

She pulled up just before he ejaculated.

Perfect. Daniel would only have to know that she was making an appearance at a party for a playwright she used to know and her old theater crowd would bore him to death so could he watch Matthew for one hour, two hours at the most?

She rolled onto her back next to Daniel. He rolled onto his side and kissed her hair. "I love you," he said.

"I love you too," she said. So much for his little idea of shipping her off to a shrink.

Chapter Thirty-seven

She stationed herself right outside the theater a bit early for intermission and paced back and forth until the side doors opened and the audience spilled out. Dressed up in her black spaghetti-strap dress with a matching black jacket with feathery fur around the collar, she blended right in with all the other ticket holders. She was about to casually stroll inside and swing by the vicinity of fifth row center when Eric Hughes emerged from the theater. They looked at each other at the same time, with matching surprise.

"Oh my god."

"I don't believe it."

"This is beyond coincidence."

"It must be fate."

"Must be." He paused. "You look lovely."

"Thank you."

"The play is amusing, don't you think?"

"Very funny."

Lots of heads were turning. Camille, if only for the moment, got to bask in his celebrity glow.

Then Mimi appeared. "There you are." Gave her a look. "Do I know you?"

"I saw your apartment the other day. . . ."

"Oh, yes. Well, sorry, but we've already accepted an offer."

"Nothing is final yet, dear."

"I'd rather not prolong this business, darling."

"I'd rather not discuss this now, luv."

"Fine," Mimi said. "I'm getting in line for bonbons."

"Good luck," Eric said.

Camille raised her eyebrows. It wasn't exactly her place to ask him why he was there with his soon-to-be ex-wife, but . . .

"We bought these tickets six months ago," he explained. "In happier times. Neither of us wanted to give up our seat. . . ."

"So you decided to suffer next to each other so you could enjoy the play."

"Exactly. And you are here with . . . ?"

"Sad to say, I was going to come with my sister, but we bought the tickets before her . . ."

"Poor thing."

"I could've asked someone else. But . . ." she sighed, "no one can take her place. It just didn't feel right. So I donated her ticket to the Theater Development Fund. It seemed the right thing to do."

"Quite." He paused for a moment. And then he leaned over and whispered in her ear. "Would you consider having dinner with me?"

The question was popped so suddenly, she had to pretend not to be surprised. "Thank you. But I don't think that will be possible."

"I assure you, it's quite over with Mimi."

"It's not that. It's just . . . my life is very complicated right now."

"Would you consider giving me your phone number?"

She panicked. She couldn't have him phoning her. "Actually, I've been staying at my brother-in-law's. While my sister is in the hospital. I don't really like to take calls there. He likes to keep the line open in case the doctor calls with any news. . . ." She tried to think of some better excuse, but he looked so disappointed. "But I suppose I could give you my cell number."

"Are you sure? You look alarmed."

"It's fine, really."

"I'm not a crook. Just an overrated actor."

She smiled, but she couldn't look him in the eye. This was too confusing. As she gave him her number, Camille felt like she'd lost all motor coordination around her mouth.

He wrote it on his program and she hoped the people who kept sneaking looks at them didn't think she was doing anything so base as getting his autograph. She felt as if she'd already committed adultery. Not that she was going to commit adultery.

"Well, we'd better return to our seats. May I escort you?"

She nodded toward the double doors. "Mimi is probably looking for you."

"Let her look. Shall we?"

"You go ahead."

He bowed his head. "As you wish."

She bowed back and watched him go inside. She hadn't anticipated being the object of curiosity. But a few people seemed to be staring at her, trying to figure out if she was someone they should recognize. She was sorry to disappoint them. After a few moments they started drifting back into the theater. It was time for her to go home, but she didn't want anyone to notice—not that it would matter—so just in case anyone was still watching, she took out her cell phone, pressed some buttons, and said hello. Then she tried to appear like she'd just been told . . . her sister had come out of her coma! "I'll be right there." She put the phone in her purse, looked at the theater doors with regret, and made herself accept the fact that she was not going to get to see the second act. No, she must head for the subway. Because at a time like this, it was very important to be at your sister's side.

"How was the party?" Daniel asked, when she got home.

"Fun!"

"Was it nice to see your old friends?"

"Still driving themselves crazy trying to get auditions, agents, stupid reviews so everyone will notice how 'special' they all are. Don't they see that theater is dead?"

"So it didn't make you miss the old days?"

"On the contrary. It made me feel so happy for my life. Did Matthew give you any trouble?" she asked as Daniel handed him to her. *Please, God, tell me he wasn't any trouble.*

"We watched the Yankees game together."

Thank you, God. "It's nice to see you bonding with him."

Camille kissed Matthew on the cheek. Then she kissed Daniel on the cheek. Her heart filled with tenderness. She hated all this deception. It would be so much easier if she could accuse Daniel of all sorts of flaws and defects to justify her actions. But the worst thing she could think was that he was preoccupied with his work. Which was also something she found attractive. She loved—was sometimes in awe of—the fact that he was so content and secure in his life and almost didn't seem to even need her. Well, no, that wasn't true. He needed her for sex and as a baby maker. But emotionally? When did he ever come to her for advice or comfort? If he had a problem with a patient he consulted with another shrink. What other troubles did he have? His only other potential problem, Camille realized with chagrin, was that he had a discontented wife who sneaked around behind his back.

She sat down to feed Matthew. He deserved better than her. She wished she could be a better wife. Why did he even want her for a wife? He could've chosen someone much more conventional, someone much more predisposed to marriage and maternity.

But then, that was another one of the things she loved about him. The fact that he had chosen her. It showed some gumption. And she wanted to reward him for his faith in her. Was she just going to fail him? Like her father had failed her?

No. She wasn't going to let that happen. She was just amusing herself, that was all. She would never be unfaithful. "Thank you for watching him," she said.

"You should take time for yourself more often. You deserve it, honey."

Deserve to be put in jail, burned at the stake, tied to a plank and lowered into the lake in Central Park . . . "Well Berthe has been great. I'm really glad I caved in on that finally."

"Me too."

The guilt was intolerable. She really wanted to make it go away. And make Daniel happy, too. If she ended up enjoying it too, that would be an added bonus. So, after Matthew "went down" at eleven o'clock, Camille snuggled up to Daniel to see if he would "come up."

"I think I might be ready," she said, running her hand up his thigh and gently cradling his balls. "It sure has been a long time."

Daniel needed no more encouragement than that. Within minutes he was eagerly straddling her with the impatience of a man who hadn't had intercourse with his wife for five (count 'em five!) months.

She let him kiss her for a while, trying not to listen for Matthew's cries. (She hadn't been sure he'd fallen completely asleep when she put him down and there was a car alarm sounding from the street.)

Before they got any farther along she asked Daniel if he had a condom, because there was no way she was going to put in her diaphragm after having healed so recently.

He smooched her cheek and trotted off to his bureau to get it.

"Are you sure this is okay?"

"Yes."

"Because I don't want you to do it before you're ready."

"Of course I'm ready," she said. "I wouldn't be doing this if I wasn't."

She was aware, and she suspected that he had to be too, that none of this was exactly "sexy" or "passionate." But intercourse was the order of the day. He was hungry and she would deliver.

Before entering her, he tried to stimulate her clitoris with his finger. But that car alarm was still going off, and Camille felt sure they probably only had a few minutes at best until Matthew woke out of the deepest first ten minutes of his nap and realized that someone's car was being broken into down below and shouldn't someone call the police? So she didn't want to slow things up by trying to achieve a state of arousal that she may or may not achieve in any event, and so she told him, "I'm ready," when in fact she wondered if she would be able to relax enough to let him in.

"Are you sure?" His solicitousness only annoyed her. He had to know (didn't he?) that she was not ready and wouldn't be ready and it was beside the point so let's just get it over with.

"Yes, I'm ready."

And he took her at her word.

"Ohhhh," she groaned, for his benefit. "Ummmmm."

She felt nothing, but figured the more he thought she was into it, the faster he might go.

He started to groan too, and move faster and faster inside of her. His finger remained on her clitoris, and she started to relax and feel aroused and she thought with giddy anticipation of receiving a phone call from Eric Hughes and would someone please turn that car alarm off? As Daniel sucked on her nipple she remembered that Matthew needed another pacifier. His new one was lost already and could this man not hurry up already? Didn't he know Matthew was going to wake up any second especially with that incessant car alarm going? And even if he didn't, this was precious time she could've been using to sleep, not that she'd be able to sleep.

Be patient, she told herself. He'd waited a long time for this and was really enjoying himself. But to keep it moving forward, she decided to narrate. "This feels so good. Oh. Honey. I missed you so much. . . ." She wasn't sure if he was going to try to draw this out, or if the impact of this long-awaited stimulation would max him out quickly. If she climaxed, maybe he would feel more inclined to climax too. "Ummmm," she said, with more volume than before, "oh, yes. . . ." She added, "Yes . . ."

She hoped that all the thrusting wouldn't disturb her episiotomy scar.

"Ohhh . . ." he said, with more excitement. It was coming, she could tell, he was coming. "Ohhh . . ."

Keep going, she thought, you can get there, she thought, you're almost there. *The Little Engine That Could. I know you can, I know you can.* But Daniel was still not at the top of his hill—perhaps the months of frustration were causing some sort of blockage—and so she pumped up the volume, rocked him with her pelvis, and faked her orgasm "Ohhhh!" (maybe it would guilt trip him into knowing that she was done); a few moments later she added another, even louder "Ohhhhhh!" that was very finely shaded (if she did say so herself) to evoke the agony and the ecstasy of the human condition, and then let the crescendo fall to a final more peaceful denouement "Ohhhhh."

She congratulated herself on a performance well done.

He seemed to get the signal, because he did speed up his thrusting a little, and she could tell he was focusing on getting his orgasm to come too, and soon it did, with three or four little explosions, moans, and groans and then he lay on her for a minute longer, the sweat congealing their bodies together, his flat chest pressed against her protruding one, vagina feeling a bit ravaged, the car alarm silent, and Matthew still thankfully asleep.

She shifted her hips a little, hoping it would encourage him to peel his torso off; he pulled out of her and then lay on his back next to her. And after a few moments of polite stillness (to give him the impression she was recovering from the incredible journey her body had just taken) she went to the bathroom to wipe off the inside of her vagina with some toilet paper. Well, at least it didn't feel too sore.

When she got back in bed, Daniel leaned over and kissed her on her forehead.

"Did you enjoy that?" he asked.

Was he questioning her performance? "Couldn't you tell?"

He smiled with pride. "I guess."

"Did you?"

"Very much. I love you."

"I love you too."

With the specter of making love with her husband lifted, and the satisfaction of having made him happy, Camille fell asleep feeling lighthearted and gay. It was the same "I am a good person" feeling she got after finally cleaning out her closet. Too bad it was just temporary. That closet would need to be cleaned out again soon enough. But for now, at least, she could feel beyond reproach. In fact, all this lying and sneaking around seemed to be helping her marriage get back on track!

She kept her cell phone extra handy. But by Monday evening, Eric Hughes still hadn't called. And Camille was starting to wonder if he ever would. Not that, by his timetable, that would be a long stretch, but she had to concede that he appeared to be a very big flirt and god only knew how many women he tried to pick up on a daily basis.

She served Daniel his dinner: steak and boiled new potatoes. Matthew sat in his rock-a-roo between them. He asked her with, she thought, forced casualness, "So exactly what friends did you say you saw Saturday night?"

"Oh, you know, Peter Heller. Cal Doyle. Charlene Herring." She mentioned people he didn't know so it would be unlikely he would check up on her, as if he would do something like that. "Why?"

"No reason. Just curious."

He'd never shown any curiosity before about her old theater friends. Did he suspect something? Or was she being paranoid. Matthew started crying. "Matthew, what's wrong?" It wasn't long before they could both smell what was wrong. That's when her cell phone rang.

"You get the phone," Daniel said. "I'll get the poop."

"Thanks." Camille went into the bedroom to take the call. It was Eric. She was, by necessity, short and quick with him. Which was a plus, really. Since she was abrupt, he could have no idea how thrilled she was to get his call. Maybe it even intrigued him. "I really can't talk now."

"Should I call back?"

"Yes. Or no. Why don't you give me your number. I'm very hard to reach."

She wrote his number on the back of an envelope and put it away in a drawer. When she returned to the dining room, she told Daniel it was a wrong number.

She would tell him the truth soon. Just not quite yet. She wouldn't be able to flirt effectively if he was in on this. Even if the flirting was just to get the part. Which, of course, was all it was.

It was the first time she'd been able to go to the midwife without Matthew. She sat in the waiting room looking at the pregnant mothers (rosy and glowing) and the mothers with newborns (shell-shocked and ragged) and felt like a veteran. It was amazing. She was becoming her own person again.

Emily pronounced her vaginal area completely healed. "Everything looks good as new," she said. "How are you feeling?"

"Better."

"How's the sex going?"

"My sex drive hasn't really returned."

"Is Matthew taking any formula?"

"Not a drop," Camille said proudly. She did feel a bit puffed up over the fact that he existed completely off her milk.

"You're with him 24/7?"

"I finally hired a baby-sitter, so I've been expressing milk for when I'm gone."

"Start him on formula," Emily said.

"But isn't breast milk better for him?"

"You don't have to wean him. Just use both. There's nothing wrong with supplementing with formula."

"I don't know. . . ." It seemed like defeat. "Why?"

"For many women, the sex drive doesn't return until they cut down on the nursing. It's mother nature's form of birth control."

"Really. So how would I do it?"

"When you skip a feeding, just express a little, to relieve your discomfort. If you're going out, put some pads in your bra to absorb any leaking. Gradually, your breasts will start getting the message, and they'll start producing less milk. And that's when you may notice your sexual desire returning. You'll most certainly buy yourself a little more freedom. That, in itself, might help."

"Well," Camille said, "it certainly is worth thinking about."

Chapter Thirty-eight

"Mimi wanted to live on the Upper East Side. Fifth Avenue in the sixties. That was her idea of heaven. But I insisted on the West Side. I wouldn't feel comfortable in those WASP enclaves. Came from rather humble beginnings myself, you know. So did she, for that matter. But she has aspirations..." He said that as if a penthouse on Riverside Drive was slumming.

"So you're selling because..."

"Bad memories. Too much space. When my current production is over, I'll be heading back to London. Start a new chapter. Put Mimi Tyler behind me."

Camille hoped they weren't going to spend the entire time talking about Mimimimimi. Not here, having drinks at the Time Café. It was five o'clock. Everyone was accounted for. Daniel was at the hospital until at least seven. Matthew was at home with Berthe and eight ounces of breast milk. And she was sitting on the green and white banquette across from Eric Hughes. Too bad the restaurant was so empty this time of day. She would've liked some adoring fans to gawk and wonder, *Who is that attractive woman with Eric Hughes?* Two young men at the bar stared at a baseball game. One middle-aged peroxide blonde drank a glass of wine and mumbled to herself. So much for her moment of glory.

"Have you had a chance to think more about the flat? Not

to pressure you, but I do believe we are about to accept an offer, so if you want to buy, you'll have to move quickly."

"I'll talk to my agent tonight." She couldn't tell him about 3C, of course. Maybe he would be out by the time they moved in and he would never have to know.

"Not that I mean to pressure you. It's just that Mimi is quite anxious to close the deal."

"Totally understandable. How are your auditions going?" Camille asked, sipping her glass of wine. A bit dizzy. She wasn't used to drinking liquor these days, and wine always made her a bit horny. Eric Hughes had ordered an entire bottle of cabernet and was more than enjoying it himself.

"Ghastly. There's another bunch on Monday and then we have to make a decision."

"Hmmmm."

Camille was dying to ask for an audition. But she wasn't ready to blow her cover. But she had to. Especially if they were deciding so soon. She couldn't let it wait. Somehow, she would have to tell him before lunch was over.

"The world is crawling with starlets and models who think they can act," he was complaining. "But where are all the properly trained actresses?"

Here.

"Hollywood is crawling with these twits who have a little success in one film or two, and then they expect people to treat them like royalty."

"It's disgusting."

"I would never marry an actress again. Especially a beautiful actress. It's the worst of both worlds."

"Well," Camille said, bristling a bit, "I don't know that you can make that generalization." But Eric Hughes was on a roll.

"I've been married to two actresses and all they ever cared about is how they looked. Their appearance was like a religion! A vocation! A life's endeavor! And their only interest was surrounding themselves with as many people as possible who would admire them."

"I can see it would be hard to be married to that—"

"They can only see themselves in other people's faces. And other people only exist in order to mirror back their desirability, their wit, their depth . . ."

"Aren't all people like that, really?"

"With actresses, it's more extreme."

"I think you're being unfair."

"Why do you defend these creatures? I saw how lovingly you took care of your sister's baby. It's beautiful. And he's not even yours! Just imagine what a fantastic mother you're going to be when you have your own child."

"You're too kind, really. . . ."

"That's what attracted me to you in the first place."

Attracted? Did he say he was attracted to her? For being a mother?

"Do you think an actress could do what you're doing?"

"Well . . ."

"No! The actress is too worried about her beauty regimen!" He started mimicking Mimi with an exaggerated spoiled American actress voice. "I must have my facial, my massage, my sauna, my makeover, my hair styled and colored, and then I can splurge one calorie on my bottle of caffeine-free Diet Coke," he said, clearly relishing his own performance. "An actress treats herself like a work of art that should never be touched. She wants to be gorgeous and desirable, but god forbid anyone actually do anything about it."

"Well," Camille said, "I hope you find someone who knows enough to appreciate your devotion."

"As I appreciate your sincerity. Most people tell you what they *think* you want to hear so you'll do them some sort of favor."

It did not seem prudent to admit she wanted an audition right then. "Did you want to have a child with Mimi?"

"She wasn't interested."

"I'm sorry." Yes, here she was, dishing out sympathy to Eric Hughes. "That must've been so frustrating."

"Luckily she's not the last fertile woman on earth."

He gave her a very approving look. As if her current bust size made him think of lactation as opposed to, say, bawdy sex. How annoying! Was he only after her for her reproductive skills? She picked at the remnants of her spinach and avocado salad. What the hell was she doing here? What had she started? No. Finished. Because this was the end. Nothing could come of this. He obviously wanted a baby machine, and she'd never be able to admit she was an actress.

"I really should go."

"So soon?"

"I promised my sister's husband I would spend some time with the baby."

"I see. Your poor sister is still . . ."

"Actually, she's come out of it."

"How splendid!"

"Yes. We're so relieved. But she's still quite weak. I feel like I should be by her side. Anyway, thank you so much. This was lovely."

"I went on about Mimi too much, didn't I?"

"No."

"You just don't like me?"

"Of course I like you."

"But . . . ?"

Now was the moment of truth. Maybe she should just give it a shot. If she didn't tell him she was an actress now, and he had the auditions on Monday, and they decided on Tuesday, well, her big chance would be over. It was now or never. The chance, perhaps, of a lifetime. She looked up at him, but could not really look at him. "There's something I should tell you. I was going to tell you. But then it became impossible to tell you. And now I find that I don't want to tell you."

"Tell me."

"It's embarrassing."

"I promise, whatever it is, no snap judgments."

"Really?"

"Really."

"Okay. Well. The truth is . . ." This was excruciating. "I'm an actress."

It was as if she had farted into the room.

"Oh," he said. "Well that's not so bad. Would I know any of your work?"

"I'm afraid not." The room positively reeked.

"Well, it's a tough profession. So tell me. What have you done?"

Camille reeled off her credits, emphasized her summer at the Royal Academy of Dramatic Art, and ended with the *New York Times* review. "It was an incredibly good rave, Jeb Sanders gushed over me, and you suddenly find me a lot less interesting, don't you?"

"No."

"At first there was no reason to mention it. And then I started to feel ashamed of the fact."

"It's an affliction, yes, but do we blame the blind for being blind? Of course not. So I forgive you. Really. I am only just a bit disappointed in myself."

"Why?"

"As much as I enjoy talking them down . . . I love actresses. I seem, as a matter of fact, to be incorrigibly drawn to them. I had hoped, since I was attracted to you, that I might've gotten over that. But I suppose I haven't."

"You are being very gracious."

"Considering I spent the better part of the meal running down actresses, I think I owe it to you."

"No. Really. You owe me nothing."

Camille hesitated. He knew she was an actress and he still accepted her. But would he still give her the audition? If he knew she was married? Not likely. That was a risk she didn't want to take. But how was she going to get him somewhere alone so she could do the monologue? She couldn't just ask him point-blank. "This feels awkward, mixing business with pleasure." Her heart was pounding. "But I am still interested in buying your apartment. Are you sure it's too late to make an offer?"

"Nothing's written in blood."

"Maybe I should come by and take one more look."

"Maybe you should. What about the baby?"

"The baby?"

"Your sister's baby."

"Oh! The baby can wait."

"Then let's go."

He motioned to the waiter for the check. All this lying was making her sweat. Her bra felt hot and soggy, and her thighs were sticking to the banquette. She peeled herself off the plastic to get some air to circulate around her legs, but it didn't really help much. Her entire body was radiating heat.

Chapter Thirty-nine

"Would you like a cup of tea?" Eric called from the kitchen.

"That would be nice." Camille looked at a tugboat pushing a huge ship up the river. "Thank you."

"I'll start the kettle. Why don't you take another look 'round?"

"I will. Thank you."

Camille took a cursory look around the living room, the second bedroom, and then his bedroom. She lingered there. The *Seagull* script was still on his desk.

He came into the room with two cups of tea and set them down on the desk, right next to the script. "So. What do you think?" They both stood next to each other, the desk in front of them, looking out at the view.

He had to know she wanted the part. She was half hoping he would be the one to suggest she audition. But he wasn't making it easy for her. She braced herself mentally for his rejection, aware that her entire body was tensed, as if clenching her bones could form a suit of armor for her ego.

"It's lovely," she said. "I want it."

"Do you?"

"Yes."

And then, pretending she was just noticing it sitting there, she picked up the script. "Is this the play you're doing?"

"Yes."

"*The Seagull: Malibu?*"

"It's a modernized version."

"Sounds intriguing."

"Let me tell you, after spending a few years out in Hollywood this play resonates now more than ever. The pressure to compromise your art for the masses . . . the seduction of fame . . . the shallowness of it all when the vast majority of people in the world are suffering . . . As Chekhov himself said through the character of Trigorin, who was most certainly based on himself—and I use the Stoppard translation here—'I know how to write and in everything else I'm a fake, a fake to the marrow of my bones.'"

He was so pretentious. She had to stifle a giggle. But she loved it.

"Every actress wants to play Nina." He sipped his tea. "We were fortunate enough to get a young lady named Julia Stiles."

"She's very good."

"Cost enough. But should get us some attention. And she's thrilled. Yes. The actress wants to play the actress. And give her little speech about how noble it is to be in the theater. Mimi wanted the part desperately. But she really is a bit too old. And age, unfortunately, is one of those professional hazards that we all must face at one time or another. It's worse for women, of course."

"Arkadina is a wonderful part too."

"But Mimi is a bit too young for that part." He looked at her. "As you are."

"Yes . . ."

"But . . . you would be a perfect Marsha."

"I think so too," she said as calmly as possible.

"It's not a big part."

"But it's a good part."

"There's a monologue," he said. "Page twenty-six. Do it."

"Now?" she asked, pretending to be anxious. "Cold?" As if

she wasn't dying to show him what she'd so thoroughly prepared to do.

"Now," he said, sitting down on the edge of the bed. "Cold."

She stood there, amazed. This was unfolding exactly as she had imagined. He could have no idea she'd memorized the monologue. So what if it was a bit deceptive. You had to be ruthless. And she could be ruthless. And now here it was. Her chance to be ruthless.

She opened the script. Trembled. Closed her eyes and took a moment to collect herself.

Took a deep breath.

Let her body relax into the space where she stood.

And opened her eyes. Eric was not Eric, he was Trey, the successful screenwriter. And she was Marsha. Hard drinking, bitter, tough, sassy Marsha who's given up on waiting for the man she loves and has decided to marry the man who loves her. She looked at the script occasionally (as if she didn't know the speech word for word) but mostly she looked straight at Eric.

"I'm just telling you this because I bet you can use it in one of your scripts one day. I've decided to give up on love and marry Murray. That's right, I'm settling for Murray. Oh, please. Don't look so surprised. You have no idea what it's like waiting for years for something that will never happen. I'm sick of it! Forget love. At least it'll be a change. At least I'll have a whole new set of problems, because let me tell you, I'm sick of the old problems. Murray may not be exciting, but he's a good person. And he loves me. And I feel sorry for him. So don't feel sorry for me. Oh, and don't forget to send me the final draft of your screenplay, okay? And write a nice note on it. Say something nice and simple like: To Marsha, who's still living even though she's forgotten why it was she wanted to live."

She froze for a moment, her gaze fixed on Eric. She had nailed it. But would he disappoint her like she'd been disappointed so many times before? He leaned all the way back on the bed so he was looking straight up at the ceiling. He seemed to be deep in thought. And then he sat up and looked straight at her.

"Who is your agent?"

"I don't have one."

"Then I'll have to get you one. Not a very good one," he added, "since I won't want to pay you very much."

"Excuse me?"

"To be Marsha."

"Are you saying . . . you'll give me the part?"

"You don't think I should?"

"I do! Yes!"

"Then this is what we'll do. Marty and Dina are having a party this Sunday at their place up in Greenwich. They're the producers. You can read for them then. We'll see what they say. It is ultimately their decision. But they will take my opinion quite seriously."

This was not happening. "Thank you. So much. Really." Was it really happening? "I can't possibly thank you enough."

"I'm sure you'll find a way." He reached out and caressed her cheek. "That was extraordinary."

Camille felt a chill down her spine. "So this party is in Greenwich?"

"Bring your swimsuit; he has a pool. A view of the Sound. It's quite lovely."

"How divine," Camille said. But her only association to the word swimsuit was "stretch marks."

"West Harden will be there. We'll have you read a scene or two in front of the powers that be, let them put their two cents in, and we'll take it from there."

Camille smiled. West Harden had been popular in a few teen movies about five years ago and was now probably trying to establish himself as a "real actor."

"Is he doing the part of Treplev?" she asked.

"Yes. Or Trey, as he's called in our version. Marsha doesn't have any actual scenes with Trey, but I'd rather have him read with you than do it myself."

Camille knew this was getting out of control. But really, didn't she deserve this? Hadn't she paid her dues? Wasn't this how things really happened in the world? Not by doing all the right things but by being in the right place at the right time?

Right time, except for the small hitch that she would have to spend the entire day without Matthew. Which she'd never done before. And it was a weekend, so she'd have to ask Daniel to watch him. So it was impossible.

"I can't . . ." she said. "Wait."

Chapter Forty

Matthew turned away from Camille's breast as if it stunk. Berthe had given him a bottle just before she'd returned home—as if she was out to punish her—and now her breasts were hard, hot, and bursting. The milk was dripping down her belly like when a faucet needs a new washer, drip drip drip.

So she set him in his rock-a-roo, gave him his plastic bead necklace, and went to get a clean glass from the kitchen. "Did you have a nice time with Berthe today? I missed you. Did you miss me?"

She sat back on the couch and started squirting a fine stream of milk from her right breast into the glass while Matthew slobbered over his toy. What incredible news. It was unreal. She didn't believe it yet. Didn't dare to. And she had no idea how she would deal with the reality of working a Broadway show. Broadway! Everything was going to change. She would need to get a full-time baby-sitter. A live-in to cover the nights.

She would need to tell Daniel.

She would need to figure out how to ward off the romantic slash sexual advances of Eric Hughes. He would expect "re-payment." It didn't help that he was so attractive. If only this was just about talent. If only she wasn't married.

No. *Bad thought*. She loved her little family. Did not think that thought. Or if she had thought that thought, she didn't actually feel it. Or if she had felt it, she didn't *want* to feel it, and it was only temporary, fleeting, like an involuntary spasm. Family had saved her from despair. No matter what happened, she had her family. She was safe. She was not alone in the world.

If only that was enough. If only her priorities were in order—if she were a *good* person—it would be enough. She would live her life in contentment knowing that she had the most important thing of all. So stop wanting more, for god's sake. Stop wanting more!

She was not a good person. She'd been cursed by her father. This compulsion to be who she was not, to be somewhere other than where she was. Full of vanity. Ambition. Bad. Like him.

She didn't want to be bad like him!

Somehow, she would figure out a way to make this work so no one got hurt. And everyone got what they wanted. There had to be a way! In the meantime, there was no need to confess to Daniel that she might act again. On Broadway! She laughed and smiled and shook her head. She might no longer have to feel bitter about her life! This was a thought she almost dared not have. Or she would jinx it. Because it *had* always seemed to be a curse, this lack of success—a curse that had cast a shadow on her entire adult life. A punishment for her flawed personality. Because she wasn't deserving and the fates had it in for her.

But now, finally, it seemed that maybe there had never been a curse at all. Her lack of success had simply been a natural outcome of competing in a highly competitive field. And her tenacity was going to pay off. And she was *not* being punished by the gods! She *was* a deserving person. Who would get what she deserved. Amazing.

She stopped squirting and looked at Matthew. His little eyebrows arched, like his father's. "Amazing," she said to him, kissing his soft little cheek, then his other cheek, then his forehead, then his nose. "Absolutely amazing." She could almost breathe in the success. Sweet as mountain air. Buoyant as helium. Even her body felt lighter, as if she might float right up to the ceiling.

The glass was half full of milk. She swished it around. She was getting better at this. There was something very satisfying about seeing the milk accumulate. She could view her accomplishment and feel proud.

She took a moment to relive that moment of silence with Eric after she'd nailed the monologue. Even if none of this worked out, she would always know that when she'd needed to, she had performed. I, she thought, am an accomplished woman.

The supermarket. One of her favorite places to go with Matthew. The excellent selection of goodies. So many things to buy. Matthew was never bored going up and down the aisles. Steak. Zucchini. A special box of rainbow cookies from the bakery section. A six-pack of beer.

A six-pack of formula.

She held the small cans in front of her. Could she really do this? Breast-feeding was such a bond. So sweet. So intimate. So wonderful, really. Her nipples tingled. How could she give it up? Before she knew it, he'd be off to college! And this stuff with its mysterious ingredients was so expensive. The powder was much cheaper. But this was so convenient.

It really was convenient.

Was a gradual weaning the answer to all her problems?

She put the cans in the shopping cart. Matthew watched, unsuspecting.

That evening, she asked Daniel about doing a little babysitting on Sunday. "There's a benefit for the Theater Development Fund. I think I'd like to go."

Daniel had not yet spent an entire day alone with his son. Wasn't it about time? So it didn't seem like an unreasonable request. She hated to lie, but she couldn't admit the truth at this stage of the game. If she got the part, then she would tell him. There was no need to admit she was caving in to the idea of acting again (caving in to Broadway!) until it was a sure thing. She also had to make sure things were squared away with Eric. She guiltily thought of his gorgeous face. White teeth. Charming smile. That goddamned sexy accent and the way he'd caressed her cheek. He hadn't meant anything by that. Why would he be interested in her? She was a nobody. It was nothing. Just an appreciation for her acting. That's all.

"Sure," he said. "Maybe you could start volunteering there."

"I was thinking of doing something like that."

"You see? I knew a baby-sitter would be a great idea. You're getting used to going out without him. Our sex life is getting back on track. . . ."

"So I'm going to leave in the late morning," she said, wanting to make sure he realized she was talking about the bulk of the day. Greenwich was about forty-five minutes away, and she wasn't sure how long Eric would want to stay there. She'd have to get a train schedule in case she needed to make an early exit. "So I won't be back until mid to late afternoon. Okay?"

"As long as you leave enough milk."

"We have a lot. And I'll pump some extra. And . . . I got some formula."

"Really?"

"The midwife said it might be a good idea. I bought some cans."

"Formula?" Daniel looked as if she was considering exposing their baby to radioactive waste.

"She said phasing out the breast-feeding may help my sex drive come back."

"Oh. Well. Why didn't you say so."

"So the fridge will be well stocked with breast milk and formula."

"Great. We'll be fine. Don't worry about it."

Camille felt incredibly relieved. She couldn't wait until

Sunday. Marty Elliot. Dina Fischer. They were big producers. Names she'd seen for years in reviews, on programs, in *Backstage*. And she had the whole afternoon away. To pursue her own interests!

She did love both her boys. How could she ever resent having a baby? It was worth it. It was all worth it.

Hard to tell how much it was guilt or desire that led her to encourage another night of making love. But when Daniel got into bed, she turned to him and started to stroke his penis. Before she knew it, they were kissing and she was trying to decide whether to wear her hair up or down to Greenwich. How would Marsha wear her hair? Down, she thought. But it was supposed to be sunny that weekend and she might want it up off her shoulders, plus if they took a walk on the beach she didn't want it flying around her face. Seemed like years since she'd set foot in an ocean. They would walk along the shore and talk about the brilliance of setting the play in Malibu, and then she'd audition for Dina and Marty right there on the sand with the waves crashing in the background and everyone would be flabbergasted and insist on signing her immediately. Eric, spellbound by her acting talents, would fall hopelessly in love and ravish her in the beach cabana when she was changing out of her bikini and . . .

"Would you do me a favor?" Daniel asked.

"What?"

"Open your eyes."

"What?"

"I feel like you tune me out. Like you go somewhere else when we make love."

"You do?"

"Maybe you could try keeping your eyes open."

"Oh. Okay."

Daniel started to kiss her again. And she kept her eyes open. It took real effort. She really had to force herself to do it. He kept his eyes open too. It wasn't just that it interfered with her thoughts, which was disconcerting enough. It was also that it made Daniel so incredibly present. She laughed and pulled away. "This is weird."

"Lots of people kiss with their eyes closed, but I want you to be here . . . with me. . . ."

"I am."

"Are you?"

"I've never even noticed I closed my eyes."

They tried again. Again she had to fight the urge to close her eyes. When she did force them open, he was watching her, and it made her feel like a spotlight was on her and it felt—surprisingly—uncomfortable.

"I don't want to keep my eyes open."

"Too scary?"

"No. I just prefer to have them closed, that's all."

"Okay. If it makes you uncomfortable . . ."

She didn't like the idea that he was criticizing her lovemaking abilities. As if he was such a stud. I mean, really. Who did he think he was?

Eric Hughes?

Chapter Forty-one

She took the train from Grand Central. The air-conditioning was up so high she was frozen when she stepped off the train. The warmth of the sun felt good on her skin. She found her way to the parking lot. Eric wasn't there. Had he forgotten to pick her up? There were some taxis, but she didn't even have the address. Just then, he drove up in his gold Jaguar. God. She couldn't believe he took that thing out on the road where some jerk could ram into it. He commented on how "lovely" she looked and opened the car door for her. She was extra careful not to bump her head as she got in.

They followed a series of country roads lined with white stately but sterile colonials. She tried to relax and enjoy being out of the city. Eric had been staying at the house since the evening before and was going on about how Dina and Marty couldn't wait to meet her. But the small nagging worry that all her hopes and dreams would be granted or denied on this very day made her "slightly tense." He turned into a stone entrance to a driveway that was so long it could've been an additional road. It cut through a vast and well-groomed lawn to a circular driveway of a three-hundred-year-old farmhouse estate. He pulled his car next to one of many that had been left rather haphazardly in front of the house.

This was it.

Time for some of the most important mingling of her life.

She stepped out of the safe haven of the car. Clutched her $125 new-for-the-occasion straw tote from Bloomingdale's. Refrained from saying anything stupid, like *this would make an amazing bed and breakfast.* Took a deep breath. Exhaled. And reminded herself that she was no longer poor. Had nothing to be ashamed of. Could pull this off. Think Katharine Hepburn in *The Philadelphia Story.* Grace Kelly in *High Society.* Better yet: Camille Chaplin opposite Eric Hughes in (she shook her head at the silliness of it) *Broadway Debut.*

Dina Fischer was a pleasant-looking woman in her fifties with a yellowy blond pixie haircut. She wore a little tennis outfit with a pleated skirt. Hadn't they gone out in the sixties? Her tan was splattered with freckles and the wrinkles around her knees made her skin sag.

"Your house is beautiful," Camille said, as they entered the enormous living room. A massive stone fireplace dominated one wall and a brown leather sofa flanked by two matching loveseats faced it. A white horse from an antique carousel stood near floor-to-ceiling pane-glass doors that opened out onto a stone patio. Beyond the patio was a swimming pool and Jacuzzi, and beyond that was a panoramic view of the Sound.

Dina led them back out to the garden behind the house. She was chattering on about West Harden and how he was busy publicizing his new movie but would be here soon. Camille hoped that was true since she was going to have to hightail it back to Manhattan.

About ten people lounged around on white Adirondack chairs watching the others play tennis and volleyball, and swim. A waiter in black slacks and a white button-down shirt served drinks from a portable bar and there was a table with a lavish spread of hors d'oeuvres.

Eric introduced Camille to some of the people on lounge chairs and rattled off names Camille recognized as being "important people in the theater." There was also a smattering of local neighbors (and, Eric had mentioned in the car, potential investors) who enjoyed being in proximity to "important people in the theater."

Oh, yes. This was how things happened. Not by living in the East Village in a rent-controlled apartment diligently auditioning for the Norman Freeds or Sylvia Hopkins of the world. Not by taking classes and giving yourself countless pep talks to bounce back from rejections. Not by cutting your teeth on Off-Off-Broadway crap hoping to make it to Off Broadway while not daring to even think in terms of Broadway.

But by being at the party at the country house of the wealthy producers.

"And this," Eric was saying, "is Marty Elliot."

"Camille Chaplin?" Marty peered at her face. "Have I seen you in anything?"

"I don't know. Have you?"

Camille took off her sweater—was baking already—and draped it on the back of a chair Eric pulled up. She noticed him take in her figure—extra voluptuous, courtesy of Matthew—as she sat down and crossed her bare legs and wished she had at least the wisp of a tan.

"Your name does sound familiar."

"Perhaps because of my great-great-uncle."

"You don't mean . . ."

"My great-grandfather was Charlie's brother."

Camille had once read Charlie Chaplin's biography. She knew he had a brother named Sydney. She wasn't sure if that brother had any children, but she figured it was safe to assume this man didn't know either. It was worth the gamble. If one had nothing else to offer, being a blood relation to a famous figure was almost necessary to gloss your image.

"How interesting. I never did find the chap amusing," Marty said.

"Neither did my great-grandfather."

Marty laughed. "And I hate it when comics decide they have to impress everyone with being a serious actor. They all do it eventually."

"Did you see Steve Martin in *Waiting for Godot?*" Eric asked.

"A few years back at Lincoln Center," Marty said. "Dreadful."

"I thought it was quite good," Eric said.

"It's so annoying," a woman next to Marty said. "He writes for *The New Yorker*. He writes novels. He writes plays. Screenplays. Acts. Does comedy . . ."

"Plays the banjo," Camille added, intent on joining the conversation. A waiter asked her if she'd like a drink and she asked for a Mimosa.

"He never did marry," said a fiftyish woman with cherry-shaped funky earrings. "Is he gay? Because I find him very attractive."

A blonde in a bikini left the volleyball game and sat down with them. "Steve Martin? I've stayed at his house in Aspen a few times. He's very anal."

It was ludicrous. Even these successful people had to name-drop. Was there no relief? Who did Steve Martin name-drop? Steven Spielberg? Tom Hanks? Once you got that successful, there could only be the old guard to name-drop, like Paul Newman and Robert Redford. Who did they name-drop? God?

The waiter brought her drink in a frosted champagne glass. There was some conversation about Julia Stiles's most recent movie, which was doing fairly well at the box office, and what a good Nina she was going to make. Camille wondered if she was going to be at this party, but someone said she was finishing up on location in Paris, though they weren't sure if it was France or Texas.

Finally, West Harden arrived along with a big, black, bald bodyguard; a Puerto Rican stylist; and an Asian boyfriend. Going overboard with the multiculturally chic thing. But she didn't want to judge. She needed him to like her. He had a fake salon tan, blond hair with gold highlights, and was dressed in a beautiful blue linen suit over a white T-shirt and spanking white Converse sneakers. Don't be intimidated. Don't be impressed. After all, he has no acting skills and his fame is based on some incredibly stupid movies. Nevertheless . . .

"Sorry I'm late," he said. "A reporter from *Entertainment Weekly* would not stop asking me questions."

Eric introduced her as his "little discovery" and they shook hands. She refrained from listing all the movies she'd seen him in. He was surprisingly (overly?) gracious. "Thanks for coming. Replacing Mimi on such short notice is giving everyone indigestion. . . ."

"I should be thanking you for reading with me."

"Are you kidding? I came for the food." He started for the buffet and Eric pulled him by the arm.

"We're going to read first, eat later. In the library, where we can have some privacy."

Camille was the one who had indigestion as they all retreated. Eric closed the double doors, and all eyes turned to her.

To her great relief, as soon as she and West started to act, she felt at ease. Energized, really. Because, finally, after all these years, she was having a chance to do what she was trained to do in front of the people who mattered. And it wasn't luck or coincidence that had brought her here. No, sir. It was perseverance and lies.

Dan: *I have to go inside.*

Marsha: *Wait.*

Dan: *What do you want?*

Marsha: *I need to talk.*

Dan: *We've been through this.*

Marsha: *My father is an idiot. You're the only one who understands. I need you to help me decide what to do.*

Dan: *I can't tell you—*

Marsha: *You understand me more than anyone! Please help me. Or I'm going to do something really stupid. I swear. I'm going to ruin my entire life! I've been trying to deal with it myself but I can't. I'm driving myself insane.*

Dan: *What's the matter?*

Marsha: *You can't believe how much I'm suffering.* (pause) *I'm still in love with Christopher.*

Dan: *Marsha . . .*

Marsha: *I know! But I can't help myself!*

Dan: *Calm down. You're getting sunstroke. None of this is important. Just go inside. Find some shade. Relax.*

As she and West reached the end of the scene, Camille felt sorry they couldn't do the whole play right then and there. It was so fun to be acting with someone again. So fun!

Marsha: *It's not the sun, believe me. I try to talk myself out of it. I want to do what's right. But love isn't like that. You can't just tell it what to do. I'm going to wreck everything, like an idiot, because I don't appreciate what I have. And the annoying thing is, I can see what I'm doing, but I still can't stop myself.*

Camille looked into West's eyes. She could luxuriate in feeling all the confusion she really did feel. She was sorry it was the end of the scene.

Marty asked if she could do more.

"Of course," Eric said. "How about the scene with Murray?"

Eric found the spot in the script for West. Camille had this scene memorized too. They reached the end, and Camille almost felt like it was too easy. The situation resembled her own so much, she hardly even needed to act.

Murray: *Come home with me, Marsha.*

Marsha: *I'm going to spend the night here.*

Murray: *The baby must be hungry.*

Marsha: *Don't be ridiculous, the baby-sitter will feed it.*

Murray: *Three nights without his mother?*

Marsha: *Stop nagging me. The baby is fine. And this subject is boring. So would you drop it?*

Murray: *Well I'm going home.*

Marsha: *Go ahead.*

Murray: *Can I take the car?*

Marsha: *Then I'll be stuck. Why don't you just walk or take the bus?*
Murray: *Fine. But will you come tomorrow?*
Marsha: *I don't know. Just go. Call me on my cell phone if you need me.*

She felt relieved to reach the end of that one. It hit too close to home. Plus the writing was horrible. She couldn't believe what they were doing to Chekhov. But that was beside the point. Chekhov was dead, and anyway, he would understand her motives.

After a moment, Eric asked if perhaps she'd like to "go have a refreshment" while they all had a "little tête-à-tête."

"Of course," she said pleasantly, as if they weren't going to talk about her.

She left the room, but before she'd even crossed the hall, he called her back. "They'd like to hear the monologue."

She returned to the room, everyone apologized for keeping her, and she reassured them it was no trouble. She did the monologue—quite well, she thought—and they excused her once more.

She retrieved her tote bag and found a bathroom. Locked the door. And felt her breasts. She wasn't leaking. Maybe her body was going to give her a break. She looked at herself in the mirror. You did it. You won them over. They loved you. She allowed herself to smile at herself. Then she turned the gold faucet handle, splashed some water on her face and reapplied her makeup.

If anything, her challenge would be having to act opposite all these Hollywood actors who had no stage training at all and were used to having a camera pick up their slightest facial expressions and reactions. She could very well end up being the best thing in this play. They were lucky Mimi had backed out. And, she suspected, Eric knew it.

When she emerged from the bathroom, the others were still upstairs. She went outside, put on her sunglasses, sat off by herself, and watched a volleyball game in progress. About five minutes later Eric, Marty, and Dina came outside in good spirits. Everyone was smiling at her.

"We were all very impressed by your audition," Marty said.

"I don't know where you've been hiding," Dina said.

Hiding!

Eric and Dina got into a discussion about the costumes. She was probably a size too large to fit into Mimi's clothes. Mimi really, they all agreed, had gotten too skinny. Dina looked Camille up and down. "Can you lose five pounds in a week?"

"I can lose ten pounds in a week."

"We wouldn't want you to do anything unhealthy," she said.

Of course they would, if it saved them time and money. "Don't worry, I'll fit them."

"We'd love to offer you the part right now," Dina said. "But there are still some details we need to square away with the lawyers. . . . Just formality." She raised her glass in a toast. "To our new Marsha. Welcome."

Eric and Camille took a stroll around the grounds. She felt her breasts getting full, but didn't want to think about that. *I am Marsha.* If only her father could be here for this! *I am going to be on a Broadway stage.* She knew she should get home, or at least phone home, but she couldn't bring herself to. She didn't want to rush back. She wanted to be right here. *I am Marsha!*

"Thank you, Eric. Thank you so much."

"Don't thank me. You got it because you're good."

"You've been wonderful."

He stopped under a tree and took both her hands in his. "I look forward to working with you."

He bowed his head slightly. Then he stood close to her. Her hands were still in his. "I'm sorry I won't be playing Murray. We could have had some good scenes together."

"And I'd love to treat you like dirt," she teased.

"If you want to treat me like dirt, I'm happy to oblige any time."

She freaked a little. He was standing so near. This was the moment to make some kind of exit. *I think the others must be wondering . . .* But his head was inclined toward her, and then he put his finger under her chin, to gently lift her chin to make her lips more accessible. So he wanted her. Why? She wasn't good enough for him, was she? Of course she was. Why not? Her heart was pounding. She thought of Daniel. Saw his face, disapproving. She pushed him out of her mind. Pictured her and Eric, profile to profile, like a movie poster. Scarlett and Rhett about to have a passionate kiss. Under the tree. Tara. Before the war, when the white geese walked the vast green lawn.

"You are quite lovely," he said. "Did you know that?"

She looked into his eyes. They were . . . bloodshot. She noticed how big the pores were on his cheeks. Two hairs stuck out from his left nostril.

I am too close up, she thought. He's ruining it! Eric Hughes could not possibly compete with the fantasy of Eric Hughes. She stepped back. "Eric," was all she could say, shaking her head, unable to look at him.

"What, you don't find me attractive?" he said, teasing her, really. Of course she, a mere mortal, should be grateful for his kiss.

"I do. I just— Too much is happening right now."

"But it is all good, isn't it?"

"Yes. All good."

If she rejected him, would he take the part from her? How could she even think of rejecting him? She looked up at him like a woman in a trance, in rapture, in love . . . It was no longer about being attracted to him. There was, as a matter of fact, something creepy about this man who could have anyone but wanted her.

But never mind. This was about the part. Nothing was going to get in the way of that. She closed her eyes, ready to melt in with Rhett. No. Eric. Flesh and blood, larger than life Eric. His arms went around her waist. Chardonnay was on his

breath. His lips—the same lips she'd admired up on screen—
were on hers. This was really happening.

Daniel again. She pictured him in the living room jiggling a
very cranky Matthew on his hip. *How can you be so selfish?*

Go away.

Can't you settle for living your lackluster, dreary little life?

I need larger than life.

Which only exists inside your pea-size little brain . . .

So let me exist in my head.

*This isn't in your head, you're really doing it! Are you really going
to betray us? Like your father betrayed you?*

Goddamn it. Here she was making love with her fantasy,
and all she could think of was her husband! Well forget it. She
could see why her father did what he did. Who could blame
him? Life was disappointing. This time she would not be disappointed. She was kissing Eric Hughes! Belly to his belly,
chest to her chest. Her nipples against his shirt. Her nipples—
she was especially aware of them because the tips were ultra-
sensitized from all the nursing—were feeling especially tender
as he pressed her to him and suddenly it occurred to her that if
she pressed up against him any harder, milk might come seeping out and make two wet marks on his Ralph Lauren white
linen shirt!

She broke away.

"I'm—" She couldn't find any words to say and didn't want
to let him get a good look at her, so she rushed up to the patio
where she found her sweater. Grabbed it and went inside as
quickly as she could with a smile pasted on her face not even
daring to look down at her chest to see if there were two wet
patches.

She trotted up the stairs to the first bathroom she could find,
locked herself in and untied the top of her dress as quickly as
she could—by some miracle she had not seeped through the
pads—and squirted her milk down the shiny brass drain. Oh
Matthew, she thought, Matthew, Matthew, I'm so sorry. . . .

When she felt pretty sure that both breasts were drained out, she retied her halter and fixed her face. She felt, literally, drained. She checked her cell phone. Three messages. Damn. They were probably from Daniel. She didn't want to listen, didn't want to speak to him. How would she exit graciously without alienating Eric even more? She didn't want to deal with reality right then, not in this house, not yet.

She put her sweater on and went back downstairs. Tried to find Eric. He was in the kitchen talking with the woman with the cherry earrings. He immediately noticed her sweater. "Are you cold?"

"Just a bit."

"Are you ill?" he asked. "You look pale."

"I'm always pale."

"Not this pale. Sit down. Would you like a glass of water? Are you upset?"

"I'm not upset," she said in a hushed tone of voice. The others were talking away, but she felt they were listening too. Did they know already that she got the part? Did she really have it? Of course she did. He said so. He wouldn't take it from her just for not kissing him, would he? "I'm happy," she said.

"Good. I want you to be happy." He squeezed her hand and gave her a reassuring smile.

"I am a bit thirsty," she said.

"I'll fetch you some water."

Oh, hell, maybe she should just stay. Matthew and Daniel could survive without her. It was absurd to think she really had to be home. God knows Daniel had spent many days late at the office. So why couldn't she spend one day doing what she wanted to do?

Eric returned with a bottle of water and she gulped the whole thing down. It occurred to her that maybe husband and child were doing just fine and there was no reason to rush home.

"Need to make a phone call. Be right back."

And so she went up the stairs to an empty bedroom and sat on the edge of a mammoth bed and phoned home hoping to god everything was all right.

"Daniel?"

"Where are you?"

She could hear Matthew howling in the background. "What's happening?"

"Matthew won't take the formula or the breast milk!"

"Really?" He'd adapted to Berthe, no problem. She refrained from saying he must be doing something wrong.

"He won't nap; he keeps crying. Where are you?"

Damn. She knew she shouldn't have called. "I'm running a little late." She wiped her lips as if there was still a residue of Eric's kiss there.

"So get yourself into a cab and come home."

"He didn't nap at all?"

"I put him in the crib and he cries. I take him out and he cries. He's driving me crazy!"

Welcome to fatherhood. "He's not used to you," she couldn't resist saying.

"If that's the point you wanted to make, then you've made it. So come home."

"I will. As soon as possible."

"Now!"

"Okay. I'm on my way." She hung up before he could ask her any more questions and turned off the power. Then she went back down the stairs. That's when she discovered Eric, Mimi, and Dina standing in the living room laughing. As soon as they saw her, they pulled apart.

"Camille," Eric said, "there you are. Look who just arrived."

"Well!" was all Camille could manage to say.

Mimi was more direct. "What is *she* doing here?"

Dina broke the news. "I'm delighted to say that Camille is taking over the part of Marsha."

"Is she really?" Mimi smiled tightly. "The part. The apartment. What else of mine do you want?"

"She just read for Marty and Dina," Eric said. "She was fantastic."

"I'm so glad. I think I'll join the others outside. I'm in the mood for a swim. I have a flight back to L.A. tonight and want some exercise."

"I think I'll join you," Dina said, giving Eric a reassuring glance. Hopefully she would calm Mimi's ruffled feathers.

Camille had questions, but she had to stay cool. So she just smiled as Eric hooked his arm into hers.

"Are you feeling better?"

"I should head back to the city."

"Because of her? I don't even know why she's here."

"It's not that."

"She certainly wasn't invited."

"It's fine, really. If you could just get me to the train station."

"Don't be silly. I'll drive you back."

"I don't want you to leave the party because of me."

"I came to the party *because* of you."

"I think it's better if I take the train."

"Because I kissed you? Is that why you're upset?"

"I'm not upset. I just really—"

"Because I don't want you to think that I presume—"

Suddenly the glass-paned French doors leading to the garden crashed open. West's bodyguard gripped the arm of a chubby peroxide blonde bulging out of black capris and a red tube top.

"I've caught her!" the bodyguard bellowed. "Someone call the police!"

"Who is this?" Eric asked.

"Mimi's stalker! She was sneaking around in the hedges by the pool!"

The woman said nothing. Camille felt she was staring—

make that glaring—at her. A crowd gathered in the room. The woman with the cherry earrings dialed 911 on her cell phone. "I need the police," she said. "Right away, please."

Mimi appeared in the skimpiest little bikini. She really had lost too much weight, Camille swore. No one could find that attractive, could they? "What's going on?" Mimi asked.

"West's bodyguard caught your stalker," Eric said. "Evidently she was behind the hedges."

"That's not my stalker. My stalker is in jail."

"Well it's not *my* stalker," Eric said. "She's much younger than that. And prettier, I might add."

"It's not West's stalker," the bodyguard said. "Unless she's a new stalker I ain't seen yet. Who were you stalking?" he asked the woman directly.

"I'm not a stalker!" the woman announced with disgust.

A crowd was now gathering in the living room. Marty pushed his way to the front. "Then who are you?"

The woman, with her free arm, pointed straight at Camille. "I'm on to you."

For a moment, Camille thought the stalker was outing *her* as a stalker (not that she was one).

"You have a stalker?" Eric asked.

Camille shrugged. "Not that I know of."

"I'm not a goddamned stalker!" the woman yelled.

"Then what the hell are you doing here?!" Marty yelled back. The crowd was backed up out the doorway to the garden. Camille could hear people asking each other what was going on.

The woman kept her eyes on Camille. "I'm in love with your husband," she said. "And when he realizes you been lyin' and cheatin' on him, he's gonna leave you and marry me!"

Camille shrugged. "She's obviously crazy."

"I'm not crazy! You're the one who's been runnin' 'round like a whore. And you got a little baby!"

"I'm sorry for the disruption," Camille said, as she smiled, shrugged, shook her head, did every conceivable gesture she could think of to let everyone know how silly this was. "She's obviously referring to my *sister's* baby. I've been taking care of her. She's in the hospital. She fell out the window. My sister, not the baby . . ."

"All right, I've heard enough," Marty said. "Would you take her out front?"

The bodyguard started pulling the woman by the arm, but she shook free and screamed, "I'm a famous actress! Don't you recognize me? You can't treat me like this!"

That's when Camille realized. This was Daniel's patient. Marilyn Monroe.

Mimi turned to Camille. "Are you married, darling?"

"I have no idea what she's talking about. . . ."

"Someone tie her up or something," Dina said. "I want her off my property."

"I've seen everything," Marilyn went on. "And I'm gonna tell Dr. Kessler all about you. When everything is out in the open, he'll never trust you again."

Camille felt like she was having an out-of-body experience. This woman wanted her life. Her life she'd been so busy trying to escape! Now her entire scheme was only going to end up in humiliation. So what else was new? Her ambition always led to humiliation. That was her fate in life. Condemned to fail no matter how many times she bounced back, no matter how hard she tried.

Everyone was staring at her with varying degrees of amusement and suspicion. Did they believe psycho Marilyn? She shrugged and said, "This woman belongs in a mental hospital."

Unpleasant thought: Psycho Marilyn was the one telling the truth. *She* was the fake.

Was she the one who belonged in the loony bin? Maybe her entire life was an illusion. One big fat figment of her fertile imagination. Better shut up or she'd talk herself right into

Bellevue. "Believe me," she said to Eric. "I don't know what she's talking about. I've never seen or met this woman in my life."

"Congratulations." Eric gave her a hearty pat on the back. "Your very own stalker. And the play hasn't even opened. Success is more imminent than you think."

Chapter Forty-two

On the train ride back to Manhattan, Camille got such a headache. Eric had again offered her a ride, but she needed the time alone to collect herself. Her cell phone was off. She was afraid to turn it on. It was late afternoon and Daniel had to be going crazy. But she could not make contact. She had to preserve what little sanity she had left by not having to explain herself yet. She needed to be out in the world a little longer. She needed time to think.

Eric had driven her to the station after the police left. They'd arrested the woman (who would only give her name as "Marilyn Monroe") and taken her away. Camille had felt like they should be taking her away too. But no. Eric had *wanted* her to come to Connecticut. He *wanted* her in the part. Or had she been imagining that? No, of course not. But would he still want her if he knew the truth? It was all too exhausting. Maybe she should admit everything to him. But it was too great a risk. Truth could not compete with ambition, fame, glory, the need to prove something . . . but to whom? Her mother didn't really care. Her father was dead and gone. Why couldn't she let it go? Why couldn't she give it up? Was this weakness? Or was it strength?

As the train left suburbia behind and cut through the tenements of Harlem, Camille realized she could save time by getting out at the station on 125th Street. But she'd never been in that station before and wasn't sure how safe it would be. Every mile she got closer, Matthew's cries got louder in her head. She wished she could tell him her breasts were coming closer and closer. She was a bad mother, no doubt about it. Selfish and self-centered. And her innocent little baby was paying for it.

At the 125th Street stop, Camille froze with indecision. Should she get off the train here in Harlem or go down to familiar Grand Central? She noticed an old abandoned building across the street. It was roofless, and trees were finding some way to grow up out of the top and through the boarded-up arched windows. But it had beautiful decorative red brickwork and—she couldn't believe her eyes—a cement carving of a knight on the front, as if it was there to guard what remained of the dilapidated old building. She dashed off the train and trotted down the steps to the sidewalk, where a line of black limos and cabs sat waiting for customers. She slid in the back seat of a cab and the driver pulled out. This had been a good idea; she'd save at least twenty minutes.

Camille stared with relief into the plastic divider that shielded the driver from robbers and talkative passengers. Was there any way Daniel would understand? When he heard about the play (minus the small detail of the kiss) would he be supportive?

By the time the cab pulled in front of the apartment, her stomach was churning. She was faint from hunger—hadn't really eaten all day—and was dehydrated. She rode up the elevator with a tremendous craving for a bowl of cereal with ice cold milk.

She stepped off the elevator and got out her key. Stood in the hall for a moment to steel herself up for her entrance. Consider her character's motivation. Her wants. Her needs. She could not risk losing Daniel's trust. So she could not tell him the truth. Not until she had a signed contract.

Chapter Forty-three

Daniel stood in the middle of the living room jiggling Matthew on his hip. Matthew was wailing.

"Where the hell were you?"

"I'm sorry."

"What the fuck were you doing?"

Daniel had never sworn at her like that before. Matthew saw her and wailed even louder (had he cried the entire time she was gone?) He leaned so far toward her, he would've fallen on the floor if Daniel hadn't forcibly held him back.

It broke her heart.

God. To be needed and wanted so much! She immediately undid the top of her sundress and took him to the couch, even though she herself was parched. He didn't stop crying until his lips were about to latch on to her nipple—pausing to give one last cry of outrage—and then sucked greedily away like it was the last few ounces of milk left on earth. She clutched him as close to her body as she could.

Daniel stood over her. "Are you going to give me some sort of explanation?"

"Would you give me a moment here?"

"I left twenty messages on your cell phone! What have you been doing?!"

Camille looked up at him. "I've been gone seven hours. You'd think it was a lifetime!"

"When you have a screaming child, believe me—"

"Like I don't know? You think he's Mr. Peace and Quiet all day while you're at work?"

"You said you were on your way three hours ago—"

"I'm sorry."

"So where the fuck were you?"

"I don't want to talk to you now. You're too angry!" It was unnerving to hear him swear like that. And just a teensy bit attractive. . . . "Would you get me a drink of water?"

He went to the kitchen and returned with a glass. She drank the whole thing down. Water had never tasted so good.

"So?" he asked.

She paused. Repositioned Matthew on her lap. "I lost track of the time. . . ."

"Lost track of the time?"

He looked at her, incredulous. She suddenly felt defensive. "That's right. Because I was out having a *good* time. With my *friends*. Away from *here!* And I didn't want to come back. Okay? I'm sorry. I was bad. I'm a bad person."

"This doesn't seem like you," Daniel said.

She looked down at Matthew, so innocently working away at her breast. It did seem like her. It seemed exactly like her. "It felt good to get away."

"You *have* been getting away. That's why we got Berthe!"

"Yes, for short periods. But this was the first time I spent an entire day and you treat me like I'm some sort of criminal. I mean, I know I should've kept in touch better, but you're gone all the time." Camille surprised herself and started to cry real tears. "Sometimes I feel like a single mother. You're so absorbed in your work. Why do you get to continue with your life just like it always was? But for me, everything's completely changed! I know I don't make any money. And this was my choice. And I was the one who didn't even want to hire a sitter. But I thought I could do it myself. I really did. But I was wrong. I tried. But I can't. I'm no good at being a mom."

"Yes you are. You're doing a great job!"

"I'm not," she looked down at Matthew. "I'm really not. I'm such a failure."

Except, she wasn't a failure. She looked back up at Daniel. She was on the brink of success. Doing what she was meant to do. Could she tell him? How could she not tell him? But how could she?

Daniel looked at her so unsuspecting. "I'm sorry I yelled at you." Matthew, as if on cue, stopped sucking and looked at her with such innocence too, and smiled as if he had no memory of the past few hours.

She switched him to her other breast. Felt like a jerk. "I'm sorry. I should've called. That was wrong of me, not to call."

"That's okay." Daniel sat down next to her and put his arm around her. "I can see how you were glad to get out, and see your friends, and you knew if you called, I would've tried to get you home. . . ."

He was forgiving her! She hated herself.

He continued to comfort her. "Time does seem to slow down when you're with a baby."

The guilt was like a layer of hot volcanic mud on her skin.

"Daniel?"

"Yes."

"There's something you should know." She paused. Was she really going to do this? "I haven't been completely honest with you."

He waited for her to continue.

"Something strange happened today. This woman approached me. One of your patients. The one who thinks she's Marilyn Monroe."

"What?"

"She's in love with you. Evidently, you are her Joe DiMaggio." Actually, Daniel was more like Arthur Miller, but it didn't seem useful to mention that right then.

"That's not possible," Daniel said. "Her family transferred her to a private hospital upstate."

"Well then something went wrong, because she followed me. . . ."

"Honey. I'm sorry. Why didn't you tell me? What did she do?"

"She told me she's in love with you. It was very upsetting . . . as you can imagine. . . ."

"That must've been really scary for you. Did you call the police?"

"Yes."

"And?"

"They took her away."

"So you filed a report. Good. Because if this continues . . . well, hopefully it won't. I'll have to find out what happened. I'm really sorry."

Camille sniffled.

"So why didn't you tell me right away?"

"Well, you see . . . she followed me. To Connecticut."

"I thought the benefit was downtown."

Camille could feel it all unraveling. Not really by choice, but it was a relief. "I wasn't exactly at a benefit. It was a party."

"Oh?"

"This is going to seem really bizarre. Okay? But I'm just going to tell you. I had the chance to meet Eric Hughes. You know, the actor? When I was apartment hunting. And I happened to mention I was an actress. And he gave me the chance to audition for a part in this play he's doing. So I auditioned. Today. For the producers. In Connecticut. And they liked me. And they're giving me the part."

"Really?"

"Yes. On Broadway."

"Broadway?" Daniel looked more than surprised. "What did you say?"

"I know it's hard to believe. It's not a big part. But it's a good part."

"Wait." Daniel took his arm from her shoulder. "Can you run this by me again?"

"I know it's surprising."

"I'm having a little trouble . . ."

"I was at a party today. In Greenwich."

Daniel stood up and positioned himself a few feet across from her. "You were at a party today in Greenwich, Connecticut."

"At the house of some producers. That's where Marilyn Monroe followed me. And I auditioned for them. And they're going to give me the part. At least, that's what they said. I'm not quite sure whether to believe it myself."

"And you've been keeping all this from me?"

"It's like I've been in an altered state."

"So . . ."

"So I have to know if this is going to be okay with you."

"That you've been lying?"

"No. I'm wondering if it's okay with you if I get back into my acting."

It was hideous to say it out loud. Back into acting. Fuck.

He laughed and shook his head. His voice was icy. "I don't think you ever really left your acting. Did you?"

She didn't say anything to that. Just looked down at Matthew.

Daniel sighed. "I'm going out."

"Where?"

He went to the door. "A walk."

"When will you be back?"

"Later." He shut the door behind him.

Camille took Matthew off her breast. He was halfway asleep and drunk with milk. She held him up on her shoulder and he lifted his head, which wobbled a little, and came out with a large belch.

It would've been comical. If Daniel had been there to share it with her.

One of her last thoughts before drifting off to sleep that evening was the wish that Matthew wouldn't wake up until at least three hours had passed. But she suspected that since he'd had an upsetting day and hadn't eaten much, he'd be waking up sooner rather than later. That's why she was freaked out when she woke up at five o'clock in the morning and Matthew had not summoned her. He'd hardly eaten the day before; he had to be starving. Maybe the trauma had done something to him. Maybe he was unconscious!

She threw the covers off and rushed out to the living room and peered down into the crib. He seemed to be asleep. But maybe he was dead. Of course he wasn't dead. But maybe he was!

She went back to the bedroom and woke Daniel.

"Honey?"

He grunted.

"I think something's wrong with Matthew."

"What?"

"He didn't wake up. I think he might be unconscious or something. Maybe all that crying did something to his lungs."

"I'm sure he's fine. Go back to sleep."

"Won't you check on him? Please?"

Daniel groaned and got out of bed. He went to Matthew and pulled up his little white T-shirt. His plump little belly went in and out with each breath.

Daniel went back to the bed.

"He's never slept this long," Camille said, following him back in, feeling foolish.

"He's getting older."

"I guess. Thank you for checking."

Daniel grunted as he got back under the covers. Camille nestled against him. She took it as a good sign that he didn't move away. But there was no way to tell how angry he was. After he'd come back from his walk, he'd barely spoken to her. Or looked at her. The next day was Sunday, though, so at least he wouldn't escape to work without having to deal with her somehow.

Matthew had slept from eleven to five. Six hours of uninter-rupted sleep. She felt so good. So fresh. Like a whole batch of brain cells finally had the chance to repair themselves.

When Matthew finally woke up at seven, she'd been up for a half hour waiting for him. She ran in the moment she heard him. He wasn't even crying, just cooing and warbling, and he smiled a big smile at the sight of her.

"Matthew! Hello little baby. I missed you so much."

She picked him up and gave him a big kiss on the cheek. "Did you have a good sleep? We didn't see each other much yesterday, did we? You had a big, long sleep." He laughed. "Yes, because you're my little baby." She gave him a big kiss on his tummy. "I love you," she said. She gave him another kiss on his cheek. "That's right." A tear escaped. "Mommy loves you."

Chapter Forty-four

Later that morning while Matthew napped, Camille and Daniel sat down across from each other at the kitchen table and sipped from hot mugs of tea.

"So why didn't you tell me about Connecticut?"

"It was such a fluke. I wanted to wait until I had some real news, in case it didn't work out."

"You didn't think I'd understand?"

"I didn't want to admit that I was wrong. About quitting acting. I felt strong giving it up—"

"I never told you to quit."

"But you didn't want me to keep doing it either. . . ."

"I never said that."

"But it's true, isn't it?"

Daniel looked back at her without speaking. She wished she could read his mind. "The part doesn't involve any kissing," she said, cringing at the thought of Eric under the tree. "Or nudity, or even partial—"

"You know," he finally said. "I'm sorry we didn't have more time together. Before Matthew arrived. Before you got pregnant. To be with each other alone. We never really had a chance to gel."

"I guess not." She cupped her hands around her mug and wondered if he was working up to telling her their marriage was a failure. But he wouldn't try to end it, would he? Not with Matthew to think of.

"We've hardly had time for just us," he went on. "And if you start performing, we'll have even less time."

"I suppose." She kept her hands around the warmth of her mug. Maybe he was going to say he didn't want her to do it. What would she do then?

"But . . . you gotta do what makes you happy. So . . . even though I may regret this later, I guess I'm saying, yes. Take the part. Do the play."

She impulsively reached to squeeze his hand and tipped over her mug of tea. It spilled all over the tabletop. Daniel handed her a rag to wipe up the spill. "Thank you," she said, damming the liquid so it wouldn't drip onto the floor. "Thank you for understanding. It's really important to me that you understand."

She would make this up to him, she thought, as she cleaned the mess. Thank god she hadn't let things go further with Eric. She would be the perfect wife. Somehow. At least, after the play closed she would be the perfect wife. She squeezed the rag out in the sink. "Do you hate me?"

"No. I just want you to be up-front with me. We have to trust each other, right?"

"Of course. I'm sorry."

"But I guess, what I really want to say is . . . congratulations."

She turned to face him. He was smiling. He was proud of her!

"It'll be amazing to see you up there on a Broadway stage."

She stepped closer to him. "I'm sorry I didn't tell you about all of this in the first place."

"Well," Daniel said, putting his arms around her, "you've been under a lot of stress."

As Daniel hugged her, she wondered if she would've gotten this far if she *had* told him. Had all that flirting with Eric been necessary? Maybe he would've appreciated her talents without imagining her as a sex object or the future mother of his children or whatever it was that attracted him to her. It still wasn't clear how she was going to ward him off, though she most certainly would find a way. She just had to get that contract signed.

Matthew woke up crying and Daniel released her from his arms. Matthew kept crying until she sat down with him and lifted her shirt. It was such a relief to feel his little body nestled against hers. She marveled at how simple it was to satisfy his needs. And how incredibly complicated.

Chapter Forty-five

Tuesday morning. She couldn't help but fret. Not that there was any reason to worry. Nothing happened as fast as you wanted. There was no reason to think they had changed their minds. And they had to work everything out with the lawyers. Just a formality, Dina had said. But still, it would be nice to hear from Eric. She considered calling. She didn't want to seem too anxious, but he would understand. So she called. And left a brief message, trying her utmost to sound casual.

"Hi Eric. Would love to hear from you. Give a call when you have a chance."

The phone rang almost immediately after she hung up. Yes! He'd been screening, but wanted to reassure her. . . .

No. It was the loan officer from the bank. Their mortgage application had been approved. "So quickly?" she asked.

"You just need to pass the board, and the apartment will be yours."

"Great."

Great? Camille hung up the phone. She considered calling Daniel and telling him the news. But she decided not to. He still didn't know Eric Hughes lived in the same building. She was hoping that would not need to be confessed.

She felt so antsy. Berthe was coming in and she didn't know what to do with herself. She decided to call Naomi.

"I'd like to look at the apartment. Take some measurements. Would you mind?" Even though she still had the keys to Eric's apartment, she didn't have the key to the one that would be her own.

After Berthe arrived, Camille walked across town. She walked so fast, she got all the way to the West Side in record time and before she knew it, she was in front of 111 Riverside Drive. The doorman sent her up. Naomi was already there.

Camille was measuring the length of the windows when Naomi mentioned apartment 16C.

"Toni told me it's off the market."

Camille let the tape measure snap shut. "Really?"

"Evidently they're back together. Isn't that great? You get to live in the same building as a celebrity!"

"No," Camille said. "That's not great." She headed out the door to the elevator.

"Where are you going?"

"To see the view." Maybe she'd jump out the window while she was at it.

"You can't just go up to his apartment!"

The doors slid open. "Please don't follow me." There might be a scene and she didn't want an audience.

"Camille!" Naomi said as the elevator door shut. "You can't just go up there and ring his bell!"

When she rang Eric's doorbell he called from behind the door, "Who is it?"

"Camille."

A few moments later, he opened the door wearing a silk paisley robe. She hated men in silk paisley robes. "Camille. I was going to call. How nice to see you. Did the doorman buzz you up?"

Mimi came from the bedroom and sat on the arm of the sofa. She was wearing a short leopard-print silk robe. Camille hated women in short leopard-print silk robes. "Did someone invite her?"

Eric kept his gaze on Camille as he said to Mimi, "Leave the room for a moment, would you darling?"

"This is my apartment," Mimi said. "I can go anywhere I want."

"Have a heart, darling."

But Mimi had no intention of having a heart. She looked on with amusement as Eric said to Camille, "I'm afraid she's moved back in."

Camille kept her eyes on Eric's face. She was transmitting to him by brain wave: *Please don't say what I know you're going to say because you look so guilty and full of pity.*

"And I'm afraid," he continued, "she's back in the cast."

For a moment she tried to cling to the thought that he'd meant she had broken a limb for a second time and was wearing a cast again.

"I was going to call you," he said.

She wanted to break one of *his* limbs.

"I do feel horrid," he added.

Or maybe all of them.

"I know how disappointed you must be."

But he didn't know. He couldn't. Maybe if she kneeled down on the floor and threw herself completely at his mercy. All she needed was a bone. A small part. She would be Mimi's understudy. Anything. *Just don't send me home with nothing!*

"If it makes you feel any better," Eric said, "I really did think your acting was quite good."

"It doesn't make me feel better. It makes me feel worse. Because it doesn't matter. Why does it never seem to matter?" She heard her voice getting shrill. "Do you know how much I want this?!"

"How did she get up here?" Mimi asked.

"I live here," she said.

"Right." Mimi picked up the intercom to call the doorman. "Hello? Did you let someone up without buzzing us first? Because Mr. Hughes and I require very tight security and if we have to hire a bodyguard after everything I've been through it will be at the building's expense—"

"Actually," Camille said, "I have a key!" She displayed the tape measure in her hand as if it explained everything. "I'm moving in." She was now shrieking. "We'll be like one big happy family!"

"What is she talking about?" Mimi hung up the intercom. "You gave her a key to our apartment?"

"I did no such thing."

"I just bought apartment 3C. Same line. Winter views. Isn't that great, neighbor?"

"You bought an apartment in this building so you could get a part in his play?"

Camille looked intently into Eric's eyes. "It means nothing to her and everything to me."

He shrugged. "Her name does sell tickets. . . ."

"But you know I'd be better in the part."

Mimi started to laugh. "Oh, please!"

"You said so yourself!"

Mimi stopped laughing and turned to Eric. "What did you say?"

Eric took Camille by the elbow and started guiding her toward the door. "I think you'd better go—"

Camille shook her arm free. "He said he was relieved when you quit. Because you have no idea how to perform on stage."

"You told her that?"

"I said no such thing!"

"Close-ups and nude scenes are all she's good for!" Camille looked over her shoulder at Mimi. "That was a direct quote."

"She's hysterical," Eric said. "Pay no attention. Now it's time for you to go—"

Camille backed away from him. "It was the same day you told me you never wanted to be married to an actress again. Or maybe it was when you kissed me under the tree!"

"She's wacko!" Eric said. "Just another stalker. Who knew?"

"I am not a stalker!" she yelled. "I lead a rich and full life! People stalk me!"

"Cut out the theatrics, please!" Mimi said. "You didn't actually think he was interested in you as an individual, did you? He was using you to get me back. You're just another middle-aged wannabe actress. A nobody!"

"That's a tad harsh, darling. . . ."

Camille was tempted to jump Mimi, wrestle her to the ground, and bite into her thigh just like Paulette Goddard did to Rosalind Russell in *The Women*. But a small voice of sanity told her not to commit any acts of violence. She went to the door and then turned around to face them for her last lines. "I wish you bad luck with your play. I hope it closes after a week. Which it should. Because the idea is totally idiotic. I'm sorry, but *Malibu?* No one wants to say it to your face. But Chekhov would be crying. I swear. You've obviously lost all sense of integrity."

She slammed the door behind her. She had to admit to herself, as she waited for the elevator, she'd probably ruined any small chance she might've had to be Mimi's understudy.

Chapter Forty-six

As she walked through the park to go home, Camille tried to convince herself that she was not devastated. Okay, she wasn't going to be able to live out her fantasy. But fantasy by its very nature existed in the imagination. So even if she'd gotten what she wanted, she still wouldn't have felt happy, because it never would've been the way she'd always imagined. Look at Eric and Mimi. Anyone could see they weren't happy even though they were theoretically living out the very fantasy she craved. So why couldn't she stop craving it?

As she passed the lake outside Belvedere Castle, she saw someone familiar sitting on one of the benches that lined the path. It was that woman. Betty Boop. From Gymboree. With her mini-Betty Boop daughter in a stroller. Camille considered stopping, sitting down, introducing herself. But she couldn't. If she started to speak, she might break down into tears.

She knew what she needed. She needed to talk to Daniel. Tell him what happened. He was the one person in the world who would know how to make her feel better.

She couldn't wait for him to come home. But there was no choice. His patients had him now. Maybe she should call him, page him. No. She could wait. She didn't have to be so needy, not like them.

As she waited for the light to change at Fifth Avenue, she got out her phone. She did need to be needy just like them.

She called his office and got his voicemail. Left a short message. She tried to keep her voice casual, but it broke a little—so annoying—when she asked him to call her at home. But it was good she'd made the call. He would comfort her, or at least she hoped so. Maybe he'd just be disgusted with her. After all, this suffering . . . it was all about vanity, wasn't it? Selfish, egotistical pride. None of it was important. Except to her. And who was she? Nobody.

Nobody, she thought, as she considered walking up and down Madison Avenue, looking in clothing stores, consoling herself with a new dress, new makeup, new shoes. But she couldn't face the salesgirls, the mirrors, the attention all those things required! She continued on home, lucky to have a home. Even if she was nobody.

Nobody, she thought, as she nodded to the doorman of her building and he smiled and tipped his hat. It was comforting, yes, but then again it was his job to be friendly and solicitous and she wasn't the one paying the bills so what did it really have to do with her? Nothing. Because she was nobody.

She opened the door.

And there was Matthew sitting in his rock-a-roo. His face lit up the moment he saw her.

She was somebody!

Yes, as far as Matthew was concerned, she was the star of the show, no doubt about it. She gave him a big kiss on the cheek and let Berthe go home early and then sat him on her knees facing her. They gazed into each other's eyes, and he smiled at her with so much love. "Thank you," she said. Of course he could have no idea what she meant, but she couldn't say it enough. "Thank you."

Daniel called a little while later. He immediately detected the distress in her voice.

"What's wrong?" he asked. "Is it Matthew?"

"No, don't worry, Matthew is fine. It's just . . ." She started to tell him but the urge to cry overcame her, and it took a huge effort not to sob. "When are you getting home?"

"Around seven. Why?"

"I just need to talk to you."

"What happened?"

"I don't want to explain over the phone. Just . . . don't be late, okay?"

When he did finally get home, his look of concern immediately made a sob rise in her chest.

"Bad news?" he asked as he put down his briefcase and loosened his tie.

"Yes." She tried to laugh, but it came out twisted. She wondered if, on some level, he'd be pleased that she failed, considering the way she'd handled things. "So I'm not getting the part after all." She put Matthew in his rock-a-roo. Hopefully he would sit there long enough to let them have this conversation. "I was fooling myself about the whole thing. I thought I had a real chance, but I didn't."

He looked straight into her eyes. "I'm sorry."

Damn. He said it with such sincerity, it really made her want to convulse into tears. "I feel so stupid. I am such a stupid idiot. A stupid, idiotic idiot!"

"Come on. Don't be so hard on yourself."

"You don't know how many times in my life I've let my hopes get raised and then . . ."

"I'm sure you raised your hopes because they led you to believe you should, and for their own reasons they let you down. How could you not hope it would work out? I'm sorry. I know how much you want this."

It was all so hateful. And his concern made her feel like an even bigger jerk. She really wished she didn't have to care anymore. It was her father's fault, of course. He did this to her. "Do you think . . . ?"

"What?"

She took a breath. Tried to keep her voice cheerful but it

came out singsong in a wobbly sort of way. "Do you think it's ridiculous to hold a grudge with a dead person?"

"Your father?"

"Yes." Of course Daniel knew immediately what she meant. He had understood from the start. That was why she'd married him, wasn't it? And now the lump . . . the lump was back. Lodged in her throat. The lump that would not let her cry. *Cry*, she commanded herself. Cry because he is dead. It's a good reason to cry. "I'm just . . . so . . . angry with him." A single hot tear went down her cheek. She quickly wiped it away. "But it's all mixed up. Like it's confused, in my head, and I'm not sure if I'm mad at him for dying or for missing me in *Camelot* or for caring more about himself than me and I guess it's all rolled together, but it's not like it was his fault that he died, and I know that he did love . . ."

She couldn't finish her sentence. The word "me" was frozen somewhere between her brain and her mouth.

"He loved you?"

Her eyes stung. "Yes."

"You can't say it."

"No. Because I'm not really sure."

"And that feels lousy."

"And that makes me hate him. But I don't want to hate him. I want to love him. And I want . . ." She couldn't say it. She could hear it in her head, but she couldn't say it out loud.

"What?"

"I want . . ." Her throat ached from holding the words in. She took a deep breath and forced the words out. "I wish Daddy could . . ." She tried again. "I'm so mad that he's never going to—"

It was as if a gust of wind was rising from up inside her chest, and finally with one big heave she started to sob. "He'll never meet you and . . ." She hated how her voice sounded—all contorted and ugly—but she had to get it out. "Matthew."

"Com'ere," Daniel said. They both sank next to each other on the couch, and Camille leaned on his shoulder and he put his arm around her and held her and rubbed her back while she heaved and got snot and tears all over his shirt.

"Why are you so good to me?" she asked.

"You don't think I should be?"

"No."

"Well, I guess I'm an idiot," he said. "Like you."

She couldn't help but smile. The button of his white cotton shirt pressed against her lips. It was so reassuring. "I love you," she said. Not because she felt guilty. Or to please him. Or because it seemed like the right thing to say at the moment. But simply because she meant it.

That night, as soon as Matthew fell asleep, they made love. Camille tried to keep her eyes open. But it still made her feel self-conscious, so she kept them closed. But one thing was clear even in the black void inside her head. It was Daniel she was making love to. And Daniel was making love to her. And she didn't want anybody else taking their places.

Epilogue

The audition was on Forty-sixth Street. Berthe came in extra early so Camille could bathe, shave, wax, blow-dry, and dress (nothing fancy—her best jeans, a red silk shirt, and her favorite black leather boots). She took the subway down and got there with ten minutes to spare. Checked in with the stage manager, a cute young man with curly hair and small wire-rim glasses reading a thick biography of Samuel Beckett. "We're running late," he said. "It might be a half hour. Sorry."

"No problem." She gave him a smile. This was a waste of time. Just another unpaid Off-Off-Broadway showcase. About ten other actresses were already there looking over their lines.

"Did you bring a headshot?"

Camille got her new headshot out of her bag and handed it to him.

"Thanks." He looked at her, and then looked at the photo, and then back at her. After a lot of obsessing, she'd gotten her hair trimmed to shoulder length before having the picture taken. And she'd changed her name. Back. Professionally, at least.

"That's a good headshot," he said. "I hate it when people have a photo that doesn't look anything like them. What's the point?"

Marketing. Ego boost. Wishful thinking . . . "It's ridiculous," she said.

She took a seat. Waited her turn. Settled into doing an old trick that calmed her before auditions. She said sentences backward in her head. *Diapers more get to need I. Rain like looks it. Now about right good taste would coffee some.* It took such concentration, she forgot to be nervous.

Lisa got off the elevator. "Camille?!"

"You're auditioning?"

"Yep."

So here they both were. Still at it.

"What d'ya know. Well, you look great," Lisa said.

"So do you."

After checking in with the stage manager, Lisa sat down next to Camille. "So did you ever buy Eric Hughes's apartment?"

"No, but we ended up buying one in the same building, a few floors down. Much more affordable."

"Does it have the views?"

"Not really. But you know what? I like being closer to the ground. You can see the people walking by on the street. You aren't so far removed."

"But can you see the river?"

"Yes. As the trees lose their leaves, we're starting to see it through the branches." Camille was looking forward to watching the river come out of hiding.

"Cool. Well congratulations. Eric Hughes's apartment was fantastic," Lisa said. "I almost considered buying it myself."

Camille didn't mention that it was back on the market. She wouldn't mind resuming her friendship with Lisa, but she didn't want her living in the same building. Naomi had told her Eric and Mimi were going ahead with the divorce, and she'd read in *Backstage* that the opening of *The Seagull: Malibu* had been delayed due to "artistic differences." At least she could enjoy imagining that she'd helped break them up.

The stage manager called out her name. "Camille Chiarelli?"

"Chiarelli?" Lisa asked.

Maybe it was harder to spell and pronounce and remember.

But it was her name. The one she grew up with. And Chaplin certainly hadn't brought her any luck.

She rose from her seat. "That's me."

She went through the door into a large room with a shiny wood slat floor, white walls, no window, and took her place in front of five strangers sitting behind a folding table. The director introduced himself and asked her to begin. She took a moment and looked at each one of the faces staring back at her. Then she smiled and reminded herself to breathe. As uncomfortable as this experience was, these people, she knew, were on her side. There was, after all, a common goal. They wanted to be transported to another world. And she wanted to take them there.